TREE OF SIGHS

LUCRECIA GUERRERO

Bilingual Press/Editorial Bilingüe

Publisher
Gary Francisco Keller

Executive Editor
Karen S. Van Hooft

Associate Editors
Adriana M. Brady
Brian Ellis Cassity
Amy K. Phillips
Linda K. St. George

Address
Bilingual Press
Hispanic Research Center
Arizona State University
PO Box 875303
Tempe, AZ 85287-5303
(480) 965-3867

TREE OF SIGHS

LUCRECIA GUERRERO

Bilingual Press/Editorial Bilingüe
Tempe, Arizona

Library of Congress Cataloging-in-Publication Data

Guerrero, Lucrecia.
    Tree of sighs / Lucrecia Guerrero.
        p. cm.
    ISBN 978-1-931010-73-3 (hardcover : alk. paper) — ISBN 978-1-931010-74-0 (pbk. : alk. paper)
    1. Self-realization in women—Fiction. 2. Mexicans—United States—Fiction. 3. Women—Identity—Fiction. 4. Grandmothers—Fiction. 5. Mexican American women—Fiction. I. Title.
    PS3557.U342T74 2011
    813'.54—dc22
                                                          2010048110

PRINTED IN THE UNITED STATES OF AMERICA

Front cover art: Nuestra Señora de la poesía *(1994) by Alfredo Arreguín*

Cover and interior design by Bill Greaves

dedicado a mi niño precioso
Lorenzo V. Peagler

and the other children claimed by the mean streets

CONTENTS

ACKNOWLEDGMENTS

I'd like to give thanks to the many people who have helped and supported me in bringing *Tree of Sighs* to the page. I thank my familia for their love and support. Jerry Holt has listened patiently during my moments of doubt and offered me both feedback and inspiration. Thanks to my "hermanos" César González, Ralph Keyes, and Luis A. Urrea for their belief in my writing and for bringing it to the attention of others. And how can I say how much I appreciate the encouragement and inspiration that I have received at the Antioch Writers' Workshop: the faculty, participants, and dedicated board have been instrumental in my development as a writer. I am grateful to the Spalding MFA program, particularly Julie Brickman, who helped me see the big picture, and Neela Vaswani, who went the extra mile for me; both women generously gave of their time and talent. I thank friends and fellow writers who gave me feedback along the way: Verna Austen, Chuck Derry, Susan Streeter Carpenter, Judy Dapolito, Ben Grossberg, Lee Huntington, Katrina Kittle, and Rachel Moulton. A big thank you to the good people at Bilingual Press and a special thanks to editor Linda St. George for her patience and her careful and diligent eye. There have been many, many friends and writers who have given of their time and I thank them all. In addition, I am indebted to the Montgomery County Culture Works and the Christopher Isherwood Foundation for their support of *Tree of Sighs*—and artists in general.

OUT
OF
THE
BLUE

ONE

BROCKTON, INDIANA, 2000

Up until the day Violet telephoned from out of my past, I'd thought I was over that business of reinventing myself. Fifteen years ago, I settled into being Grace Thornberry, and I promised myself that, by God, I'd come to the end of a string of identities that I'd adopted along the way. It's not like I had set out to be a chameleon like Madonna—the singer, I mean. Nobody can beat that woman for forging a new mold every time her career goes a little shaky or she spots a patch of loose skin. Anyway, I'm no celebrity. For years, I wanted only to get my life back to normal, and when I married Kenny Thornberry, I wanted to stay in that space, the way a phonograph needle gets stuck in the groove of one of those old vinyl records. That's been me, *scritch-scratch, scritch-scratch,* no need to worry about what was coming because I wasn't going. I admit that along the way there have been times— like when I watch Oprah on TV and she has some program about someone coming to terms with haunting memories—that I've had a fleeting thought of the family I'd started out with. But then I remind myself that some things are best left alone.

I've had more than enough excitement in my life, thank you very much. After all, I was born, in a manner of speaking, three different times: first in Mexico as Altagracia Villalobos; then thirteen years later, after I was orphaned and my grandmother gave me away (well, she was destitute, what else *could* she do?) to an americana, I became Grace Sloan; and in order to escape that little piece of hell on earth, I had to pretty much take on a new identity. Even a blind man could see why I'd had enough of change.

You've heard that old saying: You don't miss the water until the well goes dry? That's the way it's been whenever I did look back on my first life as Altagracia. I see now how spoiled I was, didn't truly appreciate my parents until after they were killed. I didn't think anything could be harder to endure than their death. To survive I learned to adapt. *Adapt,* Grandmother's last bit of advice to me as she passed me over to Molly Carol Sloan at The Three Little Pigs Café.

The café's name proved to be a prophecy of sorts: Like with the three pigs of the fairy tale, my life became one search after another for a safe haven. In a way, though, I think I felt I deserved every hardship. Grandmother had been right to give me away, I'd tell myself. Hadn't it been my decision to lie and in so doing change the course of my family's lives? Some might say—in fact, Grandmother did—that I killed my parents, or at least was responsible for their deaths. But no matter how much I blamed myself for my predicament, or how bad things got, I couldn't snuff out my desire to survive. I have never stopped wanting to live. I just can't make myself give up. I adapt.

Since marrying Kenny, I've more or less floated along on the surface of life, suppressing and repressing and pretending that the past was buried as deep in the ground as my parents and grandmother. Don't get me wrong; it's not that I've been catatonic or haven't had my fun. Sure I have. I just don't invite questions about my past. Accept me for the person I appear to be; that's been my motto. I've become so good at subterfuge that eventually I lost sight of who I was, who I *am*. Still, no matter how good I've become at self-delusion, I have never entirely rid myself of that nagging fear that one day I'd wake up to find all my secrets sitting on my chest like a three-hundred-pound bag of sand bursting at the seams. *Trickle,* out comes a stream of grains.

A few months ago, that three-hundred-pound bag finally landed in the form of a phone call on one of those fall days in Indiana when the sky is such a bright, crisp blue your eyes ache with the trueness of it. It was a fairly typical day: I was sitting at the kitchen table, had just laid down my daily crossword puzzle, a habit I'd gotten into before I married Kenny. There was something soothing about words, how they could transverse into a solution to a problem. At least, it worked out that way on paper.

"Altagracia?" a hoarse voice asked from the other end of the line. "It's Vi, Violet. Remember me?"

Altagracia. My God, how long had it been since I'd been called that? My mouth opened to answer Violet, but no sound came out. And of course I remembered her. How could I forget Molly Carol's sister, even after all these years? Both of them had shown up in a nightmare or two along the way, those screaming horrors that would scare poor Kenny out of his sweet slumber. When Kenny asked me about my dreams, I always lied and said that they slipped away the second I woke up. Repress, adapt. You get the picture.

"What a surprise," I managed. "How are you?" Superficial, I know, but what do you say to a ghost? I thought about hanging up, but as if guessing my thoughts, Violet cleared her throat and quickly went on.

"Not so good. My lungs," she said, forcing out words between rasping wheezes. I pictured lungs stained by menthol cigarettes, once pink globes now as yellow-brown as Violet's index and middle fingers had been back when I'd known her. Even then the smoke had coarsened her voice and given her a perpetual cough that she used to call her "bronical" problems.

She can't believe she's finally found me, Violet said. And to think how close we had been living to each other all this time. Ain't life a hoot? The doctors tell her she hasn't got long. She wants to see me. And in answer to my question, yes, she's still in Cogstown, right outside Cincinnati, only not at the trailer park. A friend in God is caring for her. She has information for me about my family. Not her sister Molly Carol and the twins. No, she said, she knows I don't want to hear about any of them. Anyway, Molly Carol's out in California. It's about my *real* family.

"They're all dead, what's to tell?" Even as I pretended not to care, my mind exploded with memories: a gaze of peacock-blue that has burned spots of like color into my brain; sad laughter revealing teeth almost too white to be real; an orchid, small and yellow with a mouth of pink.

"I guess you can't forgive me?"

I'm not God, I wanted to shout, but said nothing. Who was I to forgive? Violet would just have to learn to live without redemption. Hadn't I?

A muffled *clack-clack* came from Violet's end of the line. Something inside me softened. After all these years Violet still couldn't afford a set of dentures that fit properly.

"No," Violet said, when I didn't answer. "Didn't reckon you *could* forgive me."

"I don't think about the past." I dabbed at my moist upper lip with one hand and caught a faint whiff of vanilla on my palm.

"Well."

"I mean it. I'm happy. The past is dead, buried, I'm over it." My voice was rising.

"Gone and done with. Yeah, I know how it is." Violet coughed, a phlegmy sound that made me gag. "Hon," she said, "I'll never rest in my grave with you on my conscience."

After a moment I thought Violet had stopped breathing. Suddenly she gasped, sucking in air like someone who had been under water too long. Just like me, I thought, and felt that I, too, might suffocate. In my kitchen, I lifted my gaze from the stainless steel sink to the window.

Kenny sat in profile on a lawn chair on our deck. The day was unusually warm for late fall, and he'd gone out to soak in the sun. With his newspaper folded into a compact square so that it wouldn't rustle, he peeked over the edge at the bird feeder only two feet from him. Two cardinals, a vivid red male and a female in subtle red and brown, perched side by side on the bar. Maybe the birds felt secure in the kindness that emanated from Kenny like a warm light. That light had drawn me to him all those years ago and it's been Kenny and me ever since. Why should I allow the past to interrupt this calm-as-a-painting view?

Kenny sensed me watching him and turned in my direction. Without lowering his newspaper, he cantilevered his head slightly, his gesture asking me what I wanted. When I smiled and waved, he nodded and looked away. Too quickly, I thought. It hit me then how he'd been avoiding my eyes lately. How long had that been going on? Maybe he, too, had something to hide. But, no, I told myself, it was only my imagination. And my guilty conscience over all I'd held back from him. The man had no idea who he'd married.

Violet inhaled, exhaled, each breath an effort. I cranked open the window. The birds scattered in alarm. I'd broken the illusion of still life. Kenny glanced at me, irritated, but before I could shrug an apology, his eyes darted away to follow the cardinals, two spots of red disappearing into the heavens. Without warning, a blue jay screeched and dove toward the feeder, long, sharp beak ready to pierce any resistance. I pictured that jay's beak ripping at my bag of secrets.

My gasp must have loosened a gob of phlegm in Violet's lungs, for after one last bark of a cough, she said, "Can I count on you coming?"

"Yes." My quick response surprised me. But only for a moment. Something deep inside me had cracked. Despite all the nonsense that I'd force-fed myself over the years about my being able to forget what I refused to acknowledge about the past, somehow I'd always known that this day would come. And with my acceptance of Violet's invitation, I sensed that my journey would not stop there.

Outside where the border of my yard met with the green area beyond, the branches of the willow brushed the grass. When I shut my eyes, I could hear the rustle of the leaves from across the long expanse of time, back to where I'd begun the long path that would bring me here to what, I now understood, was just another stepping-stone to yet another new path. I couldn't foresee what awaited me, but I did know what lay behind.

TWO

MESQUITE, SONORA, MEXICO

When I was a child in Mexico—before the reign of Molly Carol—I worried about nothing more than how to circumvent my grandmother's rules and assert my independence. Those were the days of innocence, days that had not yet taught me that *freedom* can be a synonym for *freefall*.

Grandmother and I often sat outside near the twin orange trees: I studiously sprawled on the sunny wrought-iron bench and she stiffly perched on the edge of a cane rocker beneath the shade of the portico that ran the length of the yard, connecting our house to the family business, The Peacock Curios and Gifts. Grandmother had filled our courtyard with plants: potted geraniums in pinks, corals, and reds near the entrance of the house, while yucca and nopal cactuses lined the inside of the eight-foot-high wall that enclosed our property and protected us from trespassers. The concrete block barrier had been plastered with stucco and painted white to reveal invading tarantulas, scorpions, or centipedes. But the starkness also showed off the bougainvillea that tumbled over the top, dropping fuchsia flowers onto the sidewalk beyond.

In season, the blossoms of the orange trees filled the air with a citrus-sweet fragrance and *always* the waxy leaves rustled in the constant winds that blew off the Sonoran Desert. Chelo, our housekeeper, told me that the sounds of the wind blowing through the trees were lost spirits snagged on the branches and calling out. How they sighed and moaned.

They're searching, Chelo would say, and when I asked for what, she'd laugh and answer, ¿Qué sé yo? What do I know? Chelo and I never mentioned the significance of those sighs to Grandmother, because she, like our parish priest, didn't approve of "superstitious nonsense."

The crown of the orange trees peaked above the wall and when the fruit turned bright and plump, the promise of their nectar tempted the poor on the streets of Mesquite. Many could have scaled the cement barrier if Grandmother hadn't had the foresight to have the workers encase jagged shards of broken bottles and jars into the wet cement at the top. How do we decide who is to eat and who is to starve? Grandmother would say. If we feed them all, we'll be left with nothing for ourselves. She said that our first duty was to our family, our blood. Back then, I took the presence of family for granted, so her comments about its importance meant little to me. If only I had known what awaited us all.

Double doors of heavy metal opened at one side of the wall, but were kept chained and padlocked. Only the wind and dust managed to slip through the cracks around the doors and whirl down from overhead, covering everything inside our house with a fine dust that Chelo couldn't keep under control. The hot breath of God, Chelo said of the gritty wind. You, see, she would say, even his breath has a bite.

God might invade our sanctuary, but people entered only by way of The Peacock Curios. The shop opened onto a busy street of stores selling trinkets and souvenirs of varying degrees of quality to the many tourists who crossed over from Mesquite, Arizona, into its Mexican twin city where we lived. Visitors were seldom invited beyond the front of The Peacock Curios unless they were interested in viewing some of my father's paintings in the storeroom that doubled as his studio. It was even less likely that a visitor would be invited into our home. Our relationship with the neighbors was friendly but distant and formal. These two last words could also describe Grandmother's personality and her appearance.

Grandmother created some of her looks with illusion. For instance, Grandmother was tall, there's no questioning that. But her head inched even higher than all the other women in the neighborhood because of how she sat and stood, as if her spine was reaching beyond its physical capability. People complimented her on her perfect posture, which she proudly attributed to years of ballet training as a child. I surmised that much of the erectness had something to do with the stiff corset that Chelo helped her into each morning and out of in the evenings. Naturally, I would never have uttered such a thought, for in those days I was very Mexican, and understood the importance of respecting one's elders. My father was very tolerant of my willful ways, as Grandmother called them, but disrespectful behavior he would not tolerate. Not even from his little princess. Bad manners reflect badly on the family, he would warn me.

Grandmother's hair, a yellowish-brown shade, was styled into a thick French twist. What the casual onlooker didn't spot was how the bulk was achieved by carefully arranging the thinning hair over a hidden mesh roll. The color Grandmother owed to Chelo and chamomile. Every week Chelo bought a bunch of the tiny white flowers with yellow centers and boiled them in water. The infusion filled our house with a faint smell of ripe apples which would later cling to Grandmother after Chelo rinsed her freshly shampooed hair.

To keep my hair blonde, Grandmother said; although the only streaks that appeared yellow were where the gray strands absorbed the natural dye.

A little more than a year before the accident that would change our destinies, I'd been hearing Papi and Grandmother speak in raised voices, albeit behind closed doors, where they always discussed important family and business affairs. One day earlier when Grandmother and Chelo were at the bathroom sink with the chamomile tea, Papi and I crossed paths in the hallway and he glanced into the bathroom and said, "Your grandmother believes in the reality of her past more than she will admit."

He laughed after he'd made the comment, but it was little more than one of his forced chuckling sounds that I knew really signaled irritation, so I nodded and smiled, enough to show respect for him, not enough to suggest disrespect for Grandmother. I was only a kid, but in our house, as was the custom in those days, the man was the head of the family, and the women and kids did well to understand his moods and hidden meanings. But the truth was that I had no idea what he'd meant by his comment. It was one of those things that go on with adults that kids don't understand until time affords them the necessary experience. But if I was too young to grasp Papi's meaning, Grandmother was not. She straightened so fast, her sopping hair threw water every which way. She wrapped a turbaned towel around her hair and huffed away to her room, banging the door shut behind her.

Not long after that incident, on a spring day Grandmother and I sat outside surrounded by a cloud of orange-blossom scent. She held a pillowcase in her lap and I held another in mine as I prepared for a lesson in hemstitching.

She insisted that all proper young ladies should learn needle work. I strongly disagreed, but when I'd taken my protest to Papi, he'd thrown back his head and laughed, showing his rows of perfect white teeth.

He understood, he said, but reminded me that I must obey my grandmother or the devil might take me like in one of Chelo's stories about ungrateful children. Ha ha. I loved my father's laughter but sometimes wished that he wouldn't always answer my problems with a joke.

I had carefully pulled out the horizontal threads around an inch-wide border of the pillowcases, and now Grandmother demonstrated how I was to create a design with the vertical threads by gathering alternate bundles of three and five, then securing them with tiny stitches. I couldn't imagine a greater waste of time. I tried to concentrate, but my gaze kept traveling from Grandmother's hands up to her gold locket, pinned like a brooch over the breast of her dress.

"Keep your eyes on your duty, child," Grandmother said. "Don't you care that your father's head will rest on these pillowcases?"

"Yes, ma'am."

I doubted that Papi gave two beans about pillowcases. Anyway, he'd been staying out so late the last few weeks that his head wasn't spending much time on the bed linens that Grandmother hemstitched or embroidered with her own designs of morning glories and peacocks (in threads the color of her eyes). Even then, I suspected that some of the adult behind-closed-door discussions had something to do with my father's staying out late. I told myself to concentrate on my needle, in, out, in, out. But the bees buzzed around the orange blossoms, the constant drone lulling me, and I vaguely reminded myself to ask Chelo later if she thought the bees might be sipping a bit of some lost soul along with the nectar.

"Now look what you've done," Grandmother said. With her own needle, she pointed to my lopsided stitches and disorganized bundles of thread.

"I'm sorry, Grandmother. It's only that I was keeping an eye on those bees. You know how you swell up if one of them stings you. Maybe we should stop for today?" Earlier Chelo had told me that her niece Olga, who worked at the Sonora Salon of Beauty running errands and sweeping up hair, had dropped off some of the salon's throwaway movie star magazines for me. Celebrity gossip beat out ladylike sewing any time of the day.

"How considerate you are," Grandmother said in that sarcastic voice that made my eyes roll in spite of my promises to my father to control my facial expressions. She'd been so cranky lately, and so had Mamá and Papi. Something hung in the air besides the clean scent of blossoms and the spicy warmth of Grandmother's Maja cologne, but none of the adults would tell me what was going on.

Grandmother pulled a hanky from inside her bosom and patted at the moisture forming across her forehead. As she lowered her hand, she brushed her fingers across the locket. A common gesture of hers, as if she needed to make certain the locket was still there. Later, I would interpret it as a premonition of her loss.

Inside the locket there was a photo of Papi, and facing him, Grandmother. Her blue eyes focused on him, but his eyes turned slightly to one side. Even he, who couldn't start his day without his mother's blessing, had trouble holding her gaze. Years later when I tried to imagine those photos, it would become increasingly difficult to remember the features of either face clearly. Their images became ghostly, outlines etched in shifting strands of fog. Only the amazing blue of Grandmother's eyes remained clear in my mind. I would understand that my memory had chosen the symbolic over the literal: those photos were in black and white.

"It is awfully warm today," Grandmother said. "But that's to be expected when you live in a desert."

"Yes, ma'am." I was glad she'd mentioned the heat. "You're right as usual, Grandmother," I said. "The desert's soo-oo hot. Oh, by the way, you know Socorro Vargas, don't you? She's in most of my classes at Rosary." I was referring to Our Lady of the Rosary Academy, a private bilingual school where Mesquite's better families—or those who held dreams of attaining such stature—sent their daughters. "Well, Socorro's very *respectable*."

Grandmother's left eyebrow arched when I emphasized one of her favorite words, but I rattled on as if my intent had been innocent. "And so stylish," I continued. "She came in the other week with her mother to buy some Spanish mantillas? Did you notice what Socorro was wearing?"

"First, stop speaking in questions." Grandmother never missed a stitch as she spoke. "Be definite if you expect to be taken seriously. Life isn't easy for even the strongest of women." Grandmother stabbed her needle through the linen, another perfect stitch. "Second, say what you mean. And, no, you are not allowed to wear miniskirts. You are twelve years old, a child. Don't even ask, girl."

I hated how my grandmother always thought she could read my mind, especially when she almost could. "Mini skirts—*phht*." I made a dismissive wave with my hand. "Outdated. I'm talking about hot pants." I said the word in English so the connotation didn't hit so hard.

"Outside of school, all the girls—at least those who are no longer babies— are wearing them," I said. To be emphatic, I added with not a hint of question, "All the girls wear them." Actually most of the girls my age didn't wear them, but I hoped that for once I could be a trendsetter instead of waiting to make certain that the style had become acceptable by the respectable families. How could I know that this tendency of mine to want to be at the helm, to lead rather than follow, would help me survive the life that would be mine in the near future?

"*All* the girls can dress as they please. *You* are Altagracia Villalobos, and *you* will dress like a lady."

I made a huffing noise and with a quick glance around to make certain that my father wasn't watching, I, with a flick of the hand, tossed my hair back off my shoulders. Why didn't she come up with something original for once? I swung my leg back and forth so hard the edge of the bench chafed the tender skin on the back of my knee. Good. When I stood up she'd be able to see how much pain she'd caused me. It made no sense the way Grandmother was always talking about how we were different because we were Villalobos. As if we were blue bloods instead of common shopkeepers. We did sell a higher quality of merchandise than most of the other curio shops that lined our street, but still. . . . The odd thing was that the neighbors treated Grandmother with extra respect, as if her standoffishness meant something. She was always *doña* Paz to them. It would not be until I lived in the United States that I understood the strict social classes in Mexico and how difficult it was in those days to cross the lines that separated people.

Without looking up, I could feel the intensity of Grandmother's gaze. I hated and loved those blue eyes. People sometimes stopped Grandmother in the street just to compliment her on the color. A shade so startling that as a very small child, I couldn't imagine her vision not being affected and thought Grandmother must surely see the world painted as blue as I did through my blue-tinted sunglasses. More than once I'd asked her from whom she'd inherited those eyes. But Grandmother rarely spoke of her past. Asking questions about her parents or siblings was off limits. She would only clamp her jaw, exaggerating an under bite which, I thought then, made her look appropriately like a bulldog. I didn't press her, not because I feared her but because, like most children, my present tense concerned me much more than the past tense of adults.

Her blue gaze concentrated on my swinging leg now, and I stopped and sat up straight even though I wanted to slump and open my legs wide in the most unladylike posture I could manage. But if I did, she'd only make me stay in my room and on the weekend I'd miss going with Papi on the Sunday drive that he loved so much. There was nothing my father liked more than movement, even if he was only driving in circles.

"Altagracia." My name drifted out from around the side of the house, the voice soft enough for me to pretend I hadn't heard.

Out of the corner of my eye, I saw Grandmother's needle hesitate in midair. No doubt wondering if she'd actually heard anything other than the wind.

"Altagracia, Altagracia."

I turned my head slightly away from the voice and toward the front of our house. A cloud of small white butterflies fluttered about the pink flowers of the Rosa de Castilla that rambled up the outside wall near the front door (painted blue to keep out evil spirits, Chelo said). I imagined myself shrinking down to the size of my smallest fingernail, my stick-tiny legs striding the black body of one of the butterflies. Up and away, over the wall I would fly. Free to mix in the world beyond. Free to do as I wished. Free from Mamá's voice. I couldn't help but wonder if that whine was why Papi always found excuses to leave the house. After the accident, I would hear that voice on every breeze, even into the United States. The wind respects no borders.

"You hear your mother calling as well as I do," Grandmother said.

"But you said I couldn't stop, even if it is so hot I'm melting. And see, I'm not finished." I held up my sewing. "Maybe someone else could go this time?"

Grandmother's heavy silence told me what was expected of me. She seldom entered Mamá's room. When she did, she sometimes quoted from one of the French or English poets. "Water, water, everywhere, / Nor any drop to drink" was one of her favorites. I wasn't certain what she meant, but since she made her comments about Mamá and her room beneath her breath, I understood that I was to pretend that she hadn't spoken at all. Or she might mumble about Mamá's given name. "Orquídea," Grandmother would say, "it's not even Catholic."

But no matter what her feelings toward Mamá might be, Grandmother wouldn't tolerate my being disrespectful to either of my parents. Respect and good manners, she often said, didn't cost anything, yet they were the frosting on the cake of life. That frosting was sometimes too sweet for my tastes. I folded my sewing and placed it in the basket, making certain to drag out each task.

"You're a willful girl, Altagracia," Grandmother said. "The sooner you learn to conform to the rules of polite society, the better off you'll be. Believe me."

Believe me. As if she would know about anything other than being a conformist. "Hmmm," I answered.

Grandmother's eyebrow shot up again, but her attention had returned to her work. She always remained so distant, so cold, as if she had nothing to do with the world around her. How could I know that it was a defense mechanism that I too would need to learn one day?

When I walked away, I gave a flip to the hem of my skirt that I knew would reveal not only the backs of my scratched knees but even a bit of the forbidden thighs. Instead of grumbling, Grandmother sighed, a tired sound that, for a fleeting moment, made me regret my rudeness.

I entered the relative cool of the house and stopped for a moment to allow my eyes to adapt to the shadowy interior. Mamá, as if sensing my nearness, called again, the end of my name rising into a question mark this time.

Eyes closed, I lifted my arms slightly to the sides and turned my hands, palms out. I wanted to catch the breeze that ran through the house from the screen door at the back, down the hallway past the two bedrooms and bathroom on one side, kitchen and dining room on the other, and smacked into me. Up, up, and away.

"Altagracia," Mamá called. I laid my sewing basket on the inside of the parlor, taking my time.

"Your mother's calling." Chelo stepped out of the kitchen into the hallway, wiping her hands on her apron.

"Hmm," I hummed, and wondered if the whole world thought I was deaf. What a lousy day this was turning into. I wished I could slink off into a dark corner with the fan magazine that Olga had brought me.

When I entered my parents' bedroom, light from the hall reflected off the knobbed posters of the brass bed, and after I shut the door I shuffled through the darkness toward the remembered glow. At my mother's bedside I reached for the hand I knew was open, waiting to clutch my own. Mamá held her good luck charm—a vanilla bean pod from faraway Veracruz. The scent of her dreams would remain on my palm for years to come.

"I'm sorry," Mamá said.

"No, no." I stroked the trembling hand. My mother's life was one long *I'm sorry*. She apologized so often that the words became only a murmur, background noise like women praying the rosary at a wake. I silently wished she would shut up. "I love you, Mamá," I said too loudly.

The smell that lingered lately in her room, a sweetish odor that almost overpowered the vanilla—but not the fear—seemed to be heavier than usual. There was something familiar about the scent, but I couldn't place it. "Please, could we open the shutters?" I said.

Papi had attached the shutters to their bedroom windows because some days Mamá's memories couldn't bear up under the bright desert sun. I'd long ago become accustomed to my mother spending her life inside the walls of our house. Papi told me that she hadn't always been so afraid of the outside, and that before, she would not only leave the house but even accompany him on rides in the store van. But that was before Mamá, for reasons known only to her, had become convinced that she would die in a terrible car wreck.

I can hear the crash and grind of metal, Mamá would say. I can feel the heat of the flames. The light consumes me, she would finish with a sigh. My mother understood much more than I realized back then.

I cracked both sets of shutters open three inches and returned to stand next to the bed. Mamá grasped my hand so tightly I winced. She pulled on me until I sat on the edge of the bed close to her. The vanilla pod dug into my palm.

"Look how pretty the murals are in this light," Mamá said, and gestured with her hand to take in the surrounding walls. Papi, under Mamá's direction, had painted murals on all four walls of their bedroom, scenes that would help her recapture, in two dimensions, memories of her home state of Veracruz.

My brain, Mamá often said, has become parched in this place. She would wave her hand in ever widening circles that took in our house, our shop, Mesquite, and the Sonoran Desert beyond. Then tapping one temple, she would add, "Soon my memories, all that is me, will evaporate in this dry heat."

I didn't understand why she was always living in the past, why she couldn't just enjoy *now*. Of course at the time I had so little past myself that I didn't understand its lure. I loved everything of the northern part of Sonora, the prickly cactuses that gave way to pines if you traveled out of the desert valley and into the mountains; the azure skies that suddenly clouded in July and dumped so much rain that the cracked earth couldn't drink it fast enough, and after the rain, the vibrant rainbows; and at night, the constellations of stars that could be studied in the black sky.

I even liked that we lived on the border between Mexico and the United States, the twin cities split above ground by a ten-foot-high chain-link fence and connected below by tunnels built in the 1930s for the runoff of the summer rain. Papi called the two Mesquites conjoined twins and said that one couldn't survive without the other. Mamá often complained that the Mesquites were neither Mexico nor the U.S. She never could figure out the borderland culture. Grandmother, not one to complain much (What's the point? she would say), did make it clear that she wouldn't tolerate my mixing English and Spanish the way we often did on the border. Out of her earshot, every once in a while I'd sprinkle in an English noun pronounced and conjugated like a Spanish verb. I was proud to be a pocha.

"You're not even looking," Mamá said.

I twisted my head to glance around at walls that I had already gone over with her so many times that I could have described them with my eyes shut. On the wall behind me where the door was, Papi had painted the rain forest, lush jungles jeweled with the plumage of tropical birds. At the corner where that wall met with the one to the right of the bed, the tropical vegetation thinned out, giving way to the second wall painted with banana trees (Mamá always pointed out how the baby trees stayed close to their parents). On that same wall, after the banana trees came neat rows of blossomed coffee plants, and finally tendrils that snaked onto the third wall, and the orchid fields of Papantla, so thick with pods that I could almost smell the sweet vanilla. One orchid, pale yellow, had in its center human lips bright pink and opened in song or scream. Mamá often told me that she had been singing in a club when she first met Papi. He'd been drawn in by her canary-lovely voice. I stared at Mamá, face pale and puffy from lack of sun and exercise, and tried to reconcile that reality with the photos of the slim and tan girl who had been adored by many of the young veracruzanos.

On the fourth wall stood five Totonac dancers. Atop a high platform, four of the Totonac, ropes tied to their waists, prepared for their leap to earth as the fifth danced and played on his flute "Son del perdón," the dance of forgiveness.

Mamá, claiming the Totonac as her ancestors (and choosing to ignore the Spaniards whose blood so obviously also ran in her veins), often claimed that mural as her favorite. This day, when she saw where my gaze had roamed, she said, "Maybe, Daughter, you will someday fly like them."

"Or you, Mamá," I said, thinking she would like my lie. I couldn't imagine anyone less likely to fly than my mother.

Musical notes from the flute created a trail on that last wall that ended with the port city of Veracruz. My eyes drifted to that edge, and I could almost feel the heat in the whiteness reflecting off the port and its glassy sea.

"Why did I leave my home, my people?" she said, and squeezed my hand tighter. The pod dug into my palm.

Yes, why *did* you? I thought. I immediately regretted my unspoken cruelty, but Mamá's bad feelings about herself made me sad and tired. If her sorrow was catching, could her fear be also?

"I can't breathe," Mamá said, and fanned her face with her free hand. "Can't you smell death in here?"

"I've never been to a funeral."

"A funeral, yes, of course. That's exactly what that smell is. What a clever girl you are." Mamá pulled me closer, and her breath blew sour when she whispered, "It's your father who's bringing that smell home with him."

With my one hand I pried the other one away from hers. I stood up. "It's almost time for dinner. I'm going to get Papi."

"Where is he? Tell me that, if you can."

"In the shop like always." I backed away toward the door. "Probably one of the neighbors planted something new in their garden. The odor, I mean. Chelo says that if you pay attention to the wind, you can smell and hear all the secrets from miles around."

Mamá's eyes filled with tears. "Tell your father I won't live without him."

I hated when my parents gave me messages to deliver to each other, but the chore was especially bad now that Mamá's messages were becoming so strange. Once Olga had asked me in her blunt way, "Is your mother crazy?" Chelo had reached across the table and pinched Olga's arm until she yelped.

Years later the memory of my mother's voice would bring javelinas thundering into my dreams, yellow orchids tucked behind their bristly ears. But the orchids' vanilla scent would not blot out the wild boars' carnivore's breath or mute the sound of the piggy squeals. I wanted to help Mamá, but in the days to come my actions would put us on a path that would destroy her and eventually take me thousands of miles away from Mesquite and my life as Altagracia.

THREE

As soon as I closed the bedroom door, Chelo motioned for me to come to the kitchen. "How's your mother?" she asked.

"Still going on about the stink in her room," I mumbled. "If she'd open the windows up more. . . ." My words lifted away on the roll of my eyes.

"Altagracia," Chelo said, "not everyone can be strong."

"Hmm."

"If you're kind you'll never have to live with guilt and regrets."

"That's what you always say." I couldn't keep the irritation out of my voice. First Grandmother presumed to read my thoughts, and now Chelo was reminding me of the virtue of kindness when I was feeling mean. For years to come, my mind wracked with guilt over my little cruelties to those who had loved me, I would have many opportunities to lie awake with only my regrets to keep me company. I would force those thoughts deep into the folds and crevices of my brain and deny them so that I could get on with the business of existence. They say cream always rises to the top; well, so do corpses.

Sometimes misfortune and hard knocks turn a person bitter; sometimes they teach tolerance. Chelo showed more tolerance for Mamá's complaints than anyone else in the house. No muttering beneath her breath like Grandmother, who grumbled about Papi marrying a showgirl; no drumming of fingers on the table like Papi when Mamá droned on about her lost Veracruz. When I was older and thought of Chelo, I sometimes wondered if her calm expression truly reflected what she felt. Or was she only putting on a show of patient acceptance to placate the people who provided her livelihood?

"I have a surprise for you," Chelo said, and I followed behind. Her chancletas, backs broken down so that the one-time loafers served as slippers, whispered across the ceramic tile floor and slapped against her callused heels, *shh-slap, shh-slap*.

Chelo had come to live with my grandmother when Papi was a boy of eleven, and Chelo, a mere two years older, cared for him and the house. Like many girls from the villages, she'd traveled to the city in search of work and sent money back home to help support her parents and siblings. When Papi was older, Grandmother sent Chelo to seamstress school so that she would have a trade, wanting to make certain that if anything happened to her, Chelo could care for herself. But after her training, for reasons she never explained, Chelo had stayed on with the family. I didn't yet understand how frightening change could be, but even though back then I thought Chelo silly for not striking out on her own, I was also glad she hadn't left.

Chelo had looked after me since I was a baby. To me she was a wise and trusted friend who was always willing to listen no matter how busy she was. Now she reached around me to close the door to her room. The room, the size of a walk-in closet, was crowded with a narrow bed, a blonde wood dresser and matching bedside table, and a straight-backed chair with one wobbly leg. A metal rack with hangers for her three dresses, two sweaters, and a black jacket was pushed against the wall next to a framed picture of the Virgin of Guadalupe, sconces holding votive candles on either side. A narrow door led to the tiny backyard where there were cement tubs, one with a built-in washing board and the other deep for holding water. Next to the tubs a tiny room had been curtained to hide the old-fashioned metal commode with the tank and chain on the wall above it for Chelo's use.

Olga once said that Grandmother had provided Chelo with separate facilities because she didn't want a servant contaminating the family bathroom. Chelo had told her niece that if she couldn't respect the mistress of the house, then she should leave that very moment. That day, as she'd spoken, Chelo's eyes darted from me to the hallway. I couldn't help but wonder if she was more appalled by what Olga had said or by her indiscretion of having spoken against one family member in front of another. I remember wondering then what they might be saying about us when they thought no one could hear. (It didn't occur to me that I would someday have the opportunity to figuratively walk a few miles in Chelo's chancletas.)

Chelo reached beneath the mattress of her cot and pulled out a movie star magazine with Rigo Tovar on the cover. "From Olga," she said.

He wasn't one of my favorite stars, but I thanked her and asked after Olga. A few months ago I'd overheard Grandmother asking Chelo if she knew her niece was hanging around with political malcontents that considered Fidel Castro a hero. Papi and Grandmother had many political discussions and often argued over Castro. Papi admired the way Fidel stood up to the gringos, but Grandmother said his courage against the americanos was no reason to overlook that he was an atheistic communist. I wasn't really that clear on what *communist* meant, but when Papi said that Jesus himself was closer to being a communist than a capitalist, the blood drained right out of Grandmother's face. I raised a blasphemer, Grandmother said, and stomped out of the room. Mostly my thoughts of Castro were limited to his physical appearance: I thought he was handsome.

Now when Olga visited she didn't stick around long. At least she was free to do as she wished, I thought with envy. Free. Just saying the word deepened the claustrophobia caused by the small room. Air wouldn't go all the way to the bottom of my lungs. I pushed opened the door casually, I thought, and eased out of the room.

"Olga still involved in politics?" I asked.

"¿Qué sé yo?" Chelo said, the way she always did when she didn't want to commit to a topic. She followed me into the kitchen, pulled chairs out for both of us at the table, and picked up a large bowl of egg whites. Holding the bowl in her lap with one hand, she beat the mixture with two forks held together for added weight.

"Sit with me for a while. Now that you're turning into a young lady, you don't have time for Chelo anymore."

"No way," I said. But it was true. There were so many changes going on with my emotions and body lately. I'd always been so comfortable around Chelo; now I couldn't think of anything to say to her. The folded damp dish towel on the kitchen counter gave off the scent of roasted peppers that must be cooling inside for peeling. "¿Chiles rellenos?" I said. "You make the best."

I liked the way Chelo whipped the egg whites light and fluffy before fold-ing in the beaten yolks, so that the cheese-stuffed poblano pepper snuggled like a prize inside the omelet blanket. After my compliment, I thought Chelo would say how I was exaggerating, that she just threw a little of this and a smidge of the other into the mix, that her cooking wasn't any better than anyone else's.

"I once knew a girl," Chelo said, "who didn't want anyone telling her what to do." Clearly she wasn't going to allow me to get her off track this time.

"Hmm." Normally, I enjoyed nothing better than Chelo's stories. She spun tales both magical and frightening, stories of love, betrayal, and redemption, but today I suspected I was going to be taught a moral.

"Well," Chelo continued, "this girl lived alone with her widowed mother. Now understand, Miss, that the girl's mother worked very hard to give her only child everything she could. Well, there is no love to compare to a mother's love."

In spite of my suspicions, I propped my chin in my palm and settled in to find out what happened next.

"But as she grew older," Chelo continued, "the girl began to think that she knew better than her own mother. The daughter became rude and disrespectful. An ingrate, some might call her. Can you imagine?"

"Maybe the girl was misjudged," I said.

Chelo ignored me, beat those egg whites even harder, and went on, saying how the girl insisted on going to the movies one day even though her poor mother's back ached from all the laundry and ironing she'd done to earn a few pesos. "'Please prepare your poor old mother a little supper,' the mother begged her daughter." Chelo recited the mother's words in a pitiful voice.

In spite of the mother's pleas, the daughter not only grabbed her sweater and headed out, but on the way to the door, she knocked her mother down, grabbed her purse, and took out her mother's hard-earned money to pay for the movie. Only imagine such a girl! The poor mother fell sobbing to the floor—which, by the way, she had scrubbed only that morning on her hands and knees, and without a bit of help from her daughter. Chelo paused. "May God forgive the child," she murmured, and crossed herself.

"And then?" I glanced at the hallway to let her know I didn't have all day. That last comment of hers had crossed the line.

At the cinema, Chelo said, the girl sat watching some horrible American movie with sinful gringas carrying on in their loud-mouthed and unfeminine ways (which a *real* man would never put up with, so they'd probably die single and alone). Just as the girl was imagining herself behaving as boldly as the gringas, her right hand—the very hand she'd smacked her mother with and the very hand that she'd stolen the money with—began to itch. The scratching released a horrible smell of sulfur. People around her began to make rude comments. She ran out into the lobby. Coarse black hairs sprouted from her palm, growing longer and longer right before her eyes. The stench of rotten eggs filled the air.

"The devil's own stink," Chelo said, her words coming faster, building. "A woman next to the girl pulled manicuring scissors out of her purse and cut off that hair." Her voice dropped, slowed, and she held my gaze. "But just imagine, cutting it only made it grow longer."

"Look," I said, and held up my palm. "Not one single hair."

"The devil and his punishments can take many forms."

"Those egg whites look dry," I said, and pointed to the bowl. "You beat them too long."

Before Chelo could answer, the shop door slammed from across the courtyard. Chelo sucked in her breath, and her forks lay quiet at the side of the bowl. We both waited. Grandmother's high heels clickety-clicked much harder than usual on the cement walkway as she walked toward the house.

"That's all for today," Chelo whispered. As if she needed to tell me. Chelo's stories were another bit of superstition that Grandmother and the Catholic Church didn't approve of.

Grandmother stomped down the hall past the kitchen muttering to herself about the stupidity of men, and something about a woman who behaved like an alley cat. The door of her bedroom opened, then shut.

"What woman is Grandmother talking about?" I whispered.

"¿Qué sé yo?" Chelo shrugged. She stood, said that before fixing the chiles rellenos, she needed to go to my mother's room and empty the dirty clothes hamper.

This seemed an odd time for laundry to me, but I didn't care enough to ask. I jumped up to rush away.

"Altagracia," Chelo called after me, "you forgot your magazine."

"Oh, maybe you should keep it," I said in my most innocent voice. "I don't want hairs to grow on my palms from reading about movie stars." Chelo muttered something about ingrates, but I just kept going.

In the courtyard, I stopped to pick a sprig of the fuchsia bougainvillea and tucked it behind my ear. Papi would be certain to make some comment about how pretty I looked—he always knew the right thing to say to women—and considering how everyone had been so mean to me, I needed some kind words.

When I entered the back of The Peacock Curios, I paused at the narrow closed door to the side. It opened into Papi's little art studio. I twisted the doorknob, hoping for once it might be unlocked. Just then a woman's voice drifted through the thin curtains separating the studio from the front store. Something about the way she laughed made gooseflesh pop out on my arms.

Papi answered the woman, his voice lower than usual, his laughter deeper. I tiptoed forward, and holding my breath, peeped through the space between the curtain panels. A hot draft blew in from the front and carried a whiff of a heavy floral perfume. I wrinkled my nose. Then it hit me. That's why the new smell in my mother's room had been familiar. It was the scent that the Widow Valencia brought with her when she came into our store to buy a box of almendrado candy or maybe some fine lace handkerchiefs. The Widow always wore lily-scented perfume and she always hummed songs of love.

Papi and the Widow leaned toward each other from either side of the glass counter, exchanging gazes like the characters in the graphic romance novels that some of the girls at the Rosary Academy passed around to read when the nuns weren't looking. Now the Widow arched her back, grinning like a cat that had just lapped up all the morning cream and left its family to drink their coffee bitter. I hated the Widow. Yet I was mesmerized by her, the way she tilted her head to one side and brought her black pony tail over her shoulder. She stroked the length of her hair in long, easy movements with fingers tipped in pointy coral-painted nails.

I thought of *Zorba*, a movie that Olga had retold to me about some crazy Greeks. The movie sounded so exciting and I'd wanted to go, but Grandmother said no because it was on the church's list of forbidden movies. Olga had described how the men in the village followed a proud widow with their eyes and how she held them in her power. They were jealous of her, both men and women, Olga said, because they couldn't control her. In the end, though, the townspeople had stoned the widow and finally slit her throat.

Maybe those Greeks weren't so crazy after all, I thought, as I studied the Widow Valencia. But I also had a fleeting image of myself as an Amazonlike woman, long-legged and muscular in my hot pants, being chased by long-skirted conformists waving broomsticks, yelling about preserving decency.

So taken by the images playing out both inside my head and in front of me, I didn't realize how far forward I'd been leaning. Suddenly I lost my balance and stumbled out.

Papi straightened and stared at me. His expression looked much like what I imagined my own must be when Grandmother caught me eating sweets before dinner. He quickly recovered and demanded, "Are you spying on your father, girl?"

"No, Papi." I glanced at the Widow, then back to my father. "Mamá says you should come home."

The Widow turned to leave, and Papi held out one hand as if to stop her. "Wait," he said, but she was already out of his reach. She glanced back over her shoulder and laughed softly, full lips parted.

Papi's eyes locked on hers as if he'd forgotten me, and when she turned and walked away, he followed the sway of her skirt as she swished out of the store. He continued to stare at the space her body once filled.

I grew dizzy and clamped my hands onto the edge of the counter. I remembered my mother telling me about the beaches at Veracruz, how she had loved to stand at the water's edge so that each lap of the ocean's waves pulled a bit more sand from beneath the soles of her feet. I had that same sensation that day, only, for that moment, the idea of the earth shifting beneath me, of the inevitability of change, didn't amuse me.

As if on cue, Mr. Durán, our part-time helper, arrived to take over for Papi. Minutes later, Papi and I walked toward the house, and the scent of the Widow's lily perfume followed us, lingering like a poisonous vapor. I coughed and made gagging noises.

Papi stopped and gazed down into my eyes. "Listen very carefully, Altagracia. Your mother is an emotional woman. Anything upsetting could cause her harm." He placed both his hands on my shoulders, pressed down, and my knees almost buckled beneath the weight.

"Mamá says," I began, but had to stop to lick my dry lips. "Mamá says to tell you she won't live without you." When I said the words, I remember the flash of contempt for Mamá's weakness. Why couldn't she be strong like the Widow?

"There. You see what I'm saying about your mother?" His eyes went soft. "For her, everything is a tragedy. You and I," he said, "we have a secret. Don't make your mother suffer. Understand?"

I nodded, and the bougainvillea blossom, loosened from my tumble in the store, fell from my hair. I stomped my foot, and with the heel of my shoe ground the petals onto the cement until they were nothing more than fuchsia-colored bruises. I wanted Papi to see what I had done. What he had done. But when I looked up, my father had already turned his back to me and continued on his way. Although I would always consider myself more in tune with my father than with my mother, at that moment I felt connected to her by an invisible yet strong thread.

That evening Papi went out, and by the faraway look in his eyes, I think we all knew that it would be a late night out for him again.

"Where are you going?" Grandmother asked, and he answered, "Nowhere, but I'd like to believe I could go anywhere." I imagined him in our shop van, peacock painted on the side, driving in ever widening circles.

I woke up around midnight, and after I'd made a trip to the bathroom at the end of the hall, I followed a soft aura of light coming from the living room. Grandmother sat in her rocking chair, pulled next to the large window facing the courtyard, the way she did when Papi went out. Those days, she'd been missing a lot of sleep.

The brilliance of the full moon filled the room, bathing her in a silvery glow. The moon shadows emphasized the lines running from nose to mouth, and with her head hanging and chin pressing inward, the skin beneath her jaw sagged and crumpled into the beginnings of loose skin. I crept back to my room, opened my windows wide, hoping that the noise of traffic, dogs barking, and the howl of coyotes from the hills beyond would keep me awake. I wanted to hear when Papi returned. I prayed, eyes open so as not to fall asleep, that I would find a way to maintain the sanctuary of our home, keep the family together. The leaves of the orange tree murmured, but I couldn't understand the message. But even if I had, could I have done anything at that point to undo the events that seemed hell-bent on reaching disaster?

I awoke to morning birdsong and a blast of orange-blossom-scented wind rushing down the narrow corridor of yard between my room and the cement block wall. I sat up so suddenly that my head ached. From the kitchen, the sound of running water and the clink of metal told me that Chelo was preparing the morning coffee.

For years I'd enjoyed serving my parents their first cup of the day, and now, as I hopped out of bed, I crossed myself three times and prayed to

God to *please, please* let Papi be lying next to Mamá. I wanted to promise God that if my wish were granted I'd become a nun, but honesty wouldn't allow such a fib. I settled for swearing that I'd never again laugh at my classmates' descriptions of the sisters who hid behind bushes in the alley, then jumped out and snatched passing students who hadn't been attending catechism regularly.

Minutes later in the kitchen, I found Grandmother sitting with her usually busy hands lying limp in her lap. She lifted her gaze when I entered, but the blue of her eyes was clouded and the soft flesh beneath them smudged. She reminded me of the way my friend Mercedes had looked after she'd finally lost her reign as chess champion at the academy.

My body went hot and itchy. "Buenos días," I said too brightly. Grandmother stared at me as if I were a spirit.

"Buenas," Chelo said. She'd arranged her face with careful neutrality, pretending she knew nothing about what was going on in the house.

I wanted to ask if Papi had come home, but said, "What's for breakfast?" At the stove I lifted the lid off a skillet and sniffed the warm vapor of chorizo with eggs. The three other burners were covered with a saucepan of coffee, a skillet of refried beans, and another of chilaquiles. Papi's favorite breakfast.

In our house, we all catered to Papi, and we were especially sensitive to his likes and dislikes when he was unhappy or perturbed. He was the sun around which the household revolved. It was he that we all looked to for approval, studying his face when he ate to see if the dish was prepared to his liking and watchful for the slightest change in expression that might indicate problems. Not enough salt? Or worse, too much? Did he want an extra chile? Would he take a second bite of the dish? A third? If he had to ask for something, then we women felt we had failed him. It was the way of our culture. (And maybe it still is today, but how can an outsider like me say?)

In return for our adulation, Papi protected our honor, kept us safe from physical harm, lightened our daily boredom with his contagious laughter. I imagined then that he never felt fear or uncertainty. In the years to come, I would often wish that I had had the opportunity to have a conversation with my father as one adult to another. What pressures he must have felt living in a house with three females who loved him as though he were God, responsible for their well-being, their happiness.

"While you dawdle," Grandmother said, "your father's coffee goes cold."

Then he *was* home. I couldn't stop myself from smiling and shifted my weight from foot to foot as Chelo poured coffee from a saucepan through a cloth colander and into two waiting cups. Papi preferred coffee prepared the old-fashioned way. I placed the cups on a small tray lacquered with large pink and red flowers, and in my excitement to see Papi, I grabbed at the sugar bowl. I righted the bowl but not without leaving a trail of white grains across the counter.

"Watch what you're doing," Grandmother said. "Do you think money grows on trees?"

Good, I thought, she's getting back to normal. Grandmother was notorious for keeping a close eye on every penny spent. Although Chelo did the cooking, it was Grandmother who decided on our daily menus, Grandmother who made out the lists for the daily market and had Chelo place the items on the table when she returned so each one could be checked off the list. No extras, no waste. I didn't concern myself with household worries back then. I didn't have to—Grandmother made certain that all ran smoothly.

In answer to my knock, Mamá called out for me to enter, but when I slipped into the familiar darkness it was Papi's presence I felt. But just in case my senses were playing tricks on me, I pushed the door open wider with my foot so that the rectangle of light cut across the full width of the bed. Bravo! Two forms lay curled beneath the covers. Each rolled to separate sides of the bed, but the way I saw it, the space between them wasn't so great that it couldn't be breached.

One arm reached out from Papi's side and switched on the small lamp on a side table. When I bent down to press my lips to his forehead, a whiff of the Widow's perfume made my head spin. I quickly opened the shutters. "Just smell that morning air," I said.

"Nothing like the stink of exhaust fumes to start the day," Papi said.

I started to laugh, but swallowed the sound mid-throat when I saw Papi's face, grim and determined. Determined to do what? He sat, back against the headboard, and held Mamá's cup as she pushed herself up and rubbed the sleep from her puffy eyes. From allergies, I told myself.

I remembered articles that I'd seen in women's magazines, both Mexican and American, advice columns that needled careless wives about forcing their husbands away from them and into the arms of other women who understood how to make a man happy. Get up before your husband, the writers advised, give yourself plenty of time to dress, groom your hair, and apply makeup. Never, ever allow your husband to see you in your natural state. I imagined Mamá standing next to the Widow Valencia, and the comparison froze my gut into icy knots.

Recently more articles were appearing about the liberation of women, and I'd heard about how women in America were burning their bras. I wondered if my father might not like a woman like that? Olga and I certainly found those women interesting. But I couldn't see my mother as a bra burner, and anyway I needed a quick plan for Mamá to fight for Papi and snatch him out of the Widow's pointy-nailed clutches.

"Why are you staring at me like that?" Mamá said, and brushed the loose hairs from her face behind her ears.

"You're so pretty, Mamá," I said. *Could* be, I thought.

"I need to get dressed." Papi shooed me with his hand. No time for jokes today.

I shot one last glance over my shoulder at Mamá, hoping that maybe she could read in my eyes that she needed to change before she lost the man of the house for all of us. She yawned, contorting her mouth to one side instead of covering with her hand. Like a baby bird waiting to be fed, to be cared for. I wanted to run back and hug her, protect her. Papi was giving me his impatient look, though, so I left. It didn't matter—a plan had popped into my head. How simple and innocent it seemed at the time. Who could have predicted the outcome?

Soon Papi and Grandmother left for the shop, and I hurried to the bathroom and in the cabinet beneath the sink, pushed aside rolls of toilet paper and stored bars of Palmolive soap and Colgate toothpaste. I pulled out the shoebox of Mamá's old makeup, bottles of foundation in shades of beige, darker for summer, lighter for winter; tubes of lipstick in every imaginable shade.

After Mamá had her breakfast—alone as usual—in the kitchen, I followed her back to her room. "What's the big mystery?" Mamá said, and I brought the box from around my back and dropped it on the foot of her bed. "Old makeup?" she asked.

"It's Papi's birthday in a week," I reminded her. "I know the best gift you could possibly give him." I hoped that the excitement in my voice would be contagious. I'd read in one of Olga's teen magazines that the way to be popular was to be a good listener and to speak with enthusiasm. I found the latter suggestion was the easier of the two.

"I already asked your grandmother to pick out a guayabera for him. One from Veracruz would be nice." Mamá's eyes shifted to the murals, so when I spoke I almost shouted in order to keep her mind from drifting.

"Anybody can give him a shirt." I pointed to the cosmetics. "I can make you look like a movie star."

So she couldn't interrupt, I talked fast and refused to acknowledge her hurt gaze. "And you don't have to worry about a new outfit." I threw open the door to her armoire. "Wait, wait, don't say anything." With a flourish I pulled out the white silk blouse Papi had given her last Christmas. "Ta-da."

"Please stop yelling." Mamá clapped her hands over her ears. "What's gotten into you?"

"Look," I said, and ran my fingers over the yellow orchid on the left shoulder of the blouse. "Grandmother embroidered this especially for you. You could wear it with this black skirt. And a pair of high heels." It had been at least three years since my mother had taken to wearing floppy sandals rather than the stiletto heels that made her size four-and-a-half feet appear even daintier.

"All this noise. You've given me a headache," Mamá said. "Go get a cool cloth from Chelo. And have her sprinkle it with lavender water."

"Papi likes to go out." I lowered my voice but spoke very slowly for emphasis. Mamá lifted her braid over her shoulder and studied the tips as if checking for split ends. The wind was picking up outside and in spite of all the noise from the surrounding downtown, I was certain I could pick out the rustle of each individual leaf on our orange trees. The wind was growing stronger. "Be his little canary again, Mamá."

I twisted the tube of pink up, down, swiped a swath of pink across the web of skin between thumb and forefinger the way I'd seen the clerks do. "The same color of the mouth in that orchid?" I pointed to the wall.

Mamá sank onto the bed. Staring straight ahead, she said in a feathery voice, "What do you really want to tell me?"

I opened another tube of lipstick.

"Why doesn't anyone in this house tell me the truth?"

Because you don't like it? I thought, but said, "It's only that, well, lots of women flirt with Papi." My vocal chords tightened, and the words came out in a squeak.

"And?" Her eyes had a strange sheen to them, a low fever working to the surface.

"Nothing, Mamita." I sat next to her, rested my face against her back. Thump, thump, beat her heart inside its cage of ribs.

"Altagracia, finish what you started. It has to do with that smell he's been bringing into this room, doesn't it?" She turned to me and placed her hands on either side of my face. "Don't treat me like a child."

I didn't want to tell her, but her voice was so tranquil, her attitude so much more practical than usual. Maybe she was stronger than we'd all thought. I remembered the promise I'd made to Papi, but the thought of life without him made my soul ache. I imagined my heart crying fat tears of blood.

"The Widow Valencia." My throat tightened again, but I went on. "I think maybe Papi goes out with her. See, the thing is, she and Papi are similar. That is, they like to be on the go." The blood had drained from my mother's face, and my tongue went thick. But I was determined to finish. "Well," I continued, "maybe they're going to go to that new restaurant by the perimeter? Very romantic, Olga hears. Lots of couples go there."

"What are you saying?" Mamá released my face but the dry heat of her palms remained on my cheeks.

"You could go instead of the Widow," I said. "You and Papi. You have to go in the van. But nothing will happen to you, you'll see. And at the Skylight they have dancing. Like you two used to do in Veracruz." I stroked the orchid on the blouse. "You'll be twice as pretty as the Widow."

"Have you seen your father with this Widow?"

I hesitated, and Mamá's eyes began to shift toward the murals. "Yes," I said quickly, before I could stop myself. "She comes to the shop."

"Lots of people do." Mamá's gaze remained on the murals.

Was she going to continue staring at those stupid paintings while the Widow pulled Papi deeper and deeper into her web? Soon he wouldn't be able to break free. I took a deep breath, leaned in toward Mamá, and after only a moment's hesitation, whispered, "I saw them kissing. Like in the movies. Papi and the Widow were kissing."

I could almost smell and see clouds of sulfur escaping from my mouth. Mamá made a strangling noise, and when she looked up at me her eyes burned fever-bright. I swallowed the sour liquid that oozed up from my stomach.

"It was a joke, Mamá." I giggled like one of those psycho killers in a horror move. "I say stupid things."

Mamá closed her eyes and pressed her hands to her temples. "Leave me," she said, and for once I was happy to obey.

In the days that followed, although Papi went out almost every evening, he didn't spend the night away. The morning after, Chelo would empty the clothes hamper and use plenty of the brown bar soap on his shirt when she scrubbed it on the cement washboard. But the Widow's scent lingered on.

Grandmother demanded to know what my problem was since I left most of my food on my plate. She said she could hear me call out with nightmares. I was surprised to know I'd actually slept long enough to dream. More than one night, I sat in a chair next to the wall adjoining that of my parents and listened for words of anger or accusation or denial. When would Mamá tell Papi what I'd said, and in the process expose me as a snitch and a liar? First, I prayed that Mamá could keep a secret better than me, then I wished she'd tell and get it over with.

"You haven't been to your mother's room in days. Why's that?" Grandmother asked.

"She hasn't called for me," I answered truthfully. I pretended that it had all been a bad dream—the Widow and Papi, my lie to Mamá.

Papi's birthday finally came and he, Grandmother, and I were sitting around the dining room table, the Tres leches cake in the center, waiting for Mamá to join us. Papi drummed his fingers softly on the table, and Grandmother kept lifting the edge of the tablecloth and inspecting the threads of crochet that she had woven herself. She'd started a bedspread for Papi and Mamá's bed and had wanted me to help, but after unraveling so many of my messy squares, we'd put my crocheting aside for a yet undetermined time.

I stared at the white cake sitting in its container of milk and wanted to suggest that we eat before the milk went bad, but knew that my perfectly practical suggestion would be taken for rudeness.

An unfamiliar *tippity-tap* of stilettos on tile sounded in the hall, heading toward us. Papi's fingers stilled, and Grandmother turned her blue and expectant gaze toward the doorway. After what seemed like forever, Mamá appeared in the doorway, tiny and trim in her silk blouse and straight black skirt (at least an inch above her knees, I noticed), dark hair pulled back tightly from her face in the ponytail I'd suggested. Her full lips were painted into a luscious heart. But how tiny she was; the Widow took up so much more space. Mamá walked toward Papi, and in spite of those skyscraper heels, her step was so light and airy that she didn't seem to be made of flesh and bone.

Papi jumped up from his seat, tipping his chair in his rush to meet her halfway. He put an arm around Mamá's waist, and as they walked he almost lifted her off her feet. When he gazed down into her face, I could see the love in his eyes. But it was different from the way he'd looked at the Widow. Except for that, everything was happening like I'd prayed. I *had* been right to lie to Mamá.

Grandmother joined us in telling Mamá how pretty she was. Mamá blushed and said thank you, but when she lifted her fork her hand trembled.

"Is something wrong, mi cielo?" Papi said. He hadn't called her his heaven in ages.

Mamá's voice shook as much as her hand when she finally answered. "I read in the newspaper about a new restaurant opening. The Skylight, I think. They have an orchestra for dancing, they say."

"Who is *they*?" Papi said. He glanced at me, his eyes fishy with suspicion.

"I don't know, maybe I heard it on the wind," Mamá said. I silently thanked the saints that Mamá *could* keep a secret.

"Remember how we used to go dancing, Salvador?" she said.

"It's a long drive to the Skylight." Papi shared a look with Grandmother, who turned down the corners of her mouth slightly and lifted her shoulders to indicate that she had no idea what was going on.

Mamá scooted her chair back. "Are you ready?" I could hear the fear in her voice. I looked up, and she held my gaze long enough to make Grandmother turn toward me with an arched eyebrow.

"Do you think that's a good idea, Orquídea?" Grandmother said. "What about your premonition about car accidents? Not that I believe in such things, but I don't understand how you can change so suddenly."

"Superstitious nonsense; you've said so yourself, Mother," Papi said. I wondered if Grandmother didn't believe in that *nonsense* more than she would admit. He stood and offered his arm to Mamá, and she clutched onto him so tightly her fingernails dug half moons into his skin.

"May I have this dance?" Papi laughed, and his large teeth flashed white.

"You're behind this, aren't you?" Grandmother demanded after they'd left. "Children should stay out of affairs they don't understand."

"¿Qué sé yo?" The words came out as noncommittally as if I were Chelo herself. "Everything will be fine, Grandmother," I said. "You'll see."

In her rocker by the window, Grandmother leaned back and waited.

I was in a fitful sleep, dreaming of a yellow orchid, pink mouth opened in silent scream, when a *bang-bang clang* from outside thankfully startled me awake. At first I was so confused that in the darkness I couldn't figure out which way my body was turned or from where exactly all the pounding came.

The sign, I thought. The large square of metal hung over our shop, and when the wind blew it swung and clanked like crazy. I loved that sign that Papi had painted with a peacock in bright iridescent colors. Those who looked closely at the tail feathers would detect that one of the eyes was actually a human eye. Grandmother's eye watching, watching. Always afraid that the wind would someday take the sign with it into the desert, in my half-sleep, I thought that my premonition had come true.

Finally I realized the noise came from the courtyard, the metal doors that kept us safe from the outside. Feet pattered out of the kitchen and down the hall. From the front room Grandmother called out for Chelo.

"Don't open without being certain of who it is," Grandmother said. I crept down the hall to the living room. Grandmother remained in her rocker, but she'd turned it to face the front entry. I took a seat on the sofa. Grandmother didn't seem to notice me; her blue eyes stared straight ahead.

Chelo returned with two policemen trailing behind her. A chill ran through my body, and I shivered. Grandmother clutched the armrests of her rocker. I think we both knew what they would say, but we listened without speaking for fate to play itself out.

The policeman, eyes fast on the hat in his hands, told us about the accident. A truck had run a red light just as Papi pulled out of the parking lot of the Skylight and smashed into the passenger side of the Peacock Curios van. The officer cleared his throat. "The van burst into flames. I'm sorry to say the woman was trapped inside—"

A short scream escaped from my throat. In the background, Chelo murmured prayers and careless words about fate and destiny.

"My son," Grandmother said. "Is he all right?"

At St. Joseph's Hospital they explained again how Papi's life had been saved when he was thrown free, but he was in a coma. Grandmother told the doctors that they were to spare no expense to save her son. Anything and everything must be done.

"Of course, señora," the doctor said. He cleared his throat and avoided her gaze. "But it never hurts to pray."

Later Grandmother and I stood on either side of Papi's hospital bed, and when she stared across his body at me, I trembled but could not unlock my gaze from hers. In one short moment, in the blue of Grandmother's eye, I understood what it felt like to be despised.

I burst out crying. I pressed Papi's hand to my lips. "It's not my fault," I said between sobs. "It's not my fault."

"Control yourself, remember who you are. There's no point in blame, in regrets," Grandmother said. "What is, *is*. We adapt. Life goes on." Tears filled her eyes, and the blue had never shone so brightly.

I was afraid that no one could survive the grief I saw in her eyes. "Don't leave me," I said. But I think deep in my heart I understood that she already had.

FOUR

Altagracia, Altagracia, come out from wherever you are." Grandmother's words echoed off the walls and floors of our nearly-emptied house. From the tiled hallway, her footfall *clickety-clicked* (but not so sharply or with such confidence as before the accident last year) toward my parents' bedroom.

"Don't make me tell you again," Grandmother called.

I scooted back farther beneath the brass bed, pulling my arms and legs into a fetal position. Let her tell me a thousand times. I would not budge. Hiding under the bed was silly and childish, I knew, but in spite of all the schemes I'd come up with to keep us fed, last night Grandmother had come up with a plan of her own that shattered what was left of life as I'd known it: We were destitute, she said, her health was getting worse; she was going to send me away to live in the United States with an americana.

None of that, Grandmother said, when I had wailed in protest. Things will get better, I said, repeating what I had already told her hundreds of times. She answered that survivors were defined by their ability to accommodate to their circumstances, and that meant facing reality head on. After the accident, Papi had lain in a coma for eight months. Then, in spite of all the lit candles and prayers and costly medical procedures, he abandoned us. We buried him alongside Mamá at Lourdes Cemetery beneath a statue of St. Michael the Archangel. The day of the burial, Grandmother pointed to the empty space between my father and the graveled path that serpentined through the cemetery. My final resting place, she said.

And me? I said.

You'll have your own family someday. She batted her hand, as if my concerns were no more than pesky flies.

I understood why Grandmother hated me. She'd never demanded that I confess my part in the accident, but she knew that somehow I'd been behind Mamá's miraculous change of mind about car rides. The unspoken lay between us, an abscess that would not heal. I wanted to argue that Mamá had always feared dying in a car accident, so didn't that suggest that it was her destiny? Could anyone fight fate? It seemed to me that parallels, although wobbly, existed between my part in the fatal accident and Judas's role in the death of Christ. Why should Judas be hated for doing what he was destined to do? For helping Jesus fulfill *his* destiny? I had asked Sister Encarnación that same question once, long before the fall of my family, but the ruler-smack the nun gave me on the palm of my hand taught me to keep my unholy questions to myself.

But now Judas's predicament came back to haunt me. I thought about bringing this up with Grandmother, telling her that at least I did what I did out of love, not silver. But I sensed that suggesting that my father's slow and arduous death was his destiny was not the way to convince her of my innocence. And part of it, I think, was that I didn't want Grandmother to forgive me; I couldn't forgive myself. For months I'd even avoided my reflection in mirrors.

During those months of Papi's coma, Grandmother was usually by his side or with the doctors and nurses, insisting they try yet another treatment. At first, I wasn't alone in the house because I still had Chelo. But Grandmother had insisted Chelo go away when we could no longer afford to pay her. Make use of your seamstress training, Grandmother told her. Finally Chelo packed the scratchy hemp bags she'd brought with her from her village, and after holding me in a long hug that smelled of flour tortillas and cooking oil, she walked out of our lives. I don't know if I imagined it, but although her eyes were sad, her sigh seemed tinged with a relief of some sort.

By the time Papi died, inventory at The Peacock Curios had dwindled to nearly nothing. Grandmother and I spent most of our time in the house behind the locked blue door (so much for blue keeping out evil spirits). All that remained inside were the kerosene burner, my parents' brass bed, Grandmother's cane rocker, and Papi's paintings. Grandmother and I slept in the bed, I on Mamá's side and she on Papi's, her face buried in his pillow, hand clutching the gold locket she couldn't bear to part with.

Truth is, I think that after Papi died, Grandmother expected that she would lie down on that mattress and fall into his lingering scent, never to rise again. Life, I was learning, wasn't like in the romantic movies I used to like so much, the ones where the broken-hearted died still beautiful and so easily. In spite of Grandmother's dire predictions about our future, I believed that our situation would improve because really, how much worse could things get? But no matter how much I tried to convince her things would get better, Grandmother had no more interest in the shop, and anyway, there was no money to restock the shelves. She began selling off pieces of jewelry across the line to Youngo's Treasures, and furniture to Soto's Used Furniture until we had nothing left of any real value but the nearly empty buildings of the shop and house. We'd even sold the gas stove, and now cooked on a one-burner kerosene camping stove.

Not that we had much to cook. Our pantry held nothing but beans and rice. I went to work, in a manner of speaking. I walked the streets with my eyes down, scouring the sidewalks and gutters for odds and ends that I might clean up and sell: throwaway magazines that could be kept in bathrooms for reading, then wiping; pieces of cardboard and strips of rags that could be turned into play sandals for poor kids; cast-off tubes of lipstick, waxy contents worked out with a wooden matchstick and pressed into tiny jars; scraps of materials hand-sewn into doll clothes, decorated with my rough embroidery.

I walked door to door selling my wares. I never apologized for my products, for without articulating the thought, I understood the appreciation that Mexicans have for creativity and ingenuity. I made trips to the butcher and asked for scraps of fat and entrails for my dog, talked the vegetable stall man into giving me a few rotten vegetables for my chickens. I thought I had them fooled, but in retrospect, I appreciate that they offered charity while allowing me my pride.

When I came home with the pennies I earned for my creations or newspaper cones filled with scraps, Grandmother asked few questions. I began to understand how quickly she could turn away those blue eyes from seeing what she didn't want to see. I would say simply that I had found pennies in an empty lot near the house and had bought the food at a cut rate. Eventually

I became overconfident and forced Grandmother to confront her delusion. It was a mistake.

I'd been out in the alley when I saw old Mrs. Rubio throw a small box into her trash can. As soon as she went back inside her house, I slunk along the wall. A not-quite empty carton of raspberry sherbet sat on top of the waste. I reasoned that I wasn't really eating garbage. The carton protected the sherbet from the slop around it, and I'd snatched it away before even one single fly had a chance to land. In our kitchen, I was slurping the sherbet with a spoon, vaguely wondering why the purplish ice was foamy, when Grandmother walked in. She slapped the back of my head so hard the carton flew from my hands. She'd never hit me before, and I don't know which one of us was more shocked. Her eyes filled with tears. The only other time I had ever seen my grandmother cry was when my father died.

We aren't beggars, she said. Remember who you are.

Later that night I awoke with grinding stomach cramps. I vomited until only bile came up. Even now the sight or smell of sherbet turns my stomach. I blamed Grandmother for my sickness, as if her catching me eating the sherbet had somehow turned it bad. Even then I understood that my thought process was flawed, but her knowledge of my behavior made it all the more real, and both she and I were ashamed.

The next day, I picked up an old magazine and headed to the outside where Grandmother sat in her rocking chair. I leaned against the outside wall where she could see me from her peripheral vision. With long exaggerated movements, I ripped slick pages from the magazine, pictures of food—juicy steaks and French fried potatoes; crispy salads with creamy dressings; cookies and cupcakes of all sorts. I studied each picture, muttered what it was under my breath, "Hmm, cake" or "Yummy, taquitos." What good would my little melodrama be if she didn't understand? I pretended I hadn't noticed her presence, and she pretended to be lost in thought. I tore off bits of paper, placed them on my tongue the way the priest did with the Host. The paper did not dissolve. I chewed slowly, making smacking noises and rubbing circles on my tummy with one hand. I still can't say what made me indulge in such silliness. Maybe I wanted to hurt her. Maybe I wanted to show her that I had an infinite capacity for games of pretense. Who knows? But reasons aside, I believe that my behavior that day may have helped seal my fate. That night Grandmother told me about her plan to send me away with an americana.

The dust beneath the bed tickled the inside of my nose, and I held my breath to keep a sneeze from escaping. Grandmother stood at the side of the bed now, her once polished shoes pointing scuffed toes toward me. "Why are you being stubborn?" Grandmother said.

As if I'd ever obeyed without a struggle. When her feet didn't budge, I prayed that God would strike her with compassion. Or at least good sense. My head was beginning to ache from the dust. Grandmother's feet stood steady. I slid out, and Grandmother lowered herself to the edge of the bed, patted the space next to her.

"What kind of grandmother sends her only granddaughter away to a foreign country with a perfect stranger?" I demanded.

"The kind that cares about her granddaughter's welfare," she answered quickly, as if she'd already prepared an answer to an anticipated question. She told me we needed to talk, then began rambling about things I'd heard before. She rehashed our trials of the past year and said she was broken spiritually and financially and physically. She was, she said, dying.

"No, you're not," I said the way I always did when she brought up her supposedly imminent death.

She asked me if I knew who Mr. Genaro was, but before I could answer she explained that he owned Los Tres Cochinitos restaurant. I nodded and tried not to make a face. I hated even thinking about that man with his bulging green eyes and hoglike head and neck (how appropriate that his restaurant should be named The Three Little Pigs). On my way home from school, now the public Obregón Secondary rather than the private Rosary Academy, he often stood in the doorway of his restaurant when school let out so he could watch us girls pass by.

Mr. Genaro, Grandmother said, a respectable businessman, had heard of our situation. He had a friend, a Mrs. Smith who wanted to provide a home in Chicago for a deserving young girl, someone educated and refined but down on her luck and in need of some help.

When I tried to speak, Grandmother held up one hand to stop me, her words tumbling out, tripping over one another. Mr. Smith had passed away, and now Mrs. Smith was the sole provider for her two little children and needed a companion to stay with them while their mother worked. An English-speaker was preferred, so someone—lucky for me—who'd been educated in a bilingual school would be ideal. This companion would be well provided for with a good home and nice clothing. And eventually a college education.

"You'll have many opportunities in the United States," Grandmother said. "You'll go as far there as you would have here. Farther even. Doesn't half of Mexico dream of going to the United States?" She sighed. "A pretty girl like you begging, only imagine what would happen to you."

I pictured Mr. Genaro and the way his eyes lingered on the private parts of my body. "What about you?" I said. "How will you survive?"

"I don't have long to worry."

"You're *not* dying." I couldn't understand how she was willing to give up the battle.

At the curb in front of The Three Little Pigs, a new car's silver paint sparkled in the first glimmer of dawn. Ragged street urchins huddled at the front and back bumpers, guarding the car for a few pennies from the owner. The front door of the restaurant opened even before we knocked, as if Mr. Genaro had been waiting for us at the plate glass window. He shook a fist and yelled at the boys that they'd better not touch anything, then waved Grandmother and me in. Once she passed, her back to him, he stroked my hair with a greasy hand that smelled of chorizo. I ducked my head.

"Mrs. Smith," Mr. Genaro said. His massive head bobbed as he introduced us to the woman who sat at one of the square tables draped with floral-patterned oilcloth. She was dressed casually but expensively in a sleeveless white blouse and shorts that showed off her long tanned legs. I don't know for certain what I'd been expecting, maybe something like the witch from fairy tales, but this woman had no humped back, pickle chin, or even one single mole on her face. I didn't care how pretty or how nice she might be, I wasn't going anywhere with her.

I shook hands with Mrs. Smith, and she looked directly into my eyes, all the while squeezing with a grip as strong as a man's. In heavily accented Spanish, she repeated what Mr. Genaro had already explained to Grandmother about why she needed someone at home.

"Don't you worry about a thing, doña Paz," she said. "We'll be in touch, just like I promised." She pressed a folded paper into Grandmother's hand. "Here's my address in Chicago."

"Thank you," Grandmother whispered, and slipped the paper into the purse that she'd been clutching in both hands.

Mrs. Smith lifted a rectangular piece of cardboard off the table and held it up for Mr. Genaro to read. "Look what I've been preparing," she said softly, as if not to disturb Grandmother. After he silently read the words, he laughed so hard that his round cheeks pressed up against his eyes, molding them into green moon-slivers. I couldn't read the placard from my position and would only later understand his laughter.

Mrs. Smith took hold of my wrist as if to leave. No matter how much I twisted my arm back and forth, I couldn't pull free, so I stuck out my tongue at her. "Spirited little cuss, aren't you?" she said, and smiled in a way that almost made me go limp.

"Grandmother?" I said, but Grandmother studied the clasp of her purse, closed and opened it once, twice, three times.

"Now, now, none of that," Mr. Genaro said. "Don't make things difficult for your poor grandmother." He circled my upper arm with his fingers, squeezing until my flesh turned splotchy white and red.

Mrs. Smith tapped the face of her wristwatch, and with no further warning, grabbed my other arm. I pressed all my weight down into my feet, as if I could take root, but they dragged me out onto the sidewalk. "Grandmother?" I twisted my head to look over my shoulder.

The lines of Grandmother's face had fallen into a mask of formality. "Adapt, Altagracia," she said. She stared straight ahead at something above and beyond all of us. Her pupils were shrinking, constricting to the brightness of the rising sun, losing themselves in the irises of peacock blue. At the centers, black pinpoints. Too small for a memory of me to squeeze through? The thought weakened me, and with a push and shove, I was inside the car and the door slammed behind me.

While Mrs. Smith scurried around the car to the get into the driver's side, I reached for the handle. It had been removed. I pounded on the window. "Let me out of this car," I shrieked. Outside, the urchins stared at me from a distance. I'd always pitied those dirty children who roamed the streets of Mesquite. They'd never seemed quite real to me, not even during the year of our fall. I had a home, after all, a grandmother who would soon come to her senses and help us pull ourselves back up to our former position. Now, they laughed, a harsh sound that didn't seem it could be coming from children. I pounded again. "Grandmother, Grandmother!" I called, but she had already turned, her stiff back to me as she walked away.

"You see," Mrs. Smith said, as if reading my thoughts, "she's already getting on with her life." I turned to face the americana, and she grinned. "You should do the same. If you're a smart girl. You wouldn't want her to back out on a deal, would you?" Her words were soppy with sarcasm, then suddenly her face hardened and she said, "That good ol' boy Genaro won't like somebody backing out on him. Not one damn bit."

The last sentence had been cold enough to quiet me. I pressed the soles of my shoes against the floor of the car, as if I could put on the brakes. I hated Grandmother. I wanted to be with Grandmother. I hated her. But I couldn't allow harm to come to her. I had to think. *Adapt*, Grandmother had said. At least I could give the impression of adapting.

When I slid back and pressed against the passenger seat of the Volvo, my feet lifted off the car floor and the frayed hem of my school-plaid skirt inched above the perpetual tan line on my legs, exposing an expanse of thigh so pale that the brown knee and calf appeared to be an artificial appendage stuck on with no regard for harmony. I considered pulling down the skirt, but my hands, tightly clasped in my lap, refused to release their hold on one another. Who else *was* there now?

In the American Midwest the suntan that had never completely disappeared while I lived in the Sonoran Desert would fade over the course of the winter and remind me that I was no longer who I had been. But that day years ago riding in that Volvo, I had only the scantiest classroom knowledge of a U.S. city called Chicago—for I believed that to be my destination—and no inkling of the paleness that awaited me.

As the car inched toward the border crossing from Mexico into the United States, Mrs. Smith instructed me to call her Molly Carol.

"What're you staring at?" she demanded when I didn't answer.

I shrugged.

"If you want to stare at something, look at this." Molly Carol pointed to her own pretty face. Then rearranged it. The muscles slackened, eyelids drooped, lower jaw dropped, drawing the mouth slightly open. "Now, you do it," she said, laughing as if it were all a game.

I turned away, shook my head no. Molly Carol grabbed my arm, squeezed with her fingers that were almost as strong as Genaro's.

"Now you," she repeated.

Let her break my arm. I refused to wear that expression of the feeble-minded. I turned to face the windshield. Yards beyond, the customs officer waved another vehicle across the border into the U.S. Three cars to go. I could scream. Molly Carol wouldn't want to draw attention, have people ask questions and discover the Mexican kid she was smuggling in. I could break away, jump out, run back to my home. But I couldn't, of course. Grandmother had given me away. Only because she *had* to, I quickly reminded myself. I would repeat this thought many times in the years to come.

My eyes locked with Molly Carol's. The muscles of my stomach tightened while the muscles of my face relaxed, then froze into the expression I would wear for the border guards. Molly Carol reached under the seat, pulled out the white placard with twine attached that she'd brought with her from the restaurant. She hung it around my neck. I bowed my head, lowered my chin into the hollow of my neck, and read the upside down in English: *I'm retarded and can't understand or speak. Thank you for your consideration.*

The Volvo snailed forward. Molly Carol pressed one finger to her lips reminding me to remain silent. "Understand?"

I understood. With my auburn hair and European facial features, the border officials, when they glanced into the car, would not question that I could be Molly Carol's daughter. Not unless, of course, they engaged me in a conversation intended to test my accent and knowledge of the U.S. With the sign, I wouldn't be expected to answer correctly.

"This is not necessary," I said in English, enunciating each word carefully to let her see why I'd taken honors in English at the academy. "I can speak with the guard."

Molly Carol laughed. "Sorry, kid. You might fool a Mexican but not a gringo."

Even before the guard peered into the Volvo, Molly Carol said, "Whew. Another scorcher today. Oh, guess you want to know who I am. Molly Carol Sloan, American citizen. Got a long trip ahead of us. Heading home to Ohio."

Sloan? Ohio? Chicago was in Illinois, not Ohio; that much I knew.

"Both of you?" The guard glanced at me.

I stared hard at him, tried to tell him with my eyes that I didn't belong inside this car, that my home was south of the border, not north. At the same time, I tried to not think about what I would do, where I could go, if he *did* detain us.

"Yep. Me and Grace. My daughter." Molly Carol poked my shoulder until I shifted around, allowing the man full view of the placard. "Not much of a talker, as you can see." Molly Carol smiled.

"Christ. Real nice, lady." The guard pulled back as if the car suddenly smelled bad. "Takes all kinds," he muttered as we pulled away.

I twisted in my seat to take one last look at the Mexican Mesquite, and Molly Carol snapped, "No point in looking back. Keep your eyes forward."

Adapt.

"Know what your problem is?" she said. Molly Carol, I would learn, seldom asked questions that she wasn't prepared to answer herself. "By God," she said, "I've seen types like you and your snooty grandma. Think you're special, that's what it is. Well, don't *even* think you're better than this old girl."

At the time I was surprised by Molly Carol's assessment. After all, Grandmother and I now had nothing, and she was a well-off americana, but later I would learn that my new benefactor's sophisticated façade covered an insecure woman who assumed that if she felt inferior to others then it followed that they must feel superior to her. So sensitive about growing up trailer-park poor, Molly Carol scoured pictures in magazines to re-create her childhood and discover her current tastes in clothing, décor, and to define future goals. Her grammar and vocabulary, I would learn, was a work in progress. There would be days when, in spite of myself, I pitied Molly Carol when she pretended to actually be the woman she'd made up from bits of slick marketing.

How could I know then that it would not be long before I myself learned the value, the necessity of re-creating self?

CREATING
GRACE

FIVE

Once we'd crossed the border, Molly Carol sucked her teeth and focused on her driving. I felt invisible enough to lift the sign from around my neck and return it beneath the seat. Not wanting to give Molly Carol the satisfaction of seeing me cry, I pinched the bridge of my nose and opened my eyes wide. I gazed at the far mountains. Papi had always loved the mountains, said they held the promise of surprise and adventure. You never knew what lay beyond.

Inside the U.S. Mesquite, we stopped at a red light, and Molly Carol studied a group of young Americans on the sidewalk, strolling toward the Mexican border. One of them kept poking her open palm at passersby, apparently asking for spare change. "Phony-ass hippies," Molly Carol said. "Playacting at being poor folks with their raggedy clothes." She spoke in English now and would do so for the rest of the trip. Once the light turned to green, Molly Carol yelled out the open window, "I hope to hell somebody drops a pile of shit in your gimme-gimme hand."

Her vulgar language and bad manners shocked me, but I already knew better than to say as much. I turned my thoughts to what I'd left behind, to Grandmother and how she'd wanted to protect me from having to beg. But before I knew it, an unexpected image formed: Grandmother huddled against the outside wall of the Mesquite Catholic church, taking her place next to the old Yaqui woman who covered her face with a rebozo, protecting the hole where a nose should have been, as she begged from the more fortunate. By the

Yaqui's side, the once aloof doña Paz, wrapped in a black lace mantilla from better times, stretched out her hand and whispered to passersby, "Alms for the poor, alms for the poor." Some kind soul might look down and actually *see* the pretty woman begging for charity. Maybe they'd admire the amazing blue of her eyes and drop an extra coin in her palm.

Would I ever see my grandmother again? Who knew what bogus address was on the paper Molly Carol had given Grandmother along with the fake name of Smith. What other lies had she told? I'll find a way, I swore to myself. I'd find work and make lots of money—isn't that what people did when they left for the U.S.? I'd send some of that money home to Grandmother, and then when I was rich, I'd fly back to Mesquite and set us up in a family business again.

Once we were on the outskirts of Mesquite, the wind howled off the mountains and blew across the Sonoran Desert. Molly Carol eased the car off the road onto the sandy shoulder just as a dirt devil whirled toward us. The tiny tornado of grit broke, *ping-ping*, onto the nose of the car. Molly Carol flipped her middle finger at the wind.

I wanted to laugh, but her mouth was twisted in anger, and I knew she wasn't ready to see the humor in an adult acting like a bratty kid.

"Hand me my driving gloves," she said, and pointed to the dash compartment. She worked the supple leather onto her hands, as if it were important that each finger fit just so. Next she adjusted her seat and the rear view mirror. Although Molly Carol's studied behavior—as if she were an actress in front of a camera—would eventually become commonplace to me, during those first observations I almost held my breath waiting to see what she would do next.

"OK, let's get something straight right from the get-go," she said.

Get-go, another word that hadn't been on the vocabulary list in Sister Augusta's English class at the academy. Sister Augusta, who had grown up in the United States, said that she spoke to us in everyday English, but I suspect Sister spoke the English of classroom teachers. Sister Augusta had always encouraged us to do crossword puzzles to expand our vocabulary, and now, for the first time, I was prepared to take her advice. But as far as understanding Molly Carol, I would have to watch her gestures and facial expressions and pay attention to context. In the days ahead of us, my English vernacular vocabulary would increase dramatically, but in the beginning I developed headaches from the strain of trying to keep track of the ongoing conversation while trying to decipher the meanings of idiomatic expressions.

Molly Carol held up a finger (not the middle one this time). "I, *I* make the rules. Not you. *I* do the thinking. Not you. Get it?"

She could make all the rules she wanted. Getting me to follow them was another matter. I almost tossed back my hair the way I would at home, but I suspected Molly Carol wasn't the type to merely sigh in the face of impertinence or to be satisfied telling me a story about ungrateful, disobedient girls. In the depths of my brain, a little light flashed: *La Verdad, La Verdad.* A Mesquite newspaper by that name featured sensational tales with lurid details of sex and crime, the pain captured in accompanying grainy photos. I wasn't allowed to read the newspaper, but I managed to pilfer Chelo's copy more than once. In *La Verdad*, there were also many accounts of Mexicans crossing illegally into the United States. No stories of dreams-come-true, but rather horrors about individuals forced into slavery of all sorts, domestic, sex, workplace; individuals exploited by gringos and fellow Mexicans alike. A paper called *The Truth* would not lie. I'd have to be careful when I finally broke away from Molly Carol and struck out to make my fortune. I'd have to bide my time.

"I understand," I said.

Molly Carol instructed me that on the trip I was not to speak to even one single solitary person without her permission, that she would be saying anything that needed saying. She said that if I did speak, I'd be wearing my special sign again. If I tried to run, she'd call immigration and tell them that she'd found me hiding in the back of her trunk. Must have slipped in when she was getting the car washed. She hated to think what would happen to me once they threw a good-looking kid like me behind bars with a bunch of hardened criminals. "And it won't matter," she said, "if the other cons are Mexican. A con's a con. They'll do things to you, you never even dreamt of, girlie."

In the distance a saguaro, a grandfather with four arms, towered above the other cactuses. I wished it had been a few weeks later in the season so that the buds sprouting at the tops of his arms would be opened in waxy white fingers. Blossoms. When Grandmother and I had left the house that morning, I hadn't even paused to take one last look at the twin orange trees in the courtyard. I now thought of Chelo claiming that the branches snagged lost spirits. Had my parents sighed, whispered something to me as I walked away from my home forever? Outside the car, the wind howled. Was anyone trying to speak to me now?

During that first day on the road, Molly Carol stopped only for gasoline, bathroom breaks, and food. At fast-food restaurants, she ordered, and if I opened my mouth, she shut me up with a dead-eyed glare. Once at McDonald's, after we'd finished our burgers and I started to the bathroom, she jumped up from her seat to follow me. Too tired to hold back, I asked her if she really thought I was dumb enough to take off into Gringolandia without so much as a *clue* to where I was.

The corner of one of Molly Carol's eyes tightened but she said nothing. Not yet. When we returned to the car, she made certain our doors were shut and locked. Her arm shot out as fast as any rattlesnake. Her hand clamped across my lower face, palm smothering my mouth, fingers locking onto my jaw.

"Don't you ever, ever smart off at me." Her face was so close to mine, spit sprayed my eyes. "Understand?" She squeezed my jaw.

My throat tightened and I couldn't speak. I nodded, swallowed hard, pushing a chunk of pride down my throat. Hours later, I was beginning to think she wasn't going to stop for the night, but Molly Carol rubbed the muscles at the back of her neck and said we'd find a motel near Albuquerque. She started humming, as if she couldn't contain the song a moment more; she opened her mouth and released one of the sweetest voices I'd ever heard. Somebody in the song was waiting for a man called Danny Boy to return, but from what I could understand Danny Boy wasn't coming back alive. As much as I commanded myself to not cry, tears brimmed my eyes. What if I, like Danny Boy, never returned alive to Mesquite? Would Grandmother grieve for me? Would she allow me a space next to her and my parents?

Thirty minutes later, Molly Carol left the main highway and pulled into a ranch-style motel. MABEL'S AUTO-TEL, the neon sign had once advertised, but the *M* and *s* were burned out. After we'd showered, Molly Carol flipped on the television to *The Waltons* but didn't seem to be paying any more attention to the program than I was. "Here's the deal," she said during a commercial, and went over the story she would tell to others once we arrived in Cogstown, Ohio. I was to be her niece from Texas. My mother had been Mexican, my father American. Molly Carol had rescued me from going to an orphanage.

"And don't you worry," she said, "I'll be getting all the documents to prove it. Piece o' cake."

She told me about her nine-year-old twins, Holly and Travis. "Ever see a movie called *Breakfast at Tiffany's*? That Holly Golightly, she was a real go-getter.

Nobody but nobody could hold her back. Holly knew what she wanted and *boom*." Molly Carol punched her fist into an open palm. "I thought about naming Holly Audrey—like the girl that played the part? But I like how Holly rhymes with Molly. Get it?"

I'd have to be pretty dumb not to, but I kept my thoughts to myself, and nodded.

"You'll be looking after the twins, of course."

"Of course," I said. The corner of Molly Carol's eye tightened, and I smiled so as to erase the hard edge on my words. In addition to caring for the twins, she said, I would be cooking the meals and keeping house. Chelo, I thought, I was going to become Chelo. At least it wasn't as bad as the scenes of torture and murder that had been running through my mind.

"And school for me?" I asked, although I pretty much knew the answer. "You told Grandmother that—"

"I don't need you to tell me what I *told* any damn body, Miss High and Mighty. I never graduated from high school, and it's not hurt me one bit. I'm just as good as any muckity-muck."

I lowered my eyes. No point in getting her upset. I guess I appeared appropriately contrite, because Molly Carol moved onto the topic of her seventy-five-year-old house with three bedrooms, dining room, parlor, and huge kitchen. She described five acres dotted with trees, some for shade, others for their walnuts, apples, and cherries, and I wondered if I would also be expected to be a picker. Well, if she thought I'd be around for picking time, she'd better think again.

Later I would remember little of the trip to Ohio. After Albuquerque, my mind became a sort of whirlpool, everything around me being taken in, sucked up, spinning around and around in a downward spiral, like I would soon disappear down a drain. New Mexico, Texas, Oklahoma, Kansas, a jumble of asphalt highways, roaring semi trucks, ranch-style motels. Along the way the mountains began to disappear, and the stretched-out flatness of the land seemed to go on forever. I tried to tell myself that it was a good thing: the flatness allowed me to see where I was headed.

On Interstate 44, as we neared St. Louis, Molly Carol pulled off for gasoline. I'd never seen so many people of African descent together in one place. I studied their shades of skin, varying from almond to café au lait to mocha to chocolate. Many of the young, both male and female, wore their hair in huge puffs that went well with their bold eyes. *I'm Black and I'm Proud*, read one tee shirt. Defense and offense in one, like admitting they were up against something and were determined to overcome.

Late into the night of the fourth day, the two vertical lines between Molly Carol's eyebrows relaxed, and I sensed we were nearing our final destination. For miles we'd been driving past farms with acres and acres of land. Then in the near distance, an oasis of light, a convenience store, appeared at the side of the road. Just beyond, a field of lights twinkled in the darkness. Molly Carol veered the Volvo sharply onto a dirt lane between the store and the field of lights that turned out to be rows and rows of house trailers. A few shone shiny and new like the caravans driven by retired gringos on road trips through Mexico. But these were mostly rusty, and some had so many contraptions built on and around them that I understood the occupants were not planning on going anywhere.

Within moments, Molly Carol pulled alongside one of the trailers. Had she lied about the house she lived in, too? A bug-splattered light bulb glared yellow over the front door. A wooden lattice had been added onto the front of the trailer and vines of plastic leaves with bunches of frosted grapes interwove through the top and sides. In the right section of the yard, metal chairs with backs in the shape of scalloped seashells were pulled up to a table that looked like a giant empty spool of thread. At the center of the table a planter, a pig of bubble-gum pink, reflector sunglasses taped to his head, lay on his side, hoof on hip, hind legs crossed at trim ankles. Bouquets of silk sunflowers sprouted from his open side.

"Jesus H. Christ," Molly Carol muttered when she spotted the pig.

The decorated yard reminded me of some of the poorer neighbors that Papi had driven past on our Sunday drives back in Mesquite. The families had worked to make their humble homes pretty and welcoming. For the first time in days, I smiled. It occurred to me that it was wonderful the way people could create their own beauty from what was available to them. Looking back, I don't think it occurred to me, at least not consciously, that I might be recognizing a skill that I would have to learn myself.

Molly Carol poked me in the back, nudging me along the path of cement blocks leading to the lower steps of the trailer door. She knocked on the door, and a hoarse voice said from the inside, "You'll wake my husband up."

"Good trick, considering Harley's been dead for over twelve years now," Molly Carol said. For the first time since we'd met, her laughter rang true. She glanced back at me. "Ol' Vi's convinced somebody's just dying to rape her skinny carcass."

The door opened and the stink of cigarette rolled out. "You'll be the death of me yet, Sissy," the woman said. Older than Molly Carol, the trailer lady's complexion was grainy with loose skin rather than tanned and taut, but both women had delicate jaws and small, pointy noses. The stranger wore a housecoat and shower thongs that revealed nails so ingrown that the edges nearly met where they pinched the flesh of her big toes. I could almost feel her pain.

"Well, it's great to see you, too, Vi," Molly Carol said. "Oh, and I love the pig." She exaggerated a smirk just to make sure we got the sarcasm.

"I'm plain folks, Sissy. Don't claim to be better than who I am. Not like some I could name."

"Well, *excuse* me and let me live," Molly Carol said. "And being you're so plain and good, maybe you could let us in."

"I'm Violet," the woman said once we filed inside, and made a point of looking at me rather than her sister. "Sissy here calls me Vi, and I'll answer to that, too."

"Violet," I said, because it sounded similar to the Spanish *Violeta*. I dabbed at my upper lip with the back of my wrist. The tiny trailer was sticky and warm and smelled of dirty ashtray, and my head felt tight from trying to understand Violet's unfamiliar accent. An accent that I would notice Molly Carol often fell into when speaking with her sister.

"The twins is sleeping," Violet said to Molly Carol. With her chin, she gestured down the short path running from the living room area through the kitchen and to a closed door at the other end of the trailer. Violet wrapped an arm around my waist, and her grip was as strong as her sister's. She led me the few steps to a sofa that she referred to as a *couch,* another new word for me.

"Make yourself to home," Violet said. "How about a glass of Kool-Aid? Made another pitcherful for the twins—cherry's their favorite—not more than an hour ago." As she spoke, Violet pulled two glasses from a shelf over the sink then turned around and in a few steps was at the tiny refrigerator. Violet handed me and Molly Carol each a glass, then picked up the box-pack

of Salems sitting between an overflowing metal ashtray and a Bible with a
worn black cover. She tapped out a cigarette and lit it with a disposable lighter.

With a bony hand, Violet batted at the cloud of smoke lingering around
her face. "Well, seems Sissy isn't going to introduce you, so what's your name,
sweetie?" The softness in her voice matched the kindness (or was it resignation?)
in her eyes. Big and brown, they almost overwhelmed her fragile face. An old
and human version of Bambi, that's what she looked like.

"Altagracia," I said.

"How's that?" Molly Carol made little circles with her glass so that the
ice clinked against the sides.

"Grace," I whispered. I used the memory of Chelo's neutral expression as
a model to keep my own face impenetrable. I remembered how much it used
to irritate me when Chelo would wear that mask.

Violet turned to Molly Carol. "Why, she ain't more than a kid, Sissy.
Where's her people? With all your money, I can't see why you don't just hire
somebody from around here to help out."

"Miss Grace here's an orphan. That's right. There's not a friggin' soul
who'd give two cents for her." Molly Carol told Violet the made-up story about
my past. It would be months before Violet knew the truth.

Violet studied the Bible, a little frown on her face. I waited for her to
say she didn't believe Molly Carol, or to at least ask questions. She glanced
sideways at me. "Life's hard, no doubts about it," Violet said. "I reckon life's
plumb wore me out. And that's a fact."

In the months to come, hope of escape would be fanned from time to time
during visits with Violet, especially when she served food prepared especially
for me and the twins: cobblers of in-season fruit, apples, peaches, berries, dished
still-warm into deep bowls and drizzled with evaporated milk; fried green
tomatoes, crunchy with corn meal and flour on the outside and soft and tangy
on the inside; string beans cooked down with salt pork and served alongside
roasted ears of corn slathered in butter. I couldn't believe that a woman who
put that much love in her food wouldn't help a kid in need. But whenever I
would try to bring up the subject of Mesquite—even after Violet would learn
my real history—she would close her eyes, and whisper, "I'm too wore out to
think about it, and that's a fact." For whatever reason, Violet would never act
on the thoughts that I convinced myself were so clearly hovering behind the

brown of her eyes. Later I would console myself with the idea that at least life with Molly Carol had toughened me up for what was to come.

"*You're* wore out?" Molly Carol said, and opened her eyes wide to stare at Violet. Molly Carol ranted about how hard it was trying to sell houses to a bunch of muckity-mucks who thought they were better than her but how she put up with it so she could provide her kids with all the things she never had. And by God, was it asking too much to get a little just a little—that's all she wanted—appreciation for all her labors? I would learn that whenever Molly Carol's conscience acted up, she'd tamp it down with angry outbursts about how hard she had it.

Violet lit a fresh cigarette with the still-glowing butt of the first. She sucked the smoke deep into her lungs then released it with a hacking cough.

"What're you waiting for?" Molly Carol snapped, and at first I didn't realize she was talking to me. "Get in there and get the twins out of bed."

Violet laid her cigarette in the ashtray and motioned for me to follow her to the closed door at the other end of the trailer. When Violet flipped the switch, a gooseneck lamp over the bed flashed on, and two small bodies squirmed beneath a woolen blanket. Holly sat up, rubbed her eyes with one hand and with the other scratched her scalp through a mass of tangled curls the color of copper wire. Her eyes were large and yellow-green and her lips rosy and delicate, but I suspected that with age that mouth would turn as thin and straight as her mother's. I knew the kids were twins, but Holly, long legs stretched out in front of her, appeared inches taller than Travis, lying stomach down. He grunted when Violet nudged him and whispered, "Come on now, baby boy. Mommy's here to take you home."

"Who're you?" Holly said around a yawn. "Another babysitter?" She exaggerated the words so that they came out like a long groan. I don't know if I would have admitted it, but something about her attitude reminded me of my pre-accident self.

"This one's here to stay, I reckon," Violet said.

Ha, I thought.

"It's that slowpoke Travis holding up things, isn't it?" Molly Carol yelled.

With the sound of her voice, Travis, who'd been flopping around like a hooked fish, slid his legs over the side of the bed. Holly yawned again. "Get my back-pack," she said to me.

I almost told her to get it herself, but I bent down the way Chelo had so many times to pick up after me. I silently told myself that at least I'd never spoken to Chelo in such a rude way. Had I? When Travis stumbled into the front room, he stammered that he needed to pee. Molly Carol said that, by God, he'd already had his chance, and he could just hold it.

When we climbed into the Volvo that night, I was told to take the back seat with Travis. "I always ride in the front," Holly said. "On account of I get car sick if I don't." She didn't even glance toward her mother for affirmation. Holly was a girl I wanted on my side. For as long as I lived with them, Holly would be the only person that Molly Carol seemed to truly love and the only one she could never confront. She had apparently decided that Holly was the child she could most easily mold into the person she felt she herself could have been had she been given the opportunities.

On the drive to my new home, Molly Carol, who had sped over the highways for the entire trip, now drove at a sightseeing pace, and the Volvo seemed to find every bump in the road. Travis whimpered over each one. Molly Carol glanced in the rearview mirror and grinned.

"Next time you'll listen to Mommy when she tells you to go to the bathroom, won't you?"

"Yes, ma'am," Travis whispered.

When the Volvo finally slowed to a crawl and turned onto a side road, tires crunching over gravel, I pushed myself up tall in the seat and peered into the darkness. No buildings in sight, only tall shrubs, branches swaying and rustling, lined either side.

Molly Carol lowered her window and inhaled. "Just get a whiff of all those lilacs."

The scent was unfamiliar to me, but I did like its sweet freshness and filled my lungs. The branches of the tall shrubs with clustered flowers that looked eerily pale-colored in the dim light swayed in wind that blew harder by the minute. Distant thunder rumbled across the heavens.

Molly Carol lifted one finger off the steering wheel, pointed straight ahead. "Sloan Acres," she said.

I leaned forward. The heavy cloud cover blocked the stars and the moon, and my vision was limited to the beam of the headlights on the unpaved road winding among tall trees. When the car rounded the bend, a flash of lightning illuminated a two-story wooden house with a spacious porch.

"You just wait," Molly Carol said. One of these days, all this area's going to be developed, and I'll make out big time when I sell." How desperately she needed to be validated, even by a child she'd taken to be a live-in servant.

"I believe you," I said. I meant it. There was something about Molly Carol, some determination or strength that I would begrudgingly admire.

Molly Carol turned to look at me. "You listen and do as you're told, and you'll be treated just like one of the family."

I thought of little Travis, his face scrunched up with the concentration of holding his bladder. "Oh," I said, and fought the urge to laugh.

SIX

A cool breeze swept the scent of lilac across the front porch, and the smell of the unfamiliar added a drop of sweetness to the soup of fear and anxiety simmering in my stomach. Grandmother had been right: people came to the United States from all over the world to fulfill their dreams. Why not me? I remembered how before the accident I had yearned to be free of my family and all the restrictions of respectability. What an evil girl I'd been, just like in Chelo's stories. I wanted to pummel my ungrateful self with fists of righteousness. Yet I also wanted to know freedom.

I smiled to myself in the darkness, and I even softened toward Molly Carol. She probably wasn't as bad as she seemed. Adults were always cranky on long trips and took it out on the kids. Molly Carol cursed in the darkness as she tried to fit the key in the lock, and I shifted my weight from one foot to another, working the squeaks and groans of the sagging floorboards into a happy rhythm.

"Hey," Molly Carol yelled so suddenly the twins and I were startled. "You fixing on waking the dead with that racket?"

Holly and Travis stepped back and away from me. Why involve themselves in someone else's punishment? In the months to come, I would learn the value of this line of defense. I stilled my feet, breathed as softly as possible. Moving only my eyes, I scanned the surroundings. I'd had a half-baked plan of meeting folks like the ones on the television programs Molly Carol watched, the

Waltons or the Ingallses on *Little House on the Prairie*, only modern. But if there were houses nearby, they were obscured by the brush and tree-dotted lawn and the deep shadows beyond.

Molly Carol pushed open the front door and flipped a switch. We stepped directly into a living room—not even a bit of foyer—that had the same funny odor as the Abarrotes Sinaloa back in Mesquite. Papi told me it was old-people smell given off by Mr. and Mrs. Rubio, the couple that ran the little neighborhood grocery, and I'd answered that when I got old, I'd never allow myself to stink of burnt scrambled eggs. I would smell clean and fresh like Grandmother's chamomile and orange blossoms. Papi joked that I'd better not let Grandmother hear me describing her as old. My father had never been more handsome than when he laughed, and by this time I'd forgotten how much his laughter and jokes could irritate.

Books and magazines covered a large coffee table in the center of the room. Later I learned the books were on architecture and real estate and that Molly Carol read only what she called *true shit* as opposed to *made-up shit*. On either side of the table, footpaths worn into the avocado-green carpet ran between a stained sectional sofa on one side of the coffee table and a television console on the other side. The footpaths met and converged into the adjacent dining room.

"I got this place for a song," Molly Carol said.

"Oh," I said. Hadn't she already given me this information maybe a million times during the trip? She threw me a sharp stare, so I squinched my face into an expression of what I hoped would pass for questioning interest rather than what she had taken to calling my "high-and-mighty" look.

During my year with the Sloans, I would find that Molly Carol watched the obituaries for recent widows, the older the better. They were the ones most likely to listen to her advice about getting rid of property they couldn't take care of anymore. Molly Carol usually came out the winner in her business deals—all the while claiming that others were trying to cheat her. The odd thing was that many times she could convince the person she'd cheated that she'd done them a favor.

"I don't have to share my room with her, too, do I?" Holly pointed a finger at me, and I thought of Grandmother and my parents, who said that a well-bred person never, ever pointed at another human.

"Now, Holly, you know I fixed the girl a room of her own," Molly Carol said.

"Umph," Holly answered. Molly Carol reached out to pat Holly's head, but the girl flounced off, hair swinging.

For a moment, Molly Carol stood with her arm hanging in air, her eyes stricken after Holly's rebuff. "What the hell you staring at?" she snapped at me. "You planning on standing around all night with your thumb up your ass?"

I didn't understand the expression, but she gestured for me to follow her to the kitchen, and I did. I guessed my room was to be the typical maid's off-the-kitchen cubbyhole, but when Molly Carol opened a door on a side wall and turned on the light, a steep stairway led down to an ugly space with a cement floor. I had never been in a basement, and when she nudged me forward, I grabbed onto the railing with both hands.

"What the hell's wrong with you?" She pried my fingers loose, bending middle and index fingers back far enough to make me yelp.

The basement ran the length and width of the house's foundation, the windows filled with cubes of blocked glass. Molly Carol pointed to a plastic curtain in a corner at the opposite end of the room. "There's a shower and a john behind that," she said, and when I didn't understand the word, she explained that *john* meant commode. At least it wasn't outside like Chelo's facilities had been.

On one side of the curtained area were two large metal tubs and a washer and dryer, and on the other side, what appeared to be a large boxlike closet built of laminated wood paneling. Nowhere did I see any space that even remotely resembled a bedroom. With a solid hand to the small of my back, Molly Carol directed me toward the box. My room was a bit bigger than Chelo's, but like hers, furnished with odds and ends: a twin-size bed covered with a pink gingham bedspread, batting poking out through some worn spots; a metal rack on wheels for hanging clothes; a chest of drawers topped with a vase of silk roses; a pine end table next to the bed with a pink shaded lamp.

"I hope to hell you're not about to cry," Molly Carol said.

"It's only—I don't know what to say."

When Molly Carol studied my face for insult, I added, "So many pretty things."

No matter that Grandmother and Mr. Genaro had told Molly Carol about my reasonably comfortable life before the accident, she would never stop treating me as though I'd known nothing but poverty. Maybe she needed to convince herself that she wasn't taking advantage of me, but rather being charitable to an unfortunate who would be grateful for the slightest scrap.

Molly Carol left me alone, and after the door at the top of the stairs opened and shut behind her, I took deep breaths the way I remembered the doctor had instructed my mother to do when she became frightened of things she couldn't name. The darkness seemed to have a pulse, something living, breathing. My own pulse drummed in my ears. For the first time since I'd left Mesquite, I'd be alone. Freedom could be mine.

Get out, get out, a voice in my head roared. A sheen of cold sweat coated my face. I don't know how long I waited for silence to envelop the house. I lost all sense of time; it could have been five minutes or thirty.

I tiptoed up the wooden steps. The top one creaked, and I paused. Crystals of ice nicked the insides of my veins. Cold, I was so cold. I placed my hand on the knob to the door leading to the kitchen, afraid to turn it not only because she might be waiting on the other side, but because I expected it to be bolted. To this day, I don't understand why Molly Carol didn't lock me in that first night. Maybe she thought she'd paralyzed me with the fear of being exposed to the immigration officials, the *migra,* as we called them back home. Maybe she just forgot.

I pushed and the door eased open. I poked my head around the edge. Feeling my way up the stairs hadn't been so bad. The passage was defined, contained, but when I peered into the open space of the kitchen, my knees almost buckled. If the darkness of a room overwhelmed me, what would the great outdoors do?

But I was true to my willful self. Now that I'd started the escape, I was determined to carry it through. The refrigerator whirred from the direction of the far wall. Earlier, had I seen a back door next to it? I squinted and made out only a glint of metal. Now I remembered: a door, but blocked with a unit of metal shelves filled with canned goods. I turned toward the dining room, and running my fingers along the wall, I inched my way to the living room. Surely the front door would be locked from the inside. I held the knob in my hand, but before twisting I silently prayed to the Holy Mother. The dead bolt clicked out of its space. I silently mouthed the words, "Thank you, Virgencita, thank you."

The porch groaned beneath me. I hopped down the wooden steps, broke into a run on the lane, kept to the grassy borders rather than the noisy gravel. Another little voice edged inside my head, soft, still a whisper, Where will you go? What will you do? Who cared? I was free.

I glanced back over my shoulder. A second-story window was open about a foot, and the filmy curtains billowed in and out with the wind. My heart banged so loudly, I felt sure the pulse beat would be carried across the yard. At the end of the path, I crept around the last shrub, my back against it, my face to the outside world. I looked up and down the road. Now what? Left? Right? The voice in my head grew louder. Where will you go? What will you do? My God, what had I done? But it was too late. I'd broken free, and now I had no choice but to go forward.

If Molly Carol came looking for me she might figure that I'd gone back in the same direction we'd come from. I turned the opposite way, heading towards the unknown. The damp grass on the shoulder of the road soaked through the sides of my canvas shoes. My eyes filled with tears, my heart with panic. Grandmother had always told me I was too impatient, that I had to learn to wait for the right moment.

No streetlights lit the winding country road, and only the occasional car headlights cut through the blackness. Each time I heard a distant motor, I'd dart farther back from the road and near the shrubs. Scurrying noises moved away from me into the woods running parallel and only yards from me.

In Mesquite, I had never walked too far up into the hills behind the house because there had been reports of a roving pack of wild boars. Chelo told me that a bad girl had allowed some married man to take her up there for something a decent woman shouldn't even imagine. The next day a bunch of street urchins looking for a place to split the loot they'd pocketed from unsuspecting tourists came upon a blood-soaked blanket. The javelinas had left behind only a few splinters of bones, shreds of meat, and a faint aftersmell of sulfur. I'd never believed Chelo's stories, not completely, but as I crept along that shadowy and lonely road, I accepted every gory detail as fact. What sorts of exotic Ohio animals might be lurking among all that vegetation?

I prayed to God, to the Sacred Heart of Jesus, the Virgin of Guadalupe, my patron saint, the spirits of my parents, even the memory of Chelo. But mostly to Grandmother. Reliable, practical Grandmother always knew what to do. What was I thinking? She was the one who'd put me in this position. Forget the prayers. I had only myself to depend on now.

The wind picked up, turning the night chilly. My full-to-bursting bladder bounced with each step. Why hadn't I thought to go to the bathroom before setting out? I hadn't even gotten a simple thing like that right. Panic tap-danced up my spine, and my teeth chattered. A car engine hummed in the distance. The car slowed, and the headlight beams broke on my back, lighted up the grass and highway in front of me. The car purred slowly behind me. The panic dance on my spine tapped faster, louder, *rat-a-tat-tat*. Run, I should run. Which direction? The car would easily overtake me on the highway. Into the black space of those woods that seemed more and more to have a life of their own?

The car idled alongside me now. "Need a ride, honey?" The man's voice had the same oily smoothness as Mr. Genaro's.

I turned my face just enough to angle a peek, but couldn't see beyond the open window on the passenger side.

"You shouldn't be out here alone, baby doll," he said.

Wind howled through the woods, swept out and around me. Oh God, was that a whiff of sulfur? I tried to scream, but it caught in my throat and only a strange, guttural noise croaked out.

"Hey, keep it down." The saccharin had left the man's voice.

I forced another sound from my throat. "Helllllp!" I screamed, croaky but stronger. The car lurched forward a foot, stalled. I yelled again. The driver floored the gas pedal, his tires spitting gravel when he took off.

I ran all the way back to the house, stumbled up the lane. Still no lights, and the upstairs curtain blew gossamer in the breeze, a spirit snagged on the window frame. Would I be able to reenter the house without being detected? I couldn't think straight with a bursting bladder, so at the side of the house, I squatted and peed on what I would later learn was a honeysuckle vine. I tried the front door. As I suspected, it had locked behind me. Around the back, the wind sighed through the trees that must have been the fruit and nut trees that Molly Carol had told me about.

The adrenaline that had been pumping into my brain suddenly drained. I leaned my hot forehead against the cool front door, and could barely keep my legs from giving out. I was so tired. *Plumb wore out*, wasn't that the way Violet had put it? I didn't want to think anymore. I wanted to sleep, sleep. I made my way back to the front porch and curled up on the swing, pulling my legs and arms into myself to keep away the chill.

The next thing I knew someone was shaking me, yelling. But why was the woman screaming, "Grace!"? My head snapped backward, forward. Molly Carol jerked me up into a sitting position. I squinted into the weak morning light.

"Where the hell'd you think you were going?" Molly Carol's spit sprayed into my open mouth. I didn't see the hard jab to the face coming until it was too late. I fell back against the swing then pitched forward onto the porch floor. I pushed myself up onto my hands and knees. A rope of bloody mucous stretched from my nose, and I wiped at it with the back of my hand. For some reason, it seemed important to me that it not reach the porch floor. Molly Carol straddled me, wrapped my hair around her hand, yanked my head back farther than I thought it could go. She was going to slit my throat like the villagers had done to the widow in *Zorba*. I could already picture the bloody smile across my throat.

"Look at me," she said.

I tried to blink away the stars still flashing in front of my eyes. Frothy spit bubbled at the corners of Molly Carol's mouth. "Nobody, but nobody fucks with me." Air hissed from between her open lips. "I'll break that smart-ass attitude of yours, by God."

As she dragged me through the house by my hair, she yelled about everything she had to do that day, like driving the twins to school for their first day, getting them registered, but could anybody have a little consideration for Molly Carol? Hell, no. And because of my low-down sneaky ways, I was going to stay locked in the basement until she returned. I lay fetal-tight on my bed, afraid to move.

When Molly Carol came back after dropping off the twins at school, she was breathing in a regular way, no longer through her mouth, and my stomach untwisted some. But I already knew how quickly her moods could change. She directed me upstairs so I could wash off the dried blood and snot at the bathroom sink, but when she told me to wait while she unlocked her bedroom door, I didn't know what to expect. As it turned out, she wanted to make a phone call, and the only phone in the house was kept inside her room. The one room that would always be kept locked.

She pointed to an easy chair for me to sit in while she got busy on the phone. From what I understood, she wanted wrought-iron grids with locks put on all the windows and outside doors of the house. When Violet arrived, the workmen were already outside, and I was in the kitchen preparing breakfast. She pushed my hair back from my face and tenderly touched my black eye before tracing her fingers down my swollen cheek to my split lip. Tears sprang to her eyes. "You poor little thing," she said.

"Clumsy ox tripped and fell down the basement stairs while trying to sneak out in the dark," Molly Carol said. She sat at the kitchen table nursing a mug of coffee. "Serves her right. The wages of sin, and all that." She barked a phony laugh.

Violet turned her eyes away from me, but not before I saw the guilt flash faintly. Eventually I learned that one of Violet and Molly Carol's favorite sayings—and they had plenty—was that blood was thicker than water. It didn't matter how many times one of the sisters might snipe at or criticize the other, in the end they always came together as one. And they didn't believe in telling family business to outsiders. Family secrets stayed inside the house.

"The taxi guy's waiting out front," Violet said. "I need a few dollars."

Later Violet would tell me that she'd never taken out a driver's license, said traffic got on her last nerve what with vehicles (she stressed the middle syllable) buzzing this-a-way and that-a-way, folks yelling cuss words and flipping the finger. No way in heaven was she going to get behind the wheel of a car. For the year that I would be with the Sloans, each time Molly Carol tried to shame Violet into driving, I'd whisper to Violet later that if she didn't want to, it was a sign that she shouldn't. "You're pretty wise for a young 'un," Violet would say.

After Molly Carol left the kitchen, saying she had to keep an eye on the workers or they'd rob her blind, Violet insisted on getting down on her hands and knees alongside me to scrub the kitchen floor like Molly Carol had instructed earlier. Big brush for most of the floor, toothbrush for the corners and edges.

"Sissy's not so bad," Violet said. "Best not to rile her, though. She will work herself up into pitching one of her conniption fits. Been like that since she was just a kid. Some's born different, you know?" She dipped her brush into the bucket of soapy water. "You're better off here than some old orphanage, ain't that right?"

"Hmm," I said.

That night, alone in the darkness and silence of my basement room, the full reality of my situation hit me harder than Molly Carol's fist. The tears I'd been holding back burst out, and I buried my face in the pillow to keep from screaming. I cried until my nose was congested, and I had to breathe through my mouth. My already swollen eye puffed up so bad it completely shut. My thoughts were flying all over the place, a crazy jigsaw of words and images.

There was no point in trying to fit the chaos into a neat crossword, though, because pieces were missing.

I clutched my head in my hands. This must be what it felt like to go crazy. If I didn't stop thinking, I was afraid I'd fall into an abyss that I'd never be able to climb back out of. Desperate for something to keep my mind busy, I imagined movie screens on the insides of my closed eyelids. There, images of my past flickered like short films of my life. My memories were better than movies at the cinema. I could search my brain for scents: vanilla, chamomile, orange blossom, and all of Chelo's best dishes. There was no end to the sensory details. I felt Chelo's callused palm on my forehead, checking for fever; heard the click of Grandmother's crocheting needle and felt the intricate design of the lace beneath my fingertips; Papi laughed, deep and rich; and Mamá warbled like a tiny canary.

The only way I was going to survive was to keep my good memories of home. Or so I believed then. I would play reels of encores in my brain. That first night, I spent hours recalling past birthday celebrations and Christmas Eve suppers. After a while, bad memories began to intrude, and I flipped on the light and jumped out of bed. I searched through the drawer of the night table and found a pencil and writing tablet. I would write a letter to Grandmother telling her how things had gone terribly wrong. My one good eye was blurry from all the weeping, and my writing kept going over and under the straight lines. I hoped Grandmother would be able to make out my promises to be good, a forever obedient and respectful granddaughter. And I had an idea, I wrote—I could get a job as a maid in Mesquite. Surely the family would allow Grandmother to come and stay with me.

"What happened to Papi wasn't my fault," I wrote at the end of the letter. "But if you think it is, please forgive me, OK?" As a postscript, I added, "I hope you're feeling lots better. I am not so stubborn anymore. I can take care of you, you'll see."

I was only thirteen and still believed that an adult's capacity for forgiveness could come almost as easily as that of a child. I did not know then how soon my idea of returning to my old life would be shattered once and for all.

SEVEN

I waited a week before approaching Molly Carol for a stamp to mail Grandmother's letter. Instead of yelling, like I thought she might, Molly Carol grinned and said she'd stop at the post office on the way home from work. She forgot, though, and after waiting a few more days, I asked her again. Quit nagging me, she said, or I'll never get you the goddamn stamp.

Two months later, I was dishing out macaroni and cheese onto the kids' plates before calling them down to lunch, when Molly Carol walked into the kitchen, and said, "Funny you should bring up writing to good ol' Grandma."

"Oh?" I said, and forked a boiled wiener onto one of the buns. It had taken me a moment to grasp what Molly Carol was talking about, and when I did get it, I had to bite my tongue to keep from saying that what might be considered funny was that she expected people to pick up the thread of a conversation that had happened months ago. Did she really think she was that important? But then, maybe she *was*, because like I said, it only took me a flash to pick up on the topic.

Molly Carol said that only the day before she'd called Mr. Genaro to tell him how great I was doing now that I'd settled in, and lo and behold, if he wasn't the one with the real news. With an exaggerated sad tone to her voice, she said slowly, "I hate to be the one to have to tell you this, Gracie." Her eyes glittered the way they did when she was enjoying herself. "Your poor old Granny died last month."

I'd just speared another wiener from the saucepan of boiling water, and now the wiener slipped off the fork tines. Water splashed on my wrist. I jumped to the side and put out one hand in back to brace myself against the counter.

"Come off it. It's not like you didn't know she was sick." Molly Carol studied me, clearly not wanting to miss one moment of my shock and pain.

I sucked at the burn on my wrist and made certain to avert my gaze from Molly Carol's. There was no way I could disguise my hatred for her at that moment. If she had given me a stamp when I'd asked for it, my letter would have reached Grandmother before she died.

"We all gotta go sometime," Molly Carol said. She trailed a finger across the wall as she left the kitchen. "You've let the grease build up. I will not abide filth." Her voice was so cheery you'd never guess she was complaining. She reminded me that hard work was the best way to forget our troubles. Judging by how much work she did around the house, Molly Carol must have been the most trouble-free person in the world.

After the kids had their lunch, I scrubbed the walls. In a way, I didn't mind all the chores Molly Carol heaped on me—the physical movement kept me from thinking too much. That day, though, I couldn't help but remember how in Mesquite, Grandmother had said that our family wasn't built for manual labor, and didn't allow me to do any chores that might ruin my hands. I no longer had to worry what Grandmother would think of my red and roughened hands. Grandmother was dead. "Don't think about it," I kept repeating. "Think pretty."

Some of my best daydreams came while slaving away at the Sloans'. Sometimes I imagined that one of those spiders in my basement room would turn into a handsome prince who would whisk me away from my Cinderella existence. But that day, as I dipped my cleaning rag into a bucket of water and Lysol, my brain conjured up a substantial, rice-and-beans kind of dream. No, not a dream, a plan.

Freedom Run would go like this: 1. Become all that Molly Carol wanted me to be, so she would trust me enough to give me more time away from her. And the time I needed to accomplish this would give me time to better know my surroundings so I'd have a better idea of where I was heading. 2. Learn to act more American than the Americans. Just as Molly Carol worked at ridding herself of her working-class Southern accent by repeating after national newscasters with nondescript pronunciations, I would wipe out any trace of Mexico and the border from my speech. And I'd learn more idiomatic expressions. Also, I had to be careful of telltale behavior, such as waving my hands around too much when I spoke, and laughing too loudly and often. I'd seen a movie once where an American spy in Germany gave himself away by switching his fork from one hand to the other after cutting his steak. The little things could reveal as easily as the more obvious. 3. Save up money to buy a bus ticket out of Cogstown. After that, well, I didn't really know, but I figured something would come to me.

As months went by and I became increasingly compliant, Molly Carol gave me even less credit for intelligence, and the dumber she thought I was, the more she trusted me. But there wasn't enough trust in the world to loosen her grip on money. Sometimes when she dropped me and the twins off at the mall for shopping or a movie, she'd give us something for treats, but always the exact change. She knew prices even better than Grandmother had, and she demanded receipts when she picked us up. The mall trips weren't filling up the savings coffee can that I buried beneath a lilac shrub, but they sure did add to my store of information. Like when at a fried chicken place, a pimply-face clerk who always threw extra fries into my order told me the nearest Greyhound bus station was in downtown Cogstown and gave me directions on how to get there from my house address.

My coffee can never held more than loose change picked out from between sofa cushions, but I had a fallback. Whenever we ordered pizza delivery to the house or the kids needed money for school, Molly Carol disappeared into her bedroom. How to get the opportunity to break into her room? I decided to wait for a sign.

It came three weeks from my one-year anniversary with the Sloans, in the form of crayon drawings the twins brought home from school. After I poured the kids glasses of cold milk to go with their after-school oatmeal raisin cookies, I asked them about the men in little green suits and tall hats on the rough sheets of art paper. Leprechauns for St. Patrick's Day, silly, Holly said. What in the world did I think they were? In the beginning the twins had been confused by some of my questions. They couldn't understand why I didn't know things *everybody* knew.

My way of testing them, I'd say. Holly always said that was dumb. But like most kids, she enjoyed playing the know-it-all too much to not answer my questions.

St. Patrick's Day, she informed me with a flip of her ponytail, was a boring holiday for them, with no gifts or special stuff for kids, and mostly meant eating a lot of stinky cabbage and watching her mom drink too much Irish whiskey. I pulled up a chair and gave Holly my full attention. Apparently Violet came over for the dinner, but would complain the whole time about alcohol leading to sin and eternal ruination.

I knew that Molly Carol seldom drank because, from what I gathered from bits of overheard conversations, she was extremely sensitive to alcohol. "But your mom doesn't like to drink," I said, and handed Holly an extra cookie from the cookie jar I'd brought to the table with me.

"I knooow," Holly said, drawing the word out. "That's why Aunt Violet always gets mad. Then she makes Mommy take her home. Mommy stays out and drinks more. She gets back real late and don't get out of bed until the next day. Same thing every year. Bo-ring."

"One time we thought she was dead, huh, Holly?" Travis said. He glanced at the cookie jar, and I realized I hadn't given him an extra one. But he was so used to being slighted, he hadn't said anything. I handed him the biggest one I could find.

Molly Carol was always looking for a reason to yell at Travis. Often I imagined myself wearing Wonder Woman wrist cuffs that could deflect Molly Carol's mean comments away from him. I wondered if I had to spend years with that woman if I'd become another Travis, going around with a kick-me-if-you-want face like one of the mangy dogs that ran the streets of Mesquite.

She'd yell the same things at me when she lost out on a good deal at work. But it was easier for me than for Travis. She'd been working on him since he was a baby, but me, I'd had years with a family who had convinced me I was special, even when we didn't see eye to eye on things. Even Chelo had loved me like her own child. At least that's what I'd believed until I came to be a servant myself; I'd come to understand that being dependent on a family meant you sometimes said and did things that were not necessarily from the heart.

"Here," I said, and handed Travis another cookie. I turned to Holly. "So, your mommy always passes out on St. Patrick's Day? I'll bet she sleeps a long, long time, doesn't she?"

Holly stuck out her hand for another cookie. I pushed the jar over to her.

I'd just finished setting the dining room table for the St. Patrick's Day dinner when the kitchen door swung open. "Hey, everybody," Molly Carol hollered, "we're home."

She was returning from taking Violet to pick up her new dentures. Last month Violet had gone on for days about how she was up all hours of the night with a toothache unrelieved by her usual remedies—clove oil rubbed inside the blackened cavity and onto the pus-filled abscess she called a gum boil.

I despised Molly Carol so much that I would have died before admitting she had any goodness in her. Looking back, though, I can see that she did have her moments. She wasn't about to dole out cash and lose control over us, but she was capable of flashes of generosity. Like Violet's dentures. And several times Molly Carol bought boxes of canned goods from a discount grocery and bags of used clothing from the Goodwill store before taking off in her Volvo for the weekend. Violet, who would come over to stay with me and the twins, said that Molly Carol drove down to Kentucky, back to their old neighborhood. She'd park under a tree on a morning-quiet street and wait to see the faces of the folks when they opened their front doors to find the unexplained gifts sitting on their porches.

The box that I took from Violet now carried the promised corned beef boiled with cabbage, small red potatoes, and carrots. The cabbage stunk, and I had to really concentrate to keep my expression neutral. Molly Carol hated it when I crinkled my nose, said I was always going around looking like I smelled something bad, which was a sure sign I thought I was better than others. There was nothing Molly Carol hated more than a muckity-muck—except when she was trying to be one herself.

Molly Carol rocked back on her heels and studied the table I'd laid out with the snowy white cloth and napkins (Irish linens, washed and ironed by me). Three small, black ceramic cauldrons of live clover sat equidistant on a green runner down the horizontal center of the table. I'd placed the silver candlesticks, as Molly Carol had instructed, between the pots and then burned the virgin wicks of the pale green candles. Molly Carol had read in one of her magazines that it was tacky—one of her favorite words—to set out brand-new candles. Light them, the article instructed, long enough to blacken the wicks before your guests arrive. Otherwise, those guests might think that table candles weren't normally used in your family, that you'd only put them out to impress. A lesson, it seemed to me, in how to create the illusion of being someone you weren't.

Violet placed the platter of meat and vegetables at the head of the table where Molly Carol sat, pulling a bottle of John Powers & Son whiskey out of a slim paper bag. Holly rolled her eyes at no one in particular and slid into her seat next to Travis, rocking to one side then the other so her ponytail swayed back and forth. Earlier she'd asked me to tie her coppery curls with an emerald-green ribbon, and I'd had a flash of myself tucking a bougainvillea blossom behind my ear back in my old home. No matter how hard I pushed memories away—and by now, I understood that forgetting was my only salvation—once in a while one would sneak up on me.

Seated around the table, we bowed our heads. We never said grace except when Violet visited, and sometimes she'd go on so long thanking God for every single grain of salt that Molly Carol would stop her with a loud *a-hem*. Oh, excuse me, she'd say, I meant a-*men*. Today the thanksgiving was short and sweet, and Molly Carol was soon passing down plates with thick slices of meat and steaming vegetables. I'd never heard of corned beef back in Sonora, but it tasted so good I wondered if Mexico's Irish ate it too, and I just hadn't known about it.

Each time Molly Carol took a sip from her glass of iced tea, generously laced with whiskey, Violet told us about the ladies at her church and how they'd all go down to the town park to help the homeless alcoholics find God. Violet's new dentures made clacking noises as she spoke, and Travis was so fascinated that he laid down his fork and forgot to eat.

"Aunt Violet," Travis began. I slid down in my chair and tried to kick him beneath the table, but my foot couldn't find his. "Your new teeth sound funny," he said, and giggled.

Violet blushed and her hand flew to her mouth. She pulled up straight in her chair, as if to stand, but Molly Carol waved her back. All I could think was that the dinner—and the routine I'd counted on—were going up in smoke.

"Get the hell out of my sight," Molly Carol yelled at Travis, "before I ram my fist down your throat. We'll see who makes funny noises then."

Travis burst into tears and ran up the stairs. Holly stabbed a piece of carrot with her fork and nibbled at the end.

"You shouldn't have been so hard on the boy," Violet said.

"Don't blame me," Molly Carol said. "If you'd gone to a real dentist like I told you, those damn dentures would fit right." In spite of Molly Carol's warnings that Dr. Joe Stevens was a quack, Violet had insisted on him. She'd seen his ads on TV and, impressed with his Johnny Cash manliness and down-home accent, stated that she would entrust her mouthful of pain to no other, never believing that one of her own might take advantage of her.

Molly Carol kept pouring whiskey into her glass of iced tea whenever the level went more than two inches below the top edge. By the time I cleared the table and brought the latticed-topped pies, cherries and apples frozen from the summer harvest, in from the kitchen, Molly Carol was pink-faced and glassy-eyed from all that alcohol. Violet's mouth had turned down at the corners that now sunk into the grooves running from nostrils to lips.

Violet told me and Holly how she wished she had one of them movie cameras about now. If drunks could see themselves, she said, they'd know just how much they looked the fool. Molly Carol grinned and said that she who was perfect should cast the first stone, and Violet clenched her jaws tight and ground her teeth so hard you would think that one or two of those false teeth would have broken.

"Oh, let's be friends," Molly Carol said. "Eat up, and after dinner we'll sing. That ought to cheer up old sourpuss." She winked at Violet, who stared at the wall in front of her. Molly Carol knew how to work her big sister, though, and after pie, she picked up her guitar from the corner of the room and started strumming, and Violet's facial muscles started relaxing bit by bit. It didn't take long for Violet's rolled-in lips to soften and break into a smile, a really wide one to show off those blinding white dentures. Those sisters loved singing together, and they knew what they were doing, too. Alone, Molly Carol's voice was clear and lovely, but when she harmonized with her sister, you could close your eyes and imagine a couple of angels easing the pain of the world with the sheer beauty of their song.

Often times, they sang what they called "old-timey hymns," but in honor of St. Patrick, the sisters decided on Irish themed songs like *I'll Take You Home Again, Kathleen*, *When Irish Eyes Are Smiling*, and of course, *Danny Boy*. Next Violet requested *Amazing Grace*. Right in the middle of the hymn, Molly Carol ducked her head forward, swallowed, then belched. Too much sentiment embarrassed Molly Carol, and she'd find some excuse to get mad or do something gross to change the mood.

"Oh, well now, that's just blasphemous." Violet stood and brushed pie crumbs off her lap. "I will not stand for blasphemy, no ma'am, I will not. If you ever want to see my face again, Sis, you best take me home right this very minute."

"My wish is your command, Miss Violet," Molly Carol said in one of those exaggerated Southern belle accents.

Holly gave me a didn't-I-tell-you-so? look from across the room.

As soon as the sisters were out the door, I hurried Holly to bed, and let her go to sleep with her transistor radio next to her ear, the way Molly Carol never allowed. I wasn't even out of her bedroom door before Holly turned the volume way up. I imagine it disturbed her a bit that I didn't tell her to turn it down. And, Travis, well, I didn't want him waking up in the middle of the night with hunger pangs, so I took him a piece of cherry pie, which was his favorite, and even dumped two scoops of vanilla ice cream on top for good measure because I'd heard milk helped you sleep.

I rushed down to my room and stuffed one of Holly's old backpacks with a change of slacks and several tee shirts, and the panties and two bras Molly Carol had given me for Christmas. Molly Carol had been just as strict as Grandmother about clothing, but in a different way. Molly Carol insisted on button-up white blouses with what she called Peter Pan collars, pleated skirts that hung below my knees, or polyester pantsuits too baggy in the seat and jackets a size too big. It was her way of trying to make me look larger and older, I guess.

Before heading out, I tiptoed up to take a last good-bye check of the twins. I didn't really blame them for anything. There were times when I couldn't stand the sight of Holly, but deep in my heart I understood that part of it was that I was as jealous of her easy life just as Olga had been of mine back when things were good. But in spite of my good will toward her, I didn't go inside her room in case she might be awake. Her music was still blaring away. I knew sleepyhead Travis would be lost in dreams, and when I looked down at the poor little thing with his hollow eyes and his plastic tyrannosaurus rex clutched in his hand, my nose burned from the tears I held back. Who would be his cuffed Wonder Woman after I was gone? I hadn't been that effective, but at least I'd tried.

Maybe once I was far away from the house, I could make an anonymous call to Children's Services. The social worker who had come to the house snooping around a few months back after Travis kept peeing his pants in school might actually do something this time. Not like before when the stupid cow had asked Travis what kind of mother Molly Carol was with her sitting right there on the sofa next to him, her phony have-I-got-a-deal-for-you smile plastered on her face. But if I called Children's Services, might they start asking questions about the girl who used to live with the Sloans? Molly Carol would figure I'd reported her, and she'd spill the beans for sure. I'd have immigration on my trail. I decided to wait and call Children's Services once I was far away and settled.

With a flat chisel from Molly Carol's tool box, I popped open the lock on her bedroom door. The room was so neat and tidy that it hadn't taken me long to spot the metal box inside the closet. The box held not only loose paper money but legal documents. I hadn't even thought of taking along identification. Now here were both a social security card and a birth certificate for Grace Sloan, but on the papers Molly Carol and her ex-husband were listed as my parents rather than the couple she'd invented before as my parents. Grace Sloan existed.

I was anxious to begin reinventing a newer, more independent me.

EIGHT

I sat up in the taxi, fists shoved inside the pockets of my hooded sweat jacket. Counting my coin savings and Molly Carol's bills from the metal box—mostly ones and fives—I had a grand total of sixty dollars and forty-one cents. I'd never before been in charge of that much money. Molly Carol controlled the household finances even more tightly than Grandmother had. Before I could stop it, I had a sudden memory of Grandmother counting pennies in order to decide whether our daily plate of rice and beans might also include a chicken drumstick or, better yet my favorite, beefsteak milanesa.

Meat isn't good for us, Grandmother would say on days there was none. We didn't really need it to survive, she'd say, and explain how lots of manual laborers in Mexico lived their entire lives eating little more than beans, chiles, and tortillas. And look how strong they were. We talked as if we were eating poor folks' dishes because we'd suspected all along they ate healthier than us. Ha. One thing I can say for certain: a steady diet of beans and chiles can give the digestive system a real workout.

But while riding high in the taxi with those bills tight in my sweaty palms, my main concern wasn't budgets or diet. I wanted to put as much distance as possible between me and the Sloans. I'd called the taxi from Molly Carol's bedroom, instructing the dispatcher to have the driver pick me up at the Dairy Mart down the road at 1:00 a.m. When the taxi driver asked me for my destination, I said Cogstown, anywhere downtown.

The driver's eyes lingered in the rearview mirror, making me glad that my hood and Jackie O sunglasses hid a good bit of my face. Maybe he'd detected something foreign about me. Had I been forgetting to use contractions when I spoke? Had my sentences gone sing-songy? Sometimes when really nervous, I'd fall back into the up-and-down border intonation that used to drive Grandmother crazy. She said it made me sound like a cowboy from northern Mexico. Cowboys had been fine by me when I was a kid, but nowadays I didn't want to be taken for a Mexican of any kind.

During the year I lived in the suburbs of Cogstown, there weren't that many Mexicans around our area. Sometimes the TV showed stories about workers on the tomato farms or in the chicken processing plants, but I didn't run into too many of them on those scattered times when I did leave the house. Every once in a while I heard Spanish in the mall, and I'd glance at the people to see if they recognized me as a kindred soul. They never did. It was just as well.

The driver kept sneaking peeks in the mirror, which I pretended not to notice. "You undercover?" he asked. "Like Julie with the *Mod Squad*? Ever watch that show when it was on TV? You kinda look like her. Only a baby version, you know?"

"I'm no baby."

"I got a daughter about your age. Fourteen?"

"Sixteen." I gave my Grace Sloan age, but for some reason it pleased me that he'd guessed me to be Altagracia Villalobos's age. During the past year I'd developed curves, and now I told myself that if I weren't covered up with the baggy sweatshirt the driver would think me older. "Almost seventeen," I said.

"Oh yeah?" He smiled in that condescending way adults have with kids.

"I don't lie." I consciously used the contraction and kept out the singsong.

"Just making conversation."

I tugged my hood forward as far as I could. What if he called the cops? At least I had my documents to prove who I was. Other than being in a country illegally—and they wouldn't know that—I wasn't breaking any laws, was I? The sweat on my palms had gone cold, and I rubbed them against my polyester slacks.

"Any spot in particular?" the driver said, and indicated the outside with the wave of one hand.

We'd arrived in Cogstown, and I peered at the small shops and the streets lit up by old-fashioned streetlamps, big pots of candy-colored flowers hanging at the top. It looked like a movie set for a quaint little town, one of those cozy little settings where everybody was quirky and kind. And knew everyone else's business. No wonder Molly Carol always stuck to the malls for shopping and never brought us into town.

"Here's fine," I said, and pointed to Maggie's Designs, a boutique with lots of mod clothing in the brightly lit display window. The fried-chicken kid in the mall had told me the bus ticket counter was inside Dooley's Pharmacy, and a block away a big red sign dangled outside, just like he'd said.

"Here?" The driver turned to stare over the seat at me.

"I want to window shop for a little while," I said.

"It's two in the morning."

"I'm not afraid of anything," I said. In what I hoped was a very grown-up manner, I pulled out the small roll of money and started peeling off ones.

"Take some advice from an old man, sweetheart. Don't never, never flash your dough like that. You can trust me, but there's plenty out there. . . ." He folded my fingers down over the money. "This one's on me," he said.

I started to tell him I didn't need his charity, but thought of the bus ticket I had to buy, and mumbled, "Thanks."

When I opened the door, the driver, probably feeling entitled now that I'd accepted his generosity, couldn't resist some unasked-for advice. "If you're smart," he said, "you'll call your folks. Public phone's down the street. Go home, kid. Before you bite off more than you can chew."

I dawdled in front of Maggie's until the taxi disappeared from sight. A lemon-yellow pantsuit held my attention. And jeans with wide, long legs and lots of patches. I couldn't wait to start buying my own clothes. Nobody was going to tell me what to wear anymore. Nobody was going to tell me shit.

Afraid a police cruiser would suddenly appear with a nosy officer asking too many questions, I ducked into the first alley I spied and curled up inside a deep doorway. The night was cool but not cold, and above me stray stars sparkled between breaks in the cloud cover. Maybe because the town was so cute or because I was unaccustomed to freedom, I felt as though I were the heroine in a feel-good movie. Everything would turn out fine. According to Holly, Molly Carol would sleep through the morning, and if I wasn't there to wake the kids, they would sleep on until past nine. I planned to be at the bus station, waiting, when the door opened at 6:00 a.m. I didn't need to worry about Molly Carol. After all, she'd broken the law too. Months ago, Immigration might have believed that I'd stowed away in her car trunk, but now they'd want to know why she hadn't reported me sooner. And there were those false documents. But all the reasoning in the world couldn't convince me that Molly Carol wouldn't get even with me if she got the chance.

When the clerk at the Greyhound counter asked me, "Where to?" she squinted really hard at my sunglasses, like she needed to see my eyes in order to hear me. I took off my Jackie O's—the disguise wasn't worth the attention it attracted—and scanned the itinerary on the wall. Molly Carol often went to Cincinnati or Columbus, but I hadn't heard her mention Dayton often. "Dayton," I said.

"Round trip?"

"One way." I was heading to a place I'd never been and wouldn't be looking back. Beneath the fear, my nerve endings twanged with excitement. I was back to thinking in terms of Papi's mountains, and I couldn't help but think that something better awaited me over the summit.

Thirty minutes later, when the bus roared up to the outside curb, I rushed up the bus steps so fast I stumbled and almost fell before sliding into a seat halfway down the aisle. Outside a twenty-something guy was waving and yelling from down the block and running toward the bus. When he boarded, the scarf wrapped around his neck and lower half of his face slipped down. A piece of his jawbone was missing and his nose, a shapeless mass of flesh that was of a different shade than the rest of his face, looked stuck on. He glanced around as if to see if anyone had noticed. I turned away as quick as I could and stared out my side window. If he caught me looking, I was afraid I wouldn't be able to hide how sorry I felt for him. And I understood how sometimes pity could hurt a person's pride more than indifference. I wished I could tell him I thought we had a lot in common. Neither one of us was whole and we both were having to get used to being treated like we were someone other than who we were inside.

I figured him to be a Vietnam vet. Those days there were lots of young guys with limbs or other parts of their bodies missing, or you'd see the vets rolling around in wheelchairs with legs or arms that might as well have been missing for all the good they were doing. I hadn't really followed the war too closely back in Mesquite. I knew that the Widow Valencia's Chicano husband had been killed over there and I wished he never had been because then the

Widow would still be in California, which she never should have left. By the time I was at Molly Carol's the Vietnam War—*Conflict*, the government called it—was ending. Molly Carol and Violet both got all misty-eyed about men in uniform but didn't seem to know too much about the conflict itself. Molly Carol hated communists more than Grandmother had, but I still wasn't too certain what a communist was. The definition in the dictionary didn't scare me as much as those news commentators who yammered on about a domino theory. After taking Vietnam, the communists would invade California. I vaguely wondered how long it would take the Ohio domino to fall.

Violet was more interested in reading newspapers with stories about earth women who'd been raped by aliens from outer space and with photos of movie stars before and after they'd had their facelifts. She said she had enough problems of her own to worry about without being depressed by the news. The way I saw it, the world wasn't looking out for me, so I better focus on fixing my own problems before I tried solving everyone else's.

"Dayton," the bus driver called out in a loud irritated way that suggested he was repeating himself.

I stretched and looked around me. I was the only passenger left on the bus. I silently prayed that the vet would be OK. I'd stopped praying for myself after Molly Carol told me about Grandmother's death. Each day I awakened to the same situation, and it hurt too much to think God didn't care enough to help me. But praying for little Travis or the vet was different. I'd never see either one of them again, so I wouldn't know if my prayers were answered or not. It was one way to help me keep a little faith.

When I stepped onto the pavement, weary-faced people with backpacks and plastic shopping bags, stuffed to near bursting, milled around me. My stomach was churning up acidic juices, and the clouds of diesel fumes agitated me even more. Inside the depot a strong smell of pine disinfectant mixed in with traces of bus exhaust fumes. The waiting room looked dated, not in a quaint, made-up way like downtown Cogstown, but sad with scarred wooden benches and cracked-tile flooring. An old man with wrinkly, pecan-colored skin sat in a corner of one bench, a shoe box tied with string in his lap. His eyes, rheumy and blue with disease, told me he must be blind, yet he seemed to be staring right at me. He nodded slightly and said something I couldn't make out. Chelo would have said the old man's blind gaze was a sign. But of what?

Through the finger-smudged glass doors to the outside, a restaurant across the street caught my eye. Plate glass ran the length of the building and a neon sign advertised PARKER'S FAMILY RESTAURANT, BREAKFAST SERVED ALL DAY. Inside fluorescent lighting revealed two U-shaped islands of counter and stools interspersed with rows of red booths. Mostly men dressed in jeans and jackets sat at the counters, and three waitresses were buzzing around with plates stacked up their arms or coffeepots in hand to refill coffee cups. Breakfast had always seemed like the homiest of the daily meals to me, and I suddenly felt like I could eat the biggest special Parker's offered.

When I pushed open the restaurant door, a middle-aged waitress was standing at the counter behind the register handing a carryout paper bag and a thermos to a guy with a hard hat. She looked up but didn't return my smile. Another waitress, probably still in her teens, pushed through a swinging door down by the last island. Tall, with dark hair pulled into a braided pony tail, she could have passed for a sister to Socorro of the rolled-up skirts back at Rosary Academy in Mesquite.

Only this girl's face looked a little pinched with worry around the eyes, not haughty and spoiled like Socorro's. I'd never really liked Socorro that much, but now that I was so far from home and my people (I kept thinking of them that way in spite of telling myself I wouldn't) it was almost like finding a long-lost friend. Even before I sat down, she—Rose of Sharon, her name tag said—pulled a laminated menu out from the holder on the counter and held it out to me. I thanked her, plopped my backpack down on the stool against the wall, and eased onto the one next to it.

I was studying the menu and didn't notice the kid taking the stool next to me until he straddled it and said, "Hey, Rose of Sharon." He glanced at me and asked, "Don't she have the prettiest name you ever did hear?"

"Hmm," I said.

There were plenty of empty stools, so why did this kid have to sit almost on top of me? I considered taking a different seat, but he couldn't have been more than fourteen and was little-boy cute with his curly sandy hair and big dimples. I remembered the taxi driver's advice, and just in case Baby Face had any ideas of grabbing and running, I looped my hand through the straps of my backpack.

Rose of Sharon pulled two filled glasses of water from beneath the counter and sat them in front of us. "I know *you* don't need a menu, Stan," she said to the boy.

The older waitress came zipping across that floor so fast, she reminded me of the garter snakes that the twins and I used to find in Molly Carol's back yard. "Remember, no loafers," she said to Rose of Sharon, not bothering to lower her voice.

"Don't pay any attention to her," Rose of Sharon said, after the other waitress slithered away as fast as she'd appeared. "Loretta doesn't like kids. On top of that, she's bucking for head waitress, so she goes around looking for problems to report to management."

"What we're saying is," Stan said, "is that Miss Loretta's nose ain't brown on no accident."

I couldn't help but grin along with Rose of Sharon. "You're such a nut," she said. She pulled a pad out of her apron pocket and tapped her pencil on it. "One check?"

"No," I said, and started to explain that I'd never laid eyes on Stan before a minute ago.

"Yeh," Stan said. "I'm paying. Me and her's old friends. Ain't seen each other since forever, though."

I could have listened to his drawl—it sounded Southern, but different from Violet and Molly Carol's—all day, but I couldn't get the taxi driver's advice out of my head. I pulled a face as sour as Loretta's and stared hard at the menu. I ordered scrambled eggs, sausage, and toast, only because they didn't have biscuits and gravy. Even if they did they probably wouldn't be as good as Violet's. And Parker's sure wouldn't have a jalapeño to eat with my biscuits and gravy the way I usually did.

"Small Coke," Stan said. Even though no one commented, he told us he never was hungry of a morning anyways, and anybody who knew him could swear to as much. All that explaining reminded me of Grandmother when she insisted I finish up the beans, saying that she'd eaten while I was outside, that she never had cared for beans, and that an old person's digestive system just couldn't handle them.

Stan tried to make small talk while I waited for my food, but I picked up a section of the paper that one of the customers had left behind and started to read about what was going on with the trial of that rich girl Patty Hearst. There were two different parts to the article, one taking the position that she should be found guilty of bank robbery because how could she deny it when there were the photos? The opposing view screamed her innocence because she'd been brainwashed by the Symbionese Liberation Army and wasn't responsible for her actions. When the likes of Patty Hearst started worrying about my problems, I'd spend some time worrying about hers. Rich as she was, she'd probably get off scot-free anyway. What was I going to do after I left Parker's? That's what I had to think about. I was starting to feel like one of those prisoners on death row when they get their last meal.

When Rose of Sharon brought my breakfast, Stan's stomach growled long and hard. "I got a noisy belly," he said, and shrugged. "Don't mean nothing."

I felt so sorry for him I knew I would choke on that food if I didn't offer him a bite. Papi always told me I should never eat in front of another person unless I had enough to share. I asked Stan if he'd like me to ask Rose of Sharon for an extra plate so we could split, but he said no in an insulted way. I told him I'd ordered way more than I could eat and how wasting food was a sin. Hadn't he ever heard that?

He grinned, and said he reckoned he did *not* want to be held responsible for leading a fine young lady down the road to ruination. He offered to save me by accepting one triangle of toast and maybe a dab of grape jelly. He ended up eating pretty much half my breakfast. Stan laughed, and said he figured he'd been hungrier than he realized. "Now I done ate your food, guess we better get ourselves acquainted. Stan Morrison."

"Grace Sloan. I'm new in town."

"Seen you come in off the Greyhound," he said. His smile could have charmed Molly Carol. "On your own, right?"

"I'm looking for a job," I said. Something in Stan's eyes reminded of the street urchins back in Mesquite, and I wanted to make it clear that if he thought I was in the same situation, namely homeless or a beggar, he was mistaken.

"To work you got to be at least sixteen. Or get your parents to sign." Stan studied my face.

"Almost seventeen." I spoke so loudly, a man across from us looked up over his coffee. Before I could stop myself, I said, "I've got the papers to prove it, too."

"Whoa." Stan held up his hands. "I believe you. I was just saying, you know?"

When Rose of Sharon checked in to see if we wanted anything else, Stan piped up. "My friend Grace, she wants an application. And before you say anything, she's old enough. It's only today she didn't put her makeup on. I keep telling her how she looks like a little girl when she don't."

Rose of Sharon told me that I was coming at a good time since they were looking for a girl on the evening tour, and I almost hugged Stan. He was bringing me good luck. Or maybe it was that blind man back at the depot.

"I'm switching to nights myself," Rose of Sharon said. "We'd pull the same shift. Cool, yeah?" I liked the way she made my getting the job sound definite.

"And didn't you tell me you and your mom needed a roommate of the female persuasion?" Stan said to Rose of Sharon. "Well, here she is."

He was so nervy, I had to smile. And for Rose of Sharon's benefit, I tried to make it the most trustworthy of smiles. She frowned in concentration, and Stan, as if sensing her doubts, repeated how he knew me really well, I was good people new to Dayton, and he was trying to help me get settled.

Rose of Sharon blushed crimson, and said she was sure I was groovy, only her and her Mom hadn't been able to move into a bigger place like they'd wanted. "Maybe then," Rose of Sharon said. My face must have shown my panic, because she added, "Tell you what. Fill out an application, and I'll stick around a few minutes after my shift so I can give it personal to Don Hatch—that's the night manager. I'll say you're a friend a mine."

After Rose of Sharon left the application with me and I wrote my name and birth date, I stared at the lines beneath. Stan leaned to the side until our heads were almost touching. "Don't worry none. Stan the Man's got things under control." He took the pen and filled in the blanks below my name with childlike printing. "This here's my uncle Gerald's address and phone," he said. "Parker's calls, leaves a message, Gerald gives me the message, I give it to you. Pony Express, you know?"

"I owe you," I said.

"You're telling me."

At the register, Stan fished in his pockets. "Oh, man," he said, "I forgot my money back to Gerald's. Tell you what, next time's on me." Loretta snorted. Stan and I pretended we hadn't noticed, and he held the door open for me. "My mama raised me to be a gentleman," he said.

I wanted to say he wasn't even half-raised yet, so his mama still had work to do, but it was really a polite gesture so I didn't smart off. I hadn't realized how formal and polite Mexicans were until I'd been away from Mesquite and missed all those little niceties.

"So, you from around here?" I said. "I mean you don't sound like Ohio."

"Here I was thinking the same thing about you, Miss Grace. Matter of fact, something about the way you talk kindly reminds me of some particular folks I heard before down home. You know, out West. Only you ain't Texas."

The muscle at the corner of my eye twitched. I scratched at it, hoping Stan hadn't noticed. I would just ignore what he'd said.

Stan did a little hippity-hop step, jumped to the side and clicked his heels. With an outstretched hand he pointed up, down, right, left. "Eenie, meenie, miney mo. Which way do we go?" He pivoted to the left and headed toward the business area. I fell into step next to him.

"Here's the deal," he said. "You be Grace, I'll be Stan, and both of us is from right here, OK? No sense poking around, looking for what ain't there." He turned to me, opened his eyes wide and wriggled his eyebrows. "And if it ain't there," he said, "you cain't find it." I suspected Stan practiced facial expressions in the mirror the way I practiced avoiding expression, and I began to like him even more than I already did.

Downtown Dayton wasn't small town-quaint like Cogstown, but neither was it like the big U.S. cities I'd seen in American movies. As we walked, Stan nodded in greeting to a number of passing kids, and it gave me a safe feeling, like soon enough I'd have friends here too. I remembered the horror stories that Chelo used to tell me and Olga about Mexico City. Not that Chelo had ever been there, but she'd heard plenty, she said. Yes, Dayton was a good medium-size city for a starting point. Once I was settled, who knew where I might go. That little spark of excitement started buzzing through my veins again.

Along the way, Stan pointed out what he called hot spots, areas of town where a kid was more likely to get stopped by the cops. The *police*, he called them, stressing the first syllable the way Violet did, although his accent was gringo cowboy. He advised against hanging too close to fancy-looking offices because, he said, the workers got scared over nothing at all and would call the cops in a minute.

"Cops care about what the high-ups think," he said.

"The muckity-mucks?" I asked, using one of Molly Carol's favorite words.

"Damn straight."

When we reached a strip of park that ran along a grassy mound, we rested on a park bench beneath a tree. Stan pointed below. "The Miami River," he said.

"Nice," I said, and waited. I could tell there was something he wanted to tell me.

"Last summer one of ours drownded down there. James thought he'd take hisself a little swim to get the stink off. Got caught up in the current."

"I'm sorry," I said, but I hoped he'd drop the subject. Now wasn't the time for me to hear about dead kids.

"Never even knew his last name or where he come from. They didn't have no missing kid reports that matched up with ol' James. Nobody cared he was gone, I reckon." Stan shrugged, trying to convince me that James hadn't mattered to him one way or another. "That's the way it goes," Stan said after a moment. "When you're dead, you're dead. Anyways, I don't think about it."

"Leave the dead to the dead?"

"Damn straight."

I closed my eyes, and soon the traffic passing beyond a line of trees evolved into white noise. I concentrated on the rush of the wind through the trees and the flow of the river below. A breeze rustled the leaves of the giant tree next to us, and for a moment I could almost smell orange blossoms and Grandmother's Maja cologne, almost see Grandmother in her chair and the way she barely rocked when she was waiting, waiting. In her hands, crochet needles; in her lap, the bedspread she'd been working on for Papi. The one she slept with after he died. I wondered if that bedspread had been buried with her. I hoped so. I wished I could leave my dead alone the way Stan claimed.

"Open your eyes," Stan said, "but don't look at the street." He'd startled me, and I almost did exactly what he'd instructed me not to do. "You stare and they'll reckon something suspicious is going on." As Stan spoke, he pointed across the river, as if we were discussing the skyline.

"Nice and easy, Gracie," he said. "They's a cop car stopped at a red light and looking our way. Me and you's just two citizens enjoying the Lord's creations. Keep your hands in the open, let 'em see we got nothing. Prob'ly they just trying to figure our ages and should we be in school. But if they feeling all generous—or in a hurry to finish shifts—they won't bother us none."

Once they'd driven on, Stan turned to me. "For a minute there I thought you was going to fall apart on me." The mischievous twinkle had returned to his eyes. "What you need's a peanut butter sandwich," he said.

"Peanut butter?"

"Yeah, you know, to hold yourself together?"

I laughed and the tension almost left me. "I'm glad we're friends," I said.

"OK, then." Stan clunked the heels of his motorcycle boots against the cement then stood up.

"Where're we going?" I didn't try to keep the irritation out of my tone. I'd had little sleep the night before, and my sense of adventure had all but worn out. I had a job lined up, so that was settled, but what about a place to live? I'd been hoping that Stan would invite me to stay with him and his uncle.

"Gonna introduce you to some friends down to the warehouse," Stan said.

"So," I said, "your uncle live around here?"

"Gerald's is off limits 'til he gets home from work. Not that he don't trust me in the apartment by my lonesome. He thinks I need more fresh air. Always worrying about me. Like this morning? I got up late, so he wouldn't let me take not even a slice of bread with me. Don't get up in time, no breakfast. I reckon I'll learn my lesson."

I thought about when I was kid in Mesquite playing house with one of my girlfriends. We called it jugando a las mentiritas. I didn't want to *play at little lies* now. I wanted the solid reality of four walls and a door with a lock to keep out intruders. I was anxious to be the new Grace. As we walked, I sighed every once in a while just to make a point about how tired I was, but Stan was as good as I was at ignoring what he didn't want to hear.

"Home sweet home," Stan said, and pointed a block away. The warehouse was an abandoned three-story red brick with boarded windows and a huge advertisement for Bosco Coffee in fading paint on the side. Stan opened his eyes wide and wriggled his eyebrows, and I knew what was coming, and sure enough, he said, "If it ain't there, you cain't find it."

I didn't laugh this time. Since he had a home with Gerald, whose *sweet home* was this warehouse supposed to be? Not mine. At a bus stop in front of the warehouse, three teens perched on the back of a bench and passed a cigarette back and forth. The wind blew the sweet-smelling smoke towards us. Back in Mesquite, I'd sometimes gotten whiffs of that scent when Grandmother and I passed alleys on our way to go shopping. The thought of living inside that abandoned building almost made me pee, and I squeezed my thighs together.

"They's some bad dudes around here, like everywheres else," Stan said. "But now, you get yourself some amigos to watch your back, and you'll make it." He told me that he'd introduce me to the coolest freaks and, with his chin, indicated the two boys and a girl on the warehouse bench. They all had pasty skin and stringy, greasy hair, and a downwind breeze carried the musk of unwashed bodies.

"Hey," Stan called out.

The girl clipped the joint butt with a bobby pin and stretched out her arm in offering toward us. "Toke?"

Stan sniffed the air. "Suspicious," he said, "*mighty* suspicious."

We all laughed. Stan cupped his hand around the joint and after taking a big suck, held it to my mouth, but I shook my head. I'd never tried pot, and I sure didn't want to start when I had no idea of where I'd be spending the night. When Stan told the kids to introduce themselves, none of them gave their family names. It seemed somehow appropriate, as if they were disconnected from any bloodline or roots. Soon I would learn that they formed a family of their own, temporary and transitory. Sweet William shook his head of long blonde hair that made him look like a drawing of General Custer I'd seen in Holly's history book. Little Eddie picked at the yellowish crusts clinging to the base of his white eyelashes. And Tara said repeatedly how she'd chopped off her hair after tossing down a bunch of pills in different shapes and colors that some old man had given her. "I was fuckin' positive my hair was really a bunch of snakes growing right out of my scalp," Tara said.

"That's some deep shit," Sweet William said, and pulled a wry expression as if he was used to Tara making such statements. He'd been staring at me the whole time, and although his eyes were pretty—lavender-blue and fringed with thick brown lashes with blond tips—the expression was so sad and serious, they made me a little uneasy. He stared at me and asked Stan if I was his old lady.

Stan grinned as if he liked the idea. Once we'd moved on and were out of earshot, he told me that if I ever needed help, Sweet William was my man. "Only watch out," he said, " 'cause sometimes he figures hisself a ladies' man."

I didn't like the way Stan seemed to be lumping me in with these so-called freaks. "All those kids live in the warehouse?" I said. "Why don't they get a job?"

"Like you?" Stan said. He seemed a bit irritated, but shrugged as if he didn't have the answers. He warned me against shelters, said they'd turn me into the authorities for what they'd insist was my own good. He told me about a local social worker, a short dude he nicknamed Tom Thumb. Tom Thumb worked with wayward kids and took his favorites on special camping trips. "Yeh, he gives 'em something special, all right." Stan angled a look at me and wriggled his eyebrows.

"I bet there's some who really do help," I said, and wished he'd agree.

"You won't catch me trying to find out. Anyways, I like my freedom. I'd rather be dead and rotting in my grave than cooped up with a bunch of rules and such."

We were nearing a church with a big glass box sign outside. In the box was a clock and a warning: *Time's running out. Have you found the Lord?*

"I got myself saved once," Stan said wistfully. "Too many rules." The sign seemed to trigger memories for him, and he fell silent. My feet ached something terrible and I was sleepy. We'd walked many more blocks through downtown and across a bridge. Just when I was about to tell him that I'd had enough of this walking to nowhere, that I needed a goal, a destination, Stan spoke up. "I been thinking maybe you could stay with me and Gerald."

I stopped in the middle of the sidewalk and wrapped my arms around his neck. "Thank you, thank you. I won't be any trouble, you'll see."

He turned a deep red. I liked the way he could seem so innocent in spite of that dead look that sometimes hovered around his gray eyes.

"Gerald won't mind?" I said, and hoped that Stan would reassure me, but he only pointed to a white-painted brick apartment building. "When we get in," he said, "let me do the talking. Gerald's cool, but you got to know how to handle him."

I would have agreed to anything to stay out of the warehouse. Even though there was a doorbell, Stan rapped a little beat on the door with his knuckles, and the door flew open so quickly, it must have been a secret code. The man wore a towel around his waist and when he spotted me, he clutched at the towel and sucked in his breath. "Who is *this*?" he hiss-whispered.

"Ah, Grace's OK," Stan said.

Gerald stuck his head out far enough to take a quick up-and-down look at the hall before moving aside for us to enter. Once the door was closed and locked, he stood with legs straddled, arms crossed over his chest. He stared hard at Stan. "OK, mister, this better be good."

Stan told Gerald that I was an old friend passing through and needed a place to crash. "Ah, come on man, only for tonight," Stan said. He spoke in a new wheedling voice, and I looked away, embarrassed for him but not enough to walk back out the door.

Gerald bent over to pick up a cigarette lighter from the coffee table, and the towel hiked up, revealing muscular thighs. He threw back his head and exhaled cigarette smoke through his nostrils. "Did I or did I not warn you about dragging in strays?" he said.

"Ah, come on," Stan wheedled, and shuffled his feet. I never could be certain why he sacrificed his pride and risked his sanctuary for someone he'd only met that day, but when he stood his ground for me I knew that no matter what happened from then on, I would always have a tender spot for him.

"Well, you'll have to be extra nice tonight," Gerald said, and gave Stan a coy look.

Gerald made us all drinks, tall glasses of something sweet with sprigs of mint. I sat in an overstuffed chair across from the sofa where Gerald sat next to Stan. Gerald kept one hand on Stan's knee and his eyes on me. A bright red spot had come out on one of Stan's cheeks, and he focused on his drink. I was nervous, and after all that walking, thirsty, so I drank in big gulps. When my glass ran low, Gerald jumped to fix me another. "Better take it easy," Stan said, but Gerald told him that I was a big girl and that he should leave me alone.

The only alcohol I'd ever had was the traditional sip of rompope that Papi used to allow me on Christmas Eve, but these drinks tasted so good, I couldn't imagine anything bad coming from them. I liked the way I was feeling relaxed, the way my troubles didn't seem so big anymore. I don't remember much of what happened after that. There are snatches of memory: Stan holding my head over the toilet bowl, whispering not to worry, that he'd look after me. Stan placing my head on a pillow, lifting my legs onto the sofa, and covering me with a blanket.

Old-people music was playing, Frank Sinatra, I think, singing about doing it his way. I remember wishing for a point in my life where I could afford to do things any way other than the do-what-you-have-to-do-to-survive way. What a luxury to have choices. The world whirled around me. Gerald's and Stan's voices were floating somewhere behind and above me. I couldn't make out what Gerald said, but Stan whispered in a serious and determined voice, "No way, man, we ain't doing that. She's my friend."

I thickly wondered what Gerald had in mind. Then I was out.

The side of my neck had a crick in it where the top of my head had pressed into the arm of the sofa, and I'd drooled a wet spot onto the pillow. My head was spinning and all the vomiting I'd done the night before had left my stomach empty and burning. My bladder was a different story. The door to the bedroom was closed and I hated risking waking them with a toilet flush, but I couldn't hold my pee a minute longer.

I stumbled across the living room, holding onto the sofa, then the walls. After flushing, I washed my hands and face as quickly as I could, afraid that any minute Gerald would come banging on the door. Thirsty as I had ever been, I lowered my mouth next to the spigot and sloshed in handfuls of water.

"Hey, Grace," Stan whispered from the other side of the closed door. I opened the door a crack. He wore only a pair of jeans, and his chest was pale and hairless. He told me that I'd gotten a phone call last night after I'd fallen asleep. I appreciated his delicate way of putting things.

"I'm awake," Gerald sang out from the bedroom. "Can the whispering."

Purplish-red bruises ran up one side of Stan's neck, the kind Papi used to have sometimes when he'd been out with the Widow. I tried not to think about what Stan and Gerald had been doing during the night, but I was a virgin and had real curiosity about what exactly went on during the sex act. Olga had once told me that men and women did it the same way dogs did, and after that no matter how hard I tried to erase that image, I'd picture married couples humping, the female yelping once they were butt to butt and stuck together.

Stan must have noticed my interest, because he turned a bright red and lowered his eyes. "You got an interview at five today with Don Hatch," he said.

"How do you know?" I almost squealed with excitement, and wanted to hug Stan, but just then Gerald came out with a sheet wrapped around him like a toga.

"Four o'clock, not five," Gerald said. "And that brings up the matter of Stan's little boo-boo. We have a rule that no one gives out this telephone number but me. Understand?"

I nodded, and the movement made me so nauseated, I thought my head would fall off.

Even though Gerald stuck his red lips into a pout, Stan insisted that he would walk me to the bus stop. Thirty minutes later, when I climbed onto the bus, Stan told the driver where to let me off, and instructed me to look for Sweet William at the warehouse.

"If it ain't there, you cain't find it?" I said.

"Damn straight."

I glanced at the Timex that Molly Carol had given me for Christmas. Noon. I had four hours to kill before my interview. I thought of Papi and how he liked to keep moving. When he went for drives, he didn't drive in straight lines that would have taken him out of town, but rather in circles around Mesquite, circling back tighter and tighter until he eventually returned to The Peacock Curios and his family. I wanted to move in circles now, concentric circles that got wider and wider, until maybe, just maybe I could find a way out.

NINE

The bright morning light bored through my eyes into my brain, and with each bounce of the bus I swore that I would never again drink another drop of alcohol. A few of the passengers glanced at me, more to do with my frowziness than my looking like a foreigner or a runaway, I figured. I was beginning to think that people didn't care as much about missing kids as I'd believed. I finger-combed my hair and rubbed the crust from the corners of my eyes.

When I stepped out at my stop, a strong gust of wind almost knocked me over. I steadied myself and breathed in the fresh air. The sky burned so blue, it gave me hope. I could have stood with a little less sunshine under my current circumstances, but surely the sky's clarity was a sign that things were going to work out. My life with the Sloans was just another part of my past that I would forget (for I still believed then that the past could be forgotten). I would get that job at Parker's and Rose of Sharon would let me stay with her. She had been so nice, and I just knew her mother would be the same. She might even love me like a daughter, eventually. I wouldn't be an imprisoned housemaid; I'd be part of a family.

A police cruiser passed, and the officer turned his head slightly as if checking me out in the rearview mirror. I walked close to the buildings, head down, eyes on the sidewalk, hoping that I blended into the walls. I peeked up now and then to make certain that I hadn't lost my way. There were maybe five kids around the warehouse bench. A breeze lifted Sweet William's pale blond hair, making him look like a tall, ragged angel preparing to ascend into heaven. Pasty-faced Eddie still gave me the creeps with his expression of a stray dog that expected to be kicked, and when he *got* kicked would come right back for more. Like Travis. I felt mean to have such thoughts, but I didn't want any part of Eddie. I couldn't be everybody's keeper.

Sweet William spotted me and waved. When he reached my side, he bent down so that his face was close to mine. "Let's split," he said in a low voice, and I was thankful to turn my back on Eddie. "First piece of advice?" Sweet William said. "Stop walking like a mark."

I asked him what he meant, and he told me that if I continued to shuffle around with my head hanging low like a loser, I'd attract some bad dudes. It shocked me a little to think that maybe others were seeing me the way I saw Eddie. "Walk like you got someplace to go," Sweet William said. "Like you're some-fuckin-body. Even if you don't got a clue." More and more it became apparent to me that the way to survival was hiding how you really felt, putting on a face. Molly Carol understood that, and so had Chelo.

"The predator will sniff out the victim every time," Sweet William said. "That's the way of the animal kingdom." His voice had taken on that self-important tone teachers have in the classroom. Once we were out of earshot of the others, Sweet William told me that some kids might be trouble.

"All of us down here's freaks, so we got to stick together," he said. "But watch your back. You don't want nobody messing with your stuff."

Adapt, I thought. "Stan told me you'd treat me right," I said. Better remind Sweet William that we had a mutual friend. Just in case he got any ideas about messing with my stuff himself.

"Damn straight." Sweet William grinned, as if he understood I was warning him. "Speaking of messing around," he said, "how things go at Gerald's?"

"You don't think he'll kick Stan out?"

Sweet William watched me from the corner of his eye. "I'm surprised Stan took you there. Gerald's awful jealous."

"Different strokes for different folks," I said, the way I'd heard on some TV show. Then just to make it good and clear that I didn't appreciate gossip about Stan, I added a fib. "Stan says you're almost like a brother to him."

"Sure, he's my man. Stan the Man." Sweet William seemed genuinely moved. Fibs weren't always a bad thing.

I hadn't realized we'd circled the block and were turning into the alley behind the warehouse until we smacked into the stench of urine. I stopped dead.

"Hey, chill out." Sweet William pointed to the warehouse. "You are going to crash there tonight, right?"

"No," I almost shouted. "I got a job lined up, and I'm going to be rooming with a woman that works with me."

"Wow, man, like that was fast. Fuckin' impressive."

I understood Sweet William was being sarcastic, but I pretended that he was sincere. I didn't want any negative thoughts creeping into the sunny view I was determined to take of the future. I'd had enough hard luck after the accident, and then with Molly Carol. Now things were going to go my way. They had to. I was beginning to think that each time I adapted to unhappiness, I was losing a bit more of my soul.

"But just in case things don't turn out like you imagine," he said, "let me show you around my pad."

We'd reached the door of the warehouse, and I put my hand over my nose to block the stink of pee and other body wastes and secretions. As we entered, Sweet William whispered for me to stick with him and keep my mouth shut. Once our eyes adjusted to the darkness, we moved forward, so close that the hairs on our forearms brushed against each other. Inside the warehouse looked pretty much like I expected with a littering of cans, beer and wine bottles, articles of clothing, and torn, stained mattresses scattered at different corners of the floor. Something squeaked and skittered behind me. I didn't bother to ask what it was.

"Over there's my mattress," Sweet William said. "You can squeeze in with me if your plans don't work out—"

"They will."

"I believe it to be, therefore it *is*?"

"Whatever."

Outside again, Sweet William told me that he'd been thinking about leaving Ohio for someplace warm, maybe Florida or California or Texas. "Me and Stan planned on booking on out of here before he met Gerald. How about you, you sticking around?"

I shrugged like I didn't care either way, but really I was feeling like I did that day I saw Papi with the Widow: ocean waves pulling the sand from beneath my feet. A solid cement foundation, that's what I needed. At least for a while.

I told Sweet William that I wanted to hang around outside the warehouse so I wouldn't miss Stan when he joined me. But he convinced me that if Stan showed up it wouldn't be until later and that in the meantime we should keep movin', movin'. I again thought of Papi and his long drives, putting so many miles on the van that Grandmother would make comments about how it was nice that some people were so rich they didn't have to worry about the cost of gasoline.

I treated me and Sweet William to large carryout coffees from a White Tower, and as we walked toward town, the fog in my head started clearing. I remembered how Stan had said makeup would make me look older, so at a Woolworth's five & dime store, I bought mascara and a fuchsia-shade of lipstick that I'd seen older women wear. The store had a lunch counter, and to celebrate my new life, I bought us cheeseburger platters and syrup-flavored Cokes, vanilla for me, cherry for him. The lining of my stomach was still tender from all that alcohol, so I ended up ordering another Coke and pushing my plate over to Sweet William.

I was wondering where a certain ripe-body odor was coming from, when I took a deep sniff and realized I was the source. I couldn't go to my interview at Parker's smelling like a loser, so I ducked downstairs into the ladies room, brushed my teeth, then dispensed some of the powdery soap for what Violet would have called a-lick-and-a-promise sponge bath. The towels were the cloth kind that circulated, so I had to use toilet paper as a washcloth to clean the more fragrant parts of my body. The paper shredded, but at least I didn't stink anymore. Soon I'd have a new home and wouldn't need public restrooms.

When Don Hatch said Rose of Sharon had told him all about me, I wished I knew what exactly she'd said so I wouldn't make any slipups. I could tell that he liked my looks, so just in case I did mess up I smiled a lot in a way that would show my teeth, almost as white as Papi's. And I called him Mr. Hatch, since I'd always been taught to respect my elders. Grandmother said it was a sign of good breeding. But since being in the U.S., I'd noticed that sometimes good manners were mistaken for weakness, so I tried not to be overly polite. I was American now. Mexico was a part of me that had to remain a secret.

"Call me Don," Don Hatch said, and I flashed him another toothy smile.

"You look a little young," Don said. "Rose of Sharon says you're sixteen. You can prove that if anybody gives us flack?"

I reached for the false birth certificate in my backpack, but he was already standing up and moving toward a rack of metal shelves. "Looks like your size." He held up a plastic bag with a uniform. "You'll need to buy your own work shoes. No rush, you got a week."

"A week?" My mouth went dry, and the smile stuck to my teeth.

"Yeah, Monday," he said. "I thought you'd want to start up with Rose of Sharon. And since she's on vacation now because of her mom being sick. . . ." For the first time, he eyed me suspiciously. "You knew that, right?"

"Sure, we're old friends." My throat was so thick I could barely speak.

When I returned to the warehouse, Sweet William said, in his smart-alecky way, "What? Something didn't work the way you thought?" I wanted to punch him.

In the following days, Sweet William showed me the ropes even though I told him I wasn't sticking around long enough to need all the information. Just in case, he'd say. He pointed out the best dumpsters, those more likely to hold food never touched by human mouths and thrown out only because the restaurant had a policy to not give it away. Sweet William said that if a worker was caught slipping you a free sandwich that had been sitting under the warming lights for hours or a salad in a plastic container left over at the end of the day, the worker would be fired on the spot. And we had to be careful with our scavenging, because some badass managers would call the cops if they caught us.

When Stan didn't show up, I wouldn't let Sweet William out of my sight. Violet used to say that Travis stuck to me like white on rice. Well, Sweet William was my rice. I confided in him and whispered that I had a few dollars. Bread, he called it. After buying my work shoes, I bought two loaves of Wonder bread and big jars of peanut butter and jelly. We carried the food around with us in our backpacks and had PB & J sandwiches for breakfast and lunch. Dinnertime, we'd go to a fast food place or the White Tower or the lunch counter down at Woolworth's for grilled cheeses or turkey hot shots with extra gravy on the mashed potatoes.

Like everybody else, Sweet William and I slept with all our clothes on. The nights were chilly and my hoodie didn't keep me that warm, so when Sweet William put his arm around me and pulled me close, I let him. He smelled of pot and sweat, both stale and recent, but after a few days my body odor blended right in with his. It was better than the pee and vomit stink of the mattress, so I pressed my nose against his bony chest. A couple of times his hand moved down too low on my back or up too high onto my breasts, and each time I told him to stop the funny business. Finally he did.

Even with our mattress pushed into the corner (keep your back to the wall, Sweet William warned), the night noises had me shivering more than the cold. Besides the scratching and squeaking, there were grunts and groans, and I remembered again Olga telling me how people did it just like dogs. Marijuana smoke hung over our heads in a haze, and I complained to Sweet William that I thought I was getting a second-hand high. He told me he'd much rather be around a stoner than a mean drunk any time of the day. And, he said, he sure as hell could tell me a few stories about mean drunks. I thought maybe he wanted me to ask him about that comment, but I didn't want to hear any stories about him being beaten by one or the other, or both, of his parents, so I let his comment slide.

When Sweet William panhandled, most people ignored him but some told him to get a job like everybody else. One woman stopped and wagged a finger in his face, told him that she'd worked hard for everything she had and she wasn't about to give one red cent to some freeloader. I thought of Grandmother and how she'd preferred to give me up than see me reduced to begging. I wanted so badly to believe that Grandmother sending me away had been for purely altruistic reasons. Whenever I thought about how she'd never forgiven me for the accident, I had my doubts about her motivation, but I pushed those thoughts right out of my head. Now that she was dead, I felt safe in remembering things in a way more to my liking.

Sweet William was older than the other kids, so I asked him why he didn't apply at Parker's too. He told me he had. There and lots of other places. Either they wouldn't hire him on the spot, he said, or they insisted on an address and phone, or once when he did get hired, they told him the opening was at one of their chain stores in the suburbs. Even if it had been on the bus line, he said, he didn't have money for the ride.

"Don't worry," Sweet William said, "when I get down to Texas or wherever, I'll hook up with some construction work. I'd rather be out in the open spaces anyways. Cannot stand being closed up." He also didn't like getting up at set times or doing anything else on a schedule. Like Stan, he was not a fan of rules.

By the middle of the week, without my asking, Sweet William started talking about how he'd landed on the streets and told me about his parents kicking him out when he was fifteen. He'd decided to drop out of school and mostly wanted to close himself up in his bedroom and listen to Pink Floyd eight tracks. "It's not my parents' fault," Sweet William said. "I can be a real asshole. If I had a kid like me I'd probably kick him out, too." He cut his eyes in my direction, like he was waiting to hear a little bit about my background, but, as usual when I got asked personal questions, I pulled my Chelo mask.

We walked the streets through the night until dawn. We stepped in and out of the shadows. We owned the midnight hours. Every now and then, I even imagined myself hitting the road with Stan and Sweet William. Tara warned me that the darkness brought the pervs out. "They're like cockroaches," she said. "Turn off the lights and in no time the little bastards are crawling all over you."

Tara lived in East Dayton with her mother and had so many siblings, she joked that she had trouble keeping them straight. Since her mom was usually high or drunk, Tara pretty much came and went as she pleased. When she started talking about her sexual escapades, Sweet William said I was a nice girl and that Tara shouldn't be telling me that crap.

"What makes her so goddam special?" Tara said. She acted mad, but I could see how much his words had hurt. She turned on me then. "You don't fuck, you don't do drugs. You don't even cuss. What the hell do you do for fun?" This was the first time I'd heard Tara use so many curse words in such a short space. Sweet William snorted.

Before, Tara had told me that she'd gone out on her own the first time when she was ten. Her mom had walked in and caught Tara in bed with her stepdad, then kicked Tara out for being a man-stealing slut. After that, Tara lived with a foreigner (she didn't know where he came from) for awhile, but he was only in town for painting a bridge, and once that job was finished, he returned to Youngstown to his wife and three little kids, one of them Tara's age.

"He was real nice to me most of the time," Tara said. "Not every guy would let a chick stay in his motel room for a month." Well, she clarified, she did have to leave during the day, but he always let her return nights, as long as she didn't let anybody see her. Tara said that the bridge painter's taking her in had given her mom time to cool off, and she'd allowed Tara to return. Tara said all this in a nonchalant voice, as if being off the streets was no big deal.

She reminded me of some of those actresses in made-on-the-cheap movies who didn't know the first thing about acting.

When I'd first arrived at Parker's, I thought I couldn't be more desperate for a job and a home, but I'd been wrong. Just listening to Tara and some of the other kids tell their stories made me break out in a sweat of fear for what could be waiting for me.

She invited me to see Dayton's weekend nightlife. Sweet William was dead set against my going, but a few dark clouds were starting to gather in my the-future-is-a sunny-place attitude. It seemed to me that I'd better prepare myself. Just in case. But for all his cynicism, Sweet William wanted to protect me from too much street reality. I told him I appreciated all his help, but he was not my boss and I could do as I pleased. He muttered that I was an ungrateful brat, and I told him that he'd better come up with something original because I'd heard that one before.

When we reached the courthouse steps, Sweet William plopped down next to me on the top step. "You got no business being here," he said for the umpteenth time.

"I just want to observe," I said. "How else will I know what I'm up against?"

"Don't get sucked in, Grace," he said. "Next thing you know, you're not yourself anymore." I hooked my arm through his and held tight to let him know that I really did appreciate him.

Cars cruised past, drivers' faces pulled back in the shadows. Some wanted boys, others girls, and some both, but they all wanted bodies, young and dirty. For some the dirtier, the better the adventure. Naughty time. After getting dropped off from the cars, the kids would group on the steps, share stories, and joke about the fatherly ones—or grandfatherly—who gave lectures, warned about the dangers of youngsters getting in cars with strangers. Then the guy might press a burger wrapped in paper into the kid's hand or slip an extra dollar into a front jeans pocket, adding an extra squeeze to the still-sticky groin one last time before dropping the kid off on the corner. Sugar Daddy drove away, fingers curled to nose, sniffing his latest fishy memory. If you preferred a Sugar Mommy, the kids advised me, it was better to hang outside a bar or get invited to private parties.

Tara skipped down the steps, said she was going to find some action. That would be the last time I saw her. There would be rumors that some college boys from the nearby private university had taken her back to their frat house for a party. When they got there, she'd turned out to be the entertainment, and they pulled a train on her. That would be the word on the street. I never knew if it was true or not. I would tell Sweet William that if it *was* true, I hoped the cops got the guys, and he would bark a laugh and say the cops just wanted us to go away, weren't about to take the word of one of us over a bunch of rich college boys.

As far as I could tell, poverty worked as well as those iron grids on Molly Carol's windows and doors to keep a person imprisoned. The street kids kept talking about how free they were, but me, I was starting to think that I could do with a little less freedom.

On Friday of the last weekend I would be at the warehouse, I spotted Stan from a block away, hippity-hopping and clicking his heels. When he got closer, I could see the black eye and scratches on his face. He told us he'd fallen down the stairs, like the big clumsy that he was.

"Yeah," I said, "that happened to me before, too."

"Suspicious," Stan said, "*mighty* suspicious," and we all laughed too loudly.

I tried to apologize to Stan for the trouble I'd caused him, but he turned serious and made it clear that he didn't want to discuss Gerald. "I'm free again," he said. "If it ain't there, you cain't find it."

"Damn straight," Sweet William said, and told Stan he was ready to hit the road any time he was. When Stan said that there was no time like the present, my stomach curled up into a tight ball. I was going to be on my own.

In later years, I would study the faces of Anglo comedians, half expecting, or maybe hoping, that Stan had ended up making a living out of his natural funniness. I would never see him again, though, not in person, not on television, but I still like to think that Stan's sense of humor kept him going.

The guys walked me to Parker's, said they'd have one last Coke at the old watering hole. They told me they'd wait while I changed into my uniform, but they didn't order anything, and I knew they'd take off as soon as I went to the back. They'd probably had one good-bye too many in their lives. I held back my tears and hugged them. We all pretended that we'd be seeing each other again some day. I wanted to give them the ten dollars I had left, and when I insisted, they finally accepted five.

I'd known them for such a short time, but my heart ached from losing them so soon. I was mad at myself for becoming so attached. By now, I should have known better than to think I could have a lasting relationship of any sort.

The next time I met someone I really liked, I'd make sure to hold back on my emotions. No attachments. I never knew when I'd have to leave.

I stuck close to Rose of Sharon as she and the other four waitresses rushed around snapping tickets onto the order wheel. The grill cooks yelled at each other back in the kitchen, and every ten minutes or so, Melvin, the newly hired dishwasher, burst through the swinging kitchen doors and into the dining room to heft away another tub overflowing with dirty dishes. He muttered that Parker's must think they were back in the good old days and he was their Uncle Tom, but they better think again because nobody had told him anything about bussing tables when he was hired on, so they had better find a busboy quick if they wanted to keep his black ass around.

Rose of Sharon chuckled and asked me if I didn't think he was better looking than the actor Billy Dee Williams. Melvin was handsome all right, but I couldn't have cared less. Time was ticking away, and if I didn't find a new place to stay, there was only the dark warehouse waiting for me. And tonight there would be no Sweet William to wrap me in the safe shelter of his arms. My eyes watered each time I thought of him or Stan, but I refused to allow even one tear to fall. What was the point? I had to focus on my immediate needs. Finding a new safe haven, for instance.

I didn't have the time or the nerve to bring up the subject of sleeping arrangements until Rose of Sharon and I were off shift and sitting in the break room. She was counting up her tickets for the night and explaining that in the future I should watch out for anyone who might try to walk out with a ticket. "Parker's will take five dollars out of your next pay for each and every missing ticket. They figure that's the cost of an average order. Oh, and if you break anything? That's out of our paycheck, too. Isn't that a crock?"

"Yeah," I said, but really I wanted a job so desperately that I would have accepted any conditions Parker's wanted to throw at me. Survival, that was my first priority. I tried to think of some way to connect what she'd said to the night's sleeping arrangements, but my brain was in such a panic that it wouldn't work right. "Could I go home with you?" I blurted. "Just for the night? I promise I won't be any trouble."

I wanted to cover my eyes with my hands. Like at a scary movie when you can't stand to see what's going to happen next but peep between the spaces of your fingers because you can't *not* know.

Rose of Sharon frowned a little. "Gosh," she said. "We only have the one bedroom."

"Maybe you could call your mom and ask her if it's all right? Just for one night?" Believe me, it wasn't easy keeping hysteria from taking me over.

Rose of Sharon stacked and restacked her night's receipts and mumbled something about her mother working at The Shipwreck, not getting off until 2:30 a.m. and the bar's manager not allowing personal phone calls. She glanced up at me and must have seen the desperation on my face, because she patted my hand and said, "Oh, what the hay. We'll work something out."

As we rode the bus home that night, I thought of an old movie I'd watched on TV, *A Streetcar Named Desire*. At the end the character Blanche DuBois said that she'd always depended on the kindness of strangers. I was beginning to truly understand the meaning of those words.

The small clapboard house sat all alone among a grove of trees in an unlit alley behind the main street. It was like an enchanted cottage in a dark forest from the fairy tales. Inside, Rose of Sharon gave me a quick peek into each room. The house smelled Lysol-clean, but the tiny bedroom, living room, kitchen, and bath were all crowded with boxes and extra clothing she and her mother hadn't been able to squeeze into the two stuffed closets. Rose of Sharon said she was sorry they didn't have a basement, that it made things a little scary during tornado season. I told her not to worry because I'd never met a basement I liked.

The next day I woke up to the smell of coffee, and Rose of Sharon calling out calling out from the kitchen. "Come and have some cinnamon rolls with me and Mom."

Barb had black hair like Rose of Sharon's, but her skin was a sallow shade that suggested she tanned a rich brown in the summer. With her coloring and almond-shaped eyes, she looked mestiza to me, and I felt instantly comfortable with her. I pulled up a chair at the Formica-topped table (a deal from their favorite Goodwill, like the rest of their furniture, I'd learn later). Now that I was near Barb, I could see there was a grayish cast to her skin, and dark pouches beneath her eyes gave her a tired look. Her hair, so shiny and strong, contrasted with her drawn face, as if the hair had leeched all the nutrients from her body.

Right from the start, Barb told me I was welcome to anything in the fridge or cupboards and that I might want to get some boxes to make myself a little chest of drawers for my things. When I tried to thank her, she said I'd be doing them a favor. "We could use a little extra coming in, and that's a fact," she said. "But how about your family? And shouldn't you be in school?"

I gave her the same basic story that Molly Carol had told everyone in Brockton, only I gave Molly Carol as my dead mother since her name was on my birth certificate. Rose of Sharon and Barb were being so nice to me, and I wanted to be completely honest with them. But to tell them everything could not only put me in jeopardy with Immigration, but would get them in trouble for harboring a fugitive. I pushed the guilt down into the sludge of other feelings that I didn't want to acknowledge.

Barb told me that she was an orphan of sorts herself. When her mother was diagnosed with cancer of the ovaries, her father, unable to cope, ran off, and Barb was taken in by her grandmother. "From the Blackfoot people of Montana, she was," Barb said.

I had it right on the tip of my tongue to tell her about my Totonac ancestors. But what if Barb, with her Indian blood, knew that the Totonac were from Mexico?

I would stay with them for the next year without ever being made to feel that I was an intruder. In fact, Rose of Sharon and Barb grew dependent on my share of the household expenses. Especially when Barb started spending what little she had left over after the bills for medical costs. She had what she called "female problems" and didn't have enough money to see a doctor regularly. If she could scrape up enough for the visit, she didn't have the means to pay for prescriptions for iron supplements or hormones that would help the bleeding. Sometimes the flow was so bad that blood soaked through the pad reinforced with a folded hand towel pinned to her panties, and she'd go so lightheaded she couldn't even sit up, much less stand.

I stayed with her often since I seldom went out. Sometimes Rose of Sharon and I would go roller skating or to the drive-in movies with friends. But after a few months, she and Melvin started seeing each other outside of work, and I hung around the house even more. I wasn't interested in romance myself, but I wished the best for Rose of Sharon and Melvin. And they were going to need all the luck they could get—there was lots of talk about racial equality back then, but it seemed that Melvin and Rose of Sharon couldn't go anyplace without somebody screaming racial epithets at them. It was hard for me to understand why perfect strangers would give a damn about a couple of people who were minding their own business. All you had to do was look at Melvin and Rose of Sharon to know how much they loved each other, even when they were across the room from each other you could almost feel the connection between them. It almost made me want what they had, but not yet. Someday, and someday seemed far away, and I was still lost in having good times and not planning too much into the future.

But I guess I was starting to think about what lay in store for me more than I realized, because a seemingly meaningless incident got me to thinking about where I was headed. It was an ordinary night, one when a bunch of us from Parker's were out driving around after work, the new busboy Randy had the bright idea of hanging his back side out the front passenger window and mooning the whole damn world. It was one of those times when my foreignness hit me head on. Why in the world would a person show his bare butt? In Mesquite, the shame would have been on him, and most likely, he would've pulled that butt back in with a little something stuck in the bull's eye by an onlooker.

I must have allowed my face to reveal my distaste for Randy's idea, because he mumbled something about my thinking I was better than the others. "You're just like the rest of us," he said. "You'll never have a pot to piss in."

Hearing what he thought of me was almost as startling as if he'd smacked me in the head with that piss pot. Was I like them? Would my life be one hardship after another, relieved by weekend beers and vaguely rebellious behavior that did nothing to change my situation? A few weeks later, another incident cinched my vague thoughts of moving on.

Barb and I had just whipped up some old-fashioned fudge made with cocoa powder and popped a huge bowl of popcorn. I was adjusting the rabbit-ears antenna on the TV so we could get a better reception of *Bonanza*, when Melvin and Rose of Sharon walked in early from their date. Rose of Sharon was grinning so wide the corners of her mouth seemed to be reaching for her ears.

"Melvin's joined the air force," she said. "We're getting married."

Barb turned off the TV and brought out some pop so we could toast to Melvin and Rose of Sharon's dreams. Melvin said the military would allow him to get a college education and make a good life for Rose of Sharon and all the kids they planned to have. And, he said with a bit of a laugh, at least we were still involved in a war. He told Barb he hoped she'd live with them, and how she'd be a big help once Rose of Sharon got pregnant.

"And you, too," Rose of Sharon said to me. She'd misunderstood my reason for going silent.

I'd become uncomfortably close to Barb and Rose of Sharon over the last year. This was my chance for easy exit. "Don't worry about me," I said. "I've been making plans of my own." I could see the *whew* in Melvin's face, and even a little of it in Rose of Sharon's. I didn't blame them one bit.

"Didn't you tell me once about wanting to go to school like Melvin here?" Barb said.

"One of these days," I said. But I still wasn't ready to make definite plans for the future. I'd tried to after the mooning incident and Randy's comments, but at that time, the most I could muster was to strive to be a woman of the present and near-present tense. And to keep moving. I was ready for a new adventure. It was almost as if I had an addiction to adventure back then. I guess new excitement kept memories at bay.

TEN

I won't say that I enjoyed the next five years, but the time did blur into a comfortable haze of sameness. Parker's corporate offices closed their downtown restaurant, and I transferred to the North Dayton location, where I stayed for a little over a year before switching to Frisch's Big Boy chain. After a year, the buzzing itch in my veins signaled it was time for me to make a change. It had become my routine: For twelve months I'd busy myself with adapting to a new situation and people, and that preoccupation filled my mind enough to push back a slow drifting-in of memories. Then I was ready to move on.

A couple times when I thought I couldn't stand one more night of going home stinking of hamburgers and grease, I decided to get out of waitressing and take a completely different type of job. Some sort of office work, I figured. Problem was, once you're in the restaurant business, the people at the employment office keep steering you right back in that direction—easier for them to find you positions and cross you off their to-do list. I couldn't really blame them. When they asked me what sort of office I wanted, I didn't have a clue. And my clerical skills? They didn't exist.

With each new job, I took on different roommates. Let's keep in touch, we'd say, and I believe we meant to. But physical distance leads to emotional distance. That was fine with me. I'd even lost contact with Rose of Sharon and Barb once Melvin had been stationed in Germany.

I didn't make things happen; they just sort of happened *to* me. I coasted along, living from paycheck to paycheck. After I'd turned eighteen, I'd started frequenting nightclubs. There's something to be said for the comfort that alcohol and smoke-hazy darkness can provide. My life was filled with work, clubs, with breakfast afterwards at Denny's or some other all-night restaurant, then into bed—mine, or once I'd given up on my virginity, someone else's. The harder I partied and the longer I stayed awake into the night, the less daylight I had to struggle through. The bright sunlight revealed more than I wanted to see.

Don't think about it, that was my mantra. One of these days, I'd tell myself, I'll get it together. Tomorrow. Maybe. And so the years passed. I tried leaving the restaurant chains, went for an independently owned restaurant. Teddy Bear's Diner closed at five, so, for the first time, I'd be working days. Small changes, but you take change where you can find it. Just to shake up my routine even more, I rented a small trailer all for myself at a nearby court. It would be easier to bring home overnight friends. I was getting tired of leaving strange beds in the middle of the night.

My biggest attraction to the diner was Teddy Bear himself. Theodore Kopp had ridden with a motorcycle gang out in California until he lost his right foot in a traffic accident. Teddy always said he had stood 6' 3" before a chance encounter with a pickup truck cut him down to size. Getting his foot chopped off slowed him down, he said, and forced him to think about what he wanted out of life. He returned to his hometown and opened up an eatery where all were welcome to sit at his table and break bread with him. Maybe it was his way of making restitution for whatever he had done in his meaner days, things that would remain nameless but that I could sometimes spot in the shadows that flickered across his pale blue eyes.

Some rough characters came into the diner, but no one ever got out of hand for long. If one of the customers did come searching for trouble, one look at Teddy's massive biceps usually changed their minds. Not that Teddy was violent. Everybody wants to be treated with respect, Teddy always said. It worked for him. Maybe because Teddy could enforce his soft words with hard muscle.

Teddy spent most of his off-time rummaging through the stacks at Bonnett's Used Books on Fifth Street and would leave with bags of hardbacks and paperbacks: history, military, nature, mysteries, crime, westerns, fantasy. Teddy read it all. He turned Inez, the other waitress at the Diner, onto romances, and tried to tempt me, too. But for the time being, I was sticking with newspaper articles and my trusty crosswords. Reading novels meant sitting too long, and, unlike the reformed Teddy, I wanted movement. That's why I preferred working in understaffed restaurants—it kept me trotting. One book I did read at Teddy's insistence was *Sister Carrie*. There were a few slow parts that I skimmed, but mostly I liked it, and asked him why he'd wanted me to read it.

"You kind of remind me of Carrie," Teddy said. "All that yearning." He grinned at the use of the word *yearning*, which did sound funny coming from the mouth of a guy as big and tough as Teddy. I laughed, but fact was, the good times were starting to feel strained. I was pretending to be having fun more than I was actually *having* fun.

The day after that conversation, on a Thursday morning as I dressed for work, I looked at my reflection in the mirror and saw not a kid but a twenty-two year old woman. I'd junked my old Ford for thirty-five dollars when the transmission blew, and I was back to riding the city buses. While I huddled inside the sheltered bus stop across from the trailer park and waited for the number nine that would take me within a block of Teddy Bear's, the early morning shift at the small factory across the road was winding through the gates.

I could tell by the looks of the workers that it was a non-union factory. According to the TV and newspapers, we were supposed to believe that all the tax cuts President Reagan was giving to the rich and businesses were going to trickle down to us poor working slobs. So far, no go. Even though the factory workers were close to my age, their rounded shoulders hunched up toward ears, and faces soured like they'd just swallowed a breakfast of regrets, made them look old and weary. Soldiers commanded into a battle they knew would end badly. Some of them came into the diner, and I knew that many were stuck in their jobs because of responsibilities.

I'd long ago decided that I didn't want children—the burden of dependents could force you into choices that destroyed the spirit. Like a lifetime sentence at a no-benefits sweatshop. Besides, being around kids reminded me of the childhood I'd lost. It occurred to me that I was marching to the very same drummer as those unhappy people, in spite of not having children to blame for my situation. The difference between me and them, I thought, was that I was keeping myself free and unencumbered so when I *was* ready to start working towards my goals, there was nothing to stop me.

That got me thinking about my old dream of going to college. Dayton offered education choices: Wright State University, Sinclair Community College, and the University of Dayton, a Catholic school. I crossed the price-prohibitive private UD off my list first; Wright State was next to go because it was far from where I lived. Sinclair was the cheapest, and being downtown the easiest for me to get to on the bus. A few years back I'd picked up an application, but when I read it over and saw all the questions, I dropped it in the trash. I'd have to make up an education history, and what about transcripts? The more time that passed, the more rooted the fear of discovery had become.

Sometimes I even thought about returning to Mexico, but I had no family there anymore, no home. I kept telling myself that Altagracia Villalobos was dead; I was now Grace Sloan. But my new name just didn't fit right. Who was I? What had happened to me? All that adapting had turned into accepting. I didn't know how to get out of step. These thoughts only confused me. I was thankful for that day at the bus stop being a Thursday. Even though I'd been cutting down on my clubbing and drinking, Inez and I always went to The Parlor on Thursdays: ladies' night, drinks two for one. Teddy said we weren't much good to him during Friday morning breakfast rush, but he knew that we needed something to help us forget our worries. Forget.

Inez had been divorced for ten years from a man who used to leave the imprint of his work boot soles on her body. She said that now that she was forty and on her own, the only love and romance she wanted was in those paperbacks from Bonnett's. I didn't believe her. Each time a guy asked her out, her eyes would sparkle like she'd been sprinkled with love dust. Then when he stopped calling, she'd go back to spouting cynicisms about relationships. All the while, her stack of romances kept growing.

That particular Thursday night at The Parlor, we began, like always, by toasting as soon as the waitress sat down the first four glasses. "Here's to us girls having ourselves a ball," Inez said, and clicked one of her screwdrivers to my rum and Coke. With a wink, she added, "Or two." We hooted and laughed, as if she didn't say the same thing each and every ladies' night.

I made a half-hearted promise to myself to not go off with some guy that night. One-night stands had become a habit, and the next day would always be the same. My behavior would return in hot flashes of shame, and Inez would ask me what I'd done after I'd left with that guy (names were irrelevant). I'd say I couldn't remember.

Know what you mean, Inez would say. Had a few brain blizzards myself. She'd laugh and blow cigarette smoke from her tear-shaped nostrils. Yeah, Kiddo, she'd say, better to forget. How else we gonna live with ourselves?

After each night I woke up empty, still yearning for what, I didn't know. Sex had become a drug, something to dull rather than awaken the senses. That night I told myself I'd have one set of two drinks, share a few laughs with Inez, dance a tune or two, and go home early. But the men were feeling generous, and the waitress was bringing us drinks before we'd even touched the extras we had.

"Waste not, want not," Inez said. So on and so on.

It didn't take long before I was feeling mysterious, a shadow dweller, too hip and naughty for the farmers of the Midwest, and certainly too slick and slippery to be caught by gonorrhea or even AIDS. Inez was driving, so I told her to leave without me, that I would be leaving soon myself, but that I had a ride. Inez winked and told me to live it up while I could.

Friday dawn, I awakened squinting through eyelashes gummed up with left-on mascara as I tried to make out where I was. Nose to nose with some guy I could only vaguely remember, I breathed in his cheeseburger and beer halitosis. Had he worn a condom? Or had I forgotten to insist, too out of it to give a damn?

The sun smeared the greasy glass pane of a curtainless window, and the only thing that came even close to slick and slippery was the semi-dry goo that made sticky sounds when I separated my thighs. Scenes from the movie *Looking for Mr. Goodbar* flashed before me.

As I slipped out of his bed, the stranger mumbled, "Where you going, babe?" Without opening his eyes, he stretched out an arm, the blond hairs on his fair skin sparkling in a beam of sunlight.

"Be right back," I whispered. I dodged his hand, and his half-hearted attempt flopped back onto the wrinkled sheets. After gathering all the pieces of my clothing, except my panties (I had a vague recollection of giggling when the elastic popped as he'd ripped them off), I slipped into the bathroom.

I sidestepped the trash overflowing a small basket, and the soles of my bare feet gummed to the vinyl-tiled floor. My thought of a quick shower ended with a peep around the sliding door. Pubic hairs stuck to the floor and walls, golden commas, tiny curved lines that could keep a sentence going into forever. I tightened my stomach muscles to keep from heaving the night's contents, and when a few chunks of vomit made it up into my throat, I swallowed hard.

For the rest of the weekend, I hated myself for my lack of self-respect. Then, like a sign of what road I should take, Kenny came into the diner the very next Monday. I noticed those shoulders right away when he pushed open the plate glass door of Teddy Bear's.

"Don't look like your type at all, kinda square, know what I mean?" Inez said when she caught me staring. "Nice looking, though. Sort of like John Wayne, only not so tall or wide in the shoulders like the Duke." Once Inez had read in a fan magazine that Wayne's friends called him the Duke, she did likewise.

I had categorized the stranger as a Harrison Ford type, but yes, he *was* like a John Wayne character: a simple man, a man in charge, a man who could make sense of chaos. Outside, a young mother was crossing the parking lot, walking toward the Diner door, pushing a baby in a stroller with one hand while trying to hold onto a whining toddler with the other. Kenny was about to swing a leg over a stool at the counter when he spotted the woman. He rushed to open the door, and when she thanked him, he reached down and lifted the stroller over the two steps.

"No problem at all," Kenny said, and the baby looked up toward that kind voice and smiled. Who wouldn't have? Something about Kenny's movements, so sure and yet casual, revealed to me that he was accustomed to helping others, a combination of strength and gentleness. He was the man for me.

He sat at Inez's half of the counter, but, with a wink, she told me to go on ahead and take his order. He forked ham and eggs into his mouth with one hand, and with the other held the *Dayton Daily,* neatly folded, not really looking at me until I sloshed his coffee while refilling his cup. When he glanced up at my face, a light of appreciation came on inside his eyes. I sometimes wondered if I'd met him on any day other than that particular Monday, if I would have been so attracted to him.

Kenny started coming into Teddy Bear's every weekday for breakfast. "He's got it for you, kid," Inez said. "Dab some of that perfume of yours on the inside of your wrists—and hey, what the hell, don't forget a smidge down between your boobies. Woo-hoo."

I kept a bottle of Charlie cologne in my purse, and when I'd see Kenny park his pickup out front, I followed Inez's advice and dashed back to the kitchen for a quick spritz. I observed him closely—noticed what he looked at with approval or disapproval, listened to his comments on current events, anything that might reveal his inner self—and later jotted notes in a small spiral notebook. On our second date I found out about Kenny's broken engagement. He and Jennifer, his ex-girlfriend, had shared dreams of marriage and children. Then, out of nowhere, he said, Jennifer said she'd been mistaken. She wasn't ready for marriage. "How can you be mistaken about something as important as that?" Kenny asked me.

"She wasn't who you thought she was," I said.

"No sense talking about it," Kenny said. "What's the point in wallowing in what could've been?" He smiled in a sad way.

"Exactly," I said. "The past is over."

The clubs were full of people with broken hearts. There were lots of boozy complaints about bitches who took everything the poor guy had worked so hard for, or rants about lousy bastards who stole a woman's youth before dumping her for a newer model. Kenny never trashed Jennifer, and I respected him for that. After telling me about their separation, her name seldom came up. I could see it hurt him too much to talk about her. I also realized that he wanted to fill the space she'd left in his life. He said more than once that he was ready to settle down, get married, work hard, save his money, and someday start a family, which meant, he'd said, having at least three kids. I ignored that last part. I should have told him how I didn't see myself bringing kids into this lousy world, but I was so wrapped up in starting a new life, of finally feeling safe, that I said nothing. Maybe I thought that I might change my mind someday about kids. I don't know. Why we do what we do isn't always so clear-cut.

Kenny and I told each other we were in love because we both needed to hear the words. Maybe we believed them. Maybe they were true. After dating for five months, Kenny proposed, and one month later to the day, we married. Teddy gave me away. He was still trying to get used to a new prosthesis that was supposed to be way better than the old one he'd had. We leaned into each other, each helping the other stay standing. I wondered if I looked as startled and uncertain as Kenny did. For a moment I was paralyzed, like a rabbit caught in the beam of a headlight. Teddy held on tighter.

"Don't fight fate," Teddy whispered.

"Not me," I said.

Back when I'd lived with Molly Carol, one of her punishments had been to unscrew the lightbulbs in my bedroom and keep them for a day or two, at which time she felt I'd learned my lesson. It had been dark as death inside that box of a room, and when I lay on my bed and tried to sleep, it hadn't strained my imagination to think "coffin." I hardly slept those nights, afraid I'd awaken to discover I was dead. It didn't make sense, but the mind is tricky. After that, I had trouble sleeping without being sure to know that I could wake up and spot a sliver of light, if only enough to watch the shadows shift.

At Barb and Rose of Sharon's, they'd left a nightlight—a plastic angel with a broken wing—plugged into an outlet near the mirror in the bathroom to guide Barb and keep her from slipping during one of her many nightly trips to the toilet. The bathroom adjoined the living room where I slept, and if I woke up during the night I could make out that guiding light. Later, with my roommates, I was embarrassed to have a nightlight, so I'd turn down the volume on my TV and claim that I'd fallen asleep while watching. When Kenny and I honeymooned at a Day's Inn and I tried my TV trick, Kenny snapped it off, said the light would keep him awake. With Kenny, big and solid, lying next to me, falling asleep would eventually get a lot easier. Life became comfortable.

For years to come, Kenny and I would be busy, both of us working as many hours as we could. I stayed on at Teddy Bear's, and Kenny worked sixty hours or more as a supervisor in the porcelain department of a dental laboratory. He dreamt of owning his own lab and already had one in mind that he wanted to buy in Brockton, Indiana. Kenny said that Brockton would be a great place to raise kids. I got swept up in Kenny's excitement, began to picture the future. I shared his dreams for our own business, our own home, but was glad that Kenny insisted we not think about starting our family until we had secured our dreams. I used a diaphragm and he condoms. We didn't like surprises.

Now and again I scolded myself for deceiving Kenny. But, I reasoned, Kenny was mostly getting what he wanted out of life, and wasn't I his helper? My deception wasn't really hurting him. As long as he didn't find out I wasn't who he thought I was, we'd be just fine. I was thankful that Kenny didn't ask personal questions. At first I thought his lack of curiosity was because he feared what he might find out. That may have been part of it, but Kenny treated everyone with kind distance. He almost never gossiped. He accepted people for what he knew of them, and that was that. He liked the precision of numbers and machines. He did not like haze.

Kenny had always been frugal and had built up a nice savings account before we'd met, so within a year of our marriage, we bought the dental lab in Brockton. And after two years there, we moved into our dream house. There were times when I'd look around at all we'd accomplished together and I'd puff up with pride. Other times, I felt like an imposter.

One night—it was 1986 by now—we were sitting in the living room. Kenny was reading the newspaper and I was watching the evening news when Peter Jennings announced that the Immigration Reform and Control Act was official. Mexicans who'd been living and working without papers in the United States could apply for amnesty if they could prove they'd been in the country since before 1982. Citizenship would be granted for the eligible. It was my chance to not only make my presence legal, but to come clean with Kenny.

"Wow, that's something," I said, all the while trying to think ahead of how to lead Kenny into a conversation that might unravel my safety net. I had to repeat myself two times before Kenny peeked over the edge of his newspaper.

"You talking to Jennings or me?" he said.

"Amnesty for illegal aliens, they said. On the news. What do you think?"

"There's aliens here in Brockton?"

"Illegal immigrants, undocumented workers," I said. "They didn't say anything about Brockton, but the law applies for all over the country."

"Oh." Kenny glanced at the paper in his hands then back at me. "And?"

"Well, just imagine how those folks must feel—all those years of hiding, pretending. Like they've been living underground or something. Now they've got the chance to surface."

"You're making them sound like a bunch of gophers." He grinned but something in my expression made him lower the paper to his lap. "What's all this got to do with us? Are you talking about somebody at the lab?"

I could see his thoughts whirring behind his eyes, mentally sifting through the applications of our employees for anything untoward. His face was drawn. He'd been putting in ten hours a day, seven days a week at the lab. How would he react to the revelation that although he thought he'd married Grace Sloan, average American woman, he'd actually been harboring the lawbreaking Mexican Altagracia Villalobos? And Kenny aside, what about all those stories I'd heard about people who'd been tricked into admitting their illegal status with promises of help, then kicked out of the country and never allowed back in?

"Just making conversation," I said. "I'll go pop us some corn."

"Whatever," Kenny said, and smiled. He was always telling me how he got a kick out of the way I changed subjects midstream.

It wasn't long after that, on a bright summer day, Kenny stood at the outdoor grill, brushing his secret sauce on the short ribs as he'd done so many times before, when he looked up at me and said, "We did it, Gracie. All our ducks in a row. Time to start putting some buns in the oven, wouldn't you say?"

The day I'd been dreading. I had hoped that with time and security, the so-called maternal instinct would develop in me. I wasn't certain if I truly lacked that instinct or if it was merely that being around children brought back memories that I fought so hard to repress.

Kenny was flipping those burgers carefully, and his words were as evenly spaced as his strokes with the barbecue brush. I looked around our large back-yard, closed off from the side neighbors by a seven-foot privacy fence, then up at our two-story house, aluminum siding recently installed to help keep us insulated from the outside. I felt safe, protected, the way I had inside the courtyard as a child in Mesquite. Why not make Kenny happy with a baby?

The years of sweat-drenched concentration began. Pillow under my hips, diagonal tilt for slippery slide down the tube and into the sperm-entrapping pool; sperm temperature-assured by Kenny's avoidance of warm showers before sex and afterwards wearing not testicle-hugging briefs but crotch-breezy box-ers; I peeping momentarily out of my indifferent perseverance to gaze up into his face, skin slack; he, squeezing eyes shut. Fantasizing to keep the half-limp from soft-plopping out?

Just relax and nature will take its course, our doctor told us, but after years of on again, off again attempts, Kenny demanded more than clichés, so fertility drugs were suggested. Fearing multiple births, I mustered the courage to stand by my decision to refuse. I was secretly thankful when our eventual attempts at baby making hadn't taken. But without the dream of procreation, sex lost its meaning for Kenny. I found myself thinking that a jar of mayon-naise would serve him just as well.

We cared about one another and felt a responsibility to each other, to our marriage. We had adapted. We had accepted. And all without discussion. Don't say anything and things will work themselves out.

At least the lab was doing great. We'd hired two new employees recently: Jeff, a new technician in the porcelain department who took a lot of the work Kenny used to do, and in the office Lorene was so much more organized and efficient than the secretary I'd been, so I was freed for more supervisory duties.

More and more I began to wonder what I wanted to do with the rest of my life.
More and more my old self came to me in dreams. I'd see the girl Altagracia.
I was not inside her. It wasn't that she seemed a completely different person.
No, it was like seeing a part of me outside of myself.

Then out of the blue came Violet's phone call.

"Who was on the phone?" Kenny asked as he came into the kitchen from
the kitchen from the deck.

"Somebody I used to know," I said, and tore my gaze away from the window
and the willow tree beyond. Thoughts raced through my mind. I leaned back
against the sink for support. Another great opportunity to reveal my past. My
throat tightened the way it always did when I got nervous. I turned away and
drew myself a glass of warm water. I could start with explaining who Violet
was, her connection to me and go from there. Was I ready to accept the fallout?
If I'd found it difficult to be honest years ago when amnesty had been offered,
just think of the mess now. I imagined myself split open, insides exposed for
the first time, intestines slimy and white writhing in the light like earthworms
in the morning after a good rain.

"You OK?" Kenny took a step closer. "You look like you've seen a ghost."

"It's nothing," I said. Altagracia's birthday had been on December 12. It
felt right to wait and reveal my secrets then.

ELEVEN

I told Kenny to take a seat at the dining room table while I went to the kitchen for dessert. "A special cake," I said, and he furrowed his brow trying to remember what anniversary he'd forgotten.

When I returned, he grinned. "OK," he said, "I give. Why's a cake sitting in a pan of milk?"

"I got the recipe from a Mexican cookbook," I said. "It was my favorite when I was a kid. Tres leches, that's what the cake's called." I'd practiced my speech announcing my real identity, but words were tumbling about helter-skelter inside my head the way they tended to do whenever I was upset.

"That so?" Kenny put his forearms on the table and leaned forward.

"I used to be Mexican," I said, fast before I could censor myself.

"What?" Kenny glanced around the dining room, as if he half-expected a hidden camera to pop out.

"Remember that phone call? Way back in late October? You came inside, told me I looked like I'd seen a ghost?" I rattled on. "You asked me who called, I said it was someone I used to know?"

"What's that got to do with you saying you're Mexican?" He stared at the cake as if the answer might be floating on the milk.

"*Used* to be," I said. But I didn't feel Mexican. Home is where the heart is, Violet used to say when she'd talk about her childhood in Kentucky. Where was my heart? I giggled nervously.

"If this is supposed to be a joke, Grace, I don't get it." Kenny studied me as if I were an escapee from a mental institution.

I swallowed hard to force down another giggle. "Here's the thing," I said. "Violet—the woman who called—she's Molly Carol's sister. That's who Grandmother gave me to when I was a kid, an adolescent really. To Molly Carol. Not Violet." I shook my head, as if I could force my thoughts to fall into some order. "Let me start from the beginning."

"Yeah, maybe you'd better," Kenny said. He was trying to appear calm, but I could see the splotchy-red flush spreading up his throat and into his face.

"I was born in Mexico. My name is . . . Altagracia Villalobos." I pronounced my name with an American accent, but even with the English mushiness, it sounded foreign. I didn't want to watch the blood drain in and out of Kenny's face, so I closed my eyes. Just as I had when I lived in the basement of Molly Carol's house, I brought my life onto the screen of the backs of my eyelids. In spurts and pauses, I described to Kenny what I saw, giving only the main points of my life from the day of my parents' death, my days with Molly Carol, moving to the streets, years of surviving.

As I spoke, Kenny breathed shallowly, as if he were afraid to miss a word, but his breath soon became ragged, quick with anger. Every once in awhile he'd mutter, "Shit," or, "I don't believe this."

"I have false documents," I said finally. "They look real, though. . . ." My voice was raspy from talking so much, and I had to push out the last words on a croak.

"Only they're not," Kenny said. "What *seems* to be and what *is* are two different things."

"Yes," I said, and opened my eyes. The disappointment on Kenny's face nearly broke my heart. "I wanted to tell you. So many times," I said. I pinched the bridge of my nose to keep from crying. "But I felt so safe. I couldn't stand the thought of being abandoned again."

"And you couldn't trust me with this because . . . ?" Kenny's voice trembled.

"You never would have married me if you'd known I came with all this baggage." I tried to be angry, but understood I would only be deflecting my self-anger onto him, and my sentence ended on a whine.

"Thanks for your confidence, Grace. Or Altagrace . . . whatever. I don't even know what to say." Kenny lowered his head into his hands. "I guess I always knew there was something different about you. But. . . ." His fingers drummed on his temples.

I reached across the table, brushed his fingers with my own.

"Don't." He slammed back into his chair, and the legs tippled on the waxed tiles. I tried to grab his arm but he pulled away, knocking over the chair and falling onto his backside.

I fought the urge to laugh. If I began, I knew I wouldn't be able to stop. "I'm sorry, Kenny," I said. "I'm so sorry." What else was there to say?

His gray eyes, usually calm, shone so bright with tears that the color could be mistaken for blue. "I can't talk about this now," he said. "It's come out of left field. I need time to think things out."

When Kenny hadn't returned by midnight, I called the lab. Work was always his escape. I spoke with Jeff, who had stayed late to finish some porcelain crowns for Christmas smiles. No, Jeff said, he hadn't seen Kenny since he left earlier, around 9:30. I waited another hour before changing into my flannel pajamas and burrowing deep beneath the down comforter of our king-sized bed. I shifted my bent legs toward the edge and almost dropped them over the side, but couldn't bring myself to leave the downy cocoon. If the anxiety began—the change in breathing, the sudden irrational fear of being swallowed by the darkness—only then would I turn on a light.

Outside, the winter wind moaned, branches scratched at the siding. The forsythia, I realized, but thought of orange trees from long ago. I imagined their branches nudging, trying to break through the outside of my house. Hours later (the red digital numbers of the bedside clock blinked *1:30*), I finally allowed the heaviness of sleep to pull me down into myself.

The dream drifted in on orange blossom petals, and I turned toward the source of the illusive scent, a distant tree heavy with flower. The lower branches hung so low that their tips brushed the ground, feather-fanned the dry desert earth. I strained to make out the murmured words beneath the sighs but could not. Whose spirit had the branches snagged? A gust of wind whipped from one corner of my mind, and the tree creaked as the top branches stretched stiffly upward until they reached heaven, made scratching noises against a low canvas sky. A sky so blue, blue as the eye of a peacock's feather, blue as a grandmother's eye.

Far away, thunder rumbled. An approaching storm? Like the ones in summer that burst from the desert skies in such a torrent that the parched earth didn't have time to soak in the water. I squirmed, afraid lightning would strike the tree. But it was not thunder rumbling, only the mechanical roll of the garage door. When it clanked against the cement floor, I strained to follow Kenny's movements below, then finally upstairs. I peeked at the clock: *3:01*. Kenny had taken his sweet time coming back. When he eased open the bedroom door, the nape of my neck prickled beneath the intensity of his gaze. Outside the forsythia scratched. I kept my face to the window, arms at my chest, and became aware of my breasts, nipples foolishly erect. After a moment the door shut as softly as it had opened, and Kenny's footsteps moved down the hall.

The next morning neither of us mentioned his having slept in the guest room. Don't talk about it and it will go away. Old habits die hard. Kenny brewed the morning coffee as usual; I dropped two sliced bagels into the toaster and set out butter, cream cheese, and jam. Routine or not, our conversation from the day before hung over us, heavy and damp as an Indiana summer. In the coming days, we spoke only when necessary, both at home and at work. Lorene, in the office, asked me once if everything was OK, but when I snapped that I couldn't be better she didn't ask again.

By the end of the week, Kenny still hadn't returned to our bed. In the guestroom, he kept the standard-sized bed neat and tidy, and on the chest of drawers he'd lined up his nail clippers, hairbrush, and a tube of the latest hair growth concoction, and at the far end a brass coin sorter for his loose change. Years before, when he slid the stacks of coins into marked paper rolls and deposited them in a separate savings account at the bank, he'd grin and say, "For Baby's education." He'd continued organizing his change but long ago stopped saving for a baby.

Thursday Kenny stayed on at the lab to work on paperwork with Lorene on orders that needed to be delivered the next day, and I went home to start dinner. As I cooked the chicken to mix with cream of chicken soup, vegetables, and cheese for one of the casseroles that Kenny liked so much, I kept thinking how I didn't really like casseroles and if Kenny left me I probably wouldn't make them anymore. But he wasn't going to leave me. We'd been married for fifteen years. It had taken me a while to be straight with him about my past, but hadn't I finally come through?

That night I sat in the kitchen waiting for him to pull into the attached garage.

"It's ten o'clock," I said as soon as he walked into the kitchen. When he didn't answer, I told him there was a casserole in the refrigerator.

"Already ate," he said. He took his jacket off slowly, as if every muscle ached, and hung it on a peg by the door just as he had so many other times. He gazed past me to the darkness of the dining room and the stairs. "Well," he said, "it's late."

"This is silly," I said, before he could walk away from me. "You're working yourself to death just to avoid coming home."

"Is that what I'm doing? Apparently there's a lot you know that I don't, so maybe you're right."

"Gooseberry pie," I said, and pointed to the counter. "Made with the berries we froze from the bushes this past summer. You always have room for pie." I sliced the pie and held out a plate to him. "We've had some good times," I said.

"Thanks," he said, and set the plate on the kitchen table. He leaned back against the wall. "I was going to wait until morning, but what the hell."

I glanced at the pie. I wished I hadn't cut into its perfection.

"It's like we've wasted all these years," he said after a moment. "If you'd been honest. . . ." His arms were to his sides, palms flat against the wall. He drummed his fingers.

"We've been happy," I said.

"All these years. I could've found somebody who wanted what I wanted, and you . . . someone you could trust enough to reveal your secrets."

"You've found someone?" It wasn't that I thought he had, only I wanted to not talk about me. Let him be on the defensive for a while.

His skin flushed his usual marbled pink and white. "I'm not the kind who betrays his marriage vows." I opened my mouth to speak, but he held up a hand. "Our marriage wasn't strong enough to withstand this shock. I want a divorce."

"Divorce?" I'd understood that this was where the conversation was leading, but hearing the word still hit like a punch between the eyes. I forked a huge bite of pie into my mouth.

"I've divvied up—on paper, I mean—everything we own." Kenny pulled a sheet of paper, creased into neat fourths, from his front shirt pocket. "Fair split, you can see for yourself. Cars, house, business, all right here." He slid the square across the counter toward me but kept it trapped beneath his index finger. *Tap, tap, tap*, his finger drummed on the bottom line of our years together. "What do you say we just let it go?" he said.

I couldn't swallow the pie-turned-to-mush. I grabbed a paper napkin to spit it out.

"Just let it go," I repeated. Who would I become without Kenny to define my role in my latest and longest identity as Grace Thornberry, wife and business partner? In a few years I'd be forty years old. How could I re-create myself yet again?

"You know," I said, "Violet didn't just call to say hi. Did I mention that she's sick? Anyway, she wants me to come see her. She's looking for forgiveness. I can forgive."

Kenny stared at the floor. "Forgiving is one thing; forgetting's not so easy."

"I'm going to drive to Violet's," I said. "I'll stay in Cogstown for a few days. It'll give us time to think."

"Jesus," Kenny said. "Why are you making this so difficult? We both know it's over."

"Just think about it a little more," I said. "That's all I'm asking." I held out the creased paper. "Hold on to this." He wouldn't take it, so I dropped it on the counter.

In the best of weather, the drive to Cincinnati would have taken less than three hours, but I was a Midwesterner and knew that in cold weather patches of black ice could send a car into an uncontrollable skid and spin, so I took it slow, avoiding semis that could jackknife on those slick surfaces. I drove past fields that in summer would be alive with corn and soybeans but now lay sleeping beneath softly rolling mounds of snow, surfaces sparkling in the sun like sugar-sprinkled meringue, past groves of trees, branches that would burst with green in summer now bare and black against the gray winter sky.

I'd printed out MapQuest directions to the address Violet had given me and recognizing nearby streets, I knew her new home wasn't far from Molly Carol's old house. Yet once I arrived in the area, I wouldn't have recognized it. Rolling farmland and mom-and-pop restaurants and stores with old-fashioned gas stations had been replaced by strip malls, clusters of office buildings, and housing tracts made up of man-made gentle hills and ponds with the ubiquitous geyser fountain. Molly Carol must have made a hefty profit on the sale.

But being near the old house stirred up my remembered fear of Molly Carol. Why was I here? I could stay in a motel while Kenny came to his senses. Why stir up old memories? This was a question I'd asked myself over the years whenever I thought about my childhood, of the person I had once been. Yet when Violet wouldn't tell me over the phone what her news was about my family, I understood that the past had stayed with me more than I had wanted to admit.

On the phone Violet had told me she was staying with friends, but the woman who answered the door seemed anything but friendly. After quickly introducing herself as Mrs. Sharpe, she gestured for me to come in. "I hope this isn't going to take too long," she said. The door opened directly into the living room, and she stepped back to stand next to an armchair facing the television. A man was yelling for another contestant to come on down, and the crowd was cheering wildly. She pointed to the hall. "That way, first door on your right. Violet's having one of her bad days."

Violet sat in bed, clear plastic tubes running from her nostrils to a tank of oxygen next to her bed. "Well, just look at you," she said. She patted a space on the bed next to her. "I'd of knowed you anywheres, Gracie. You turned out real pretty. But then, you always was."

How should I respond? There was no telling Violet how good she looked when she seemed to be at death's door. And should I hug her, shake her hand? Curse her? "It's been a long time," I said. I pulled a weather-beaten wicker chair to a few feet from the bed.

"Ain't that the God's truth?" Violet kept stealing shy glances at me like a guilty child. "I done the best I could by you," she said.

"Sure," I said. Neither one of us seemed to know what to say. Whoops and cheers came from the television in the living room. Another audience member had been selected to join in guessing the prices of displayed items.

"Will you forgive me?" Violet spoke in such a low voice that it took me a moment to understand what she'd said. I thought about asking her if it hadn't bothered her that Molly Carol—her own damn sister, for crissakes—kept a kid as a slave, or why she'd never offered to help me get away. But I knew there were no simple answers. It no longer mattered. I would not be visiting Violet again.

"Sure," I said. I patted her puffy hand but pulled away when she tried to hold on. Violet's chin quivered.

She remained silent for a few moments, then whispered, "I purely do appreciate that, hon," she said. After another long pause, she told me that Molly Carol and Tiffany were in California. When I said nothing, Violet continued. "Grace, I know you got your heart set against Molly Carol. But Sissy ain't all bad." Violet tried to hold my gaze. "Why, you only have to see how she dotes on Tiffany. She's done good by that girl."

I wasn't up to arguing with a dying woman. "Well," I said, "is Travis with them?"

She shook her head. "Poor little Travis. He never did amount to much. Causing us one heartache after another. Drugs, trouble with the police." She broke up her words with gasps. "I don't know what happened to that boy," she said. "Sissy done all she could for him. She says he was born bad. Bless his little heart."

It was interesting the way a person could distort a memory in order to bear the guilt and pain. In the short hallway outside Violet's room, Mrs. Sharpe passed by, clearing her throat. I realized the cheering from the TV had ended.

"Well," I said. I was hungry to hear something about my family, some acknowledgment that they—and Altagracia—had existed.

"I done got myself so shook seeing you again, I almost forgot your news." Violet smiled and the plastic tubes running to her nose stretched. "Your granma, the one that give you away? She never did die like Molly Carol told you."

I was standing now, and held onto the back of the chair.

"Molly Carol only ever told you she was dead for your own good. So's you could forget all that from earlier. Start a new life. A better one." Tears sprang into Violet's eyes. "I wish I could have me a smoke about now," she said, and broke off into a hacking cough.

In the hallway Mrs. Sharpe passed again, clearing her throat. I clutched, unclutched the wicker, waiting for Violet to stop the coughing. "Molly Carol told you my grandmother's still alive?" I asked.

Violet spit phlegm into a tissue and wiped her mouth. "No, no. Only that she didn't die back then. Maybe you all can get back together?"

"Hmmm," I hummed, and held on to the back of that chair as if my life depended on it.

As I drove away from Violet's, tiny blue dots flashed behind my eyes. Was it possible to go home? Could I survive in the presence of memories? I tried to think out what to do next, which direction to take. Finally at dusk, I pulled into a motel. I would not be returning to Brockton, at least not for awhile. I phoned Kenny. Not certain of what I wanted to say, I began by telling him that Molly Carol had lied about Grandmother.

"That's the one who gave you away?" He paused. "Or was that a lie, too?"

I couldn't blame him for doubting my word, but it hurt just the same. And how to explain why I cared whether Grandmother lived or died? "She did it for my own good," I said.

"You need to get back here, Grace. Let's do something about your status in the U.S. before you go trying to reinvent the past. I don't know how you've eluded the authorities this long." Kenny's fingers drummed on the mouthpiece of the phone. "I've been making some calls. Looks like we might be able to straighten out this immigration mess."

"What's the rush?"

"Your luck could run out; you could get in serious trouble, that's the rush. And me, do you think they're going believe that all these years I had no idea of your legal status?" When I didn't answer, Kenny continued. "This immigration lawyer I spoke to says you'll probably have to write a letter of apology for living here illegally, that kind of thing," he said. "But that you're married to an American, been a tax-paying, law-abiding citizen, etcetera. All those years together, they should count for something."

"Yes," I said. Was he saying we could stay together? And if so, was that what I really wanted? For a moment, though, I did wonder what it would be like to have a relationship where I could feel free to be myself. But I'd worked so hard to become Grace Thornberry. Too much was happening too soon.

"I made an appointment for both of us to see this lawyer. We'll see what he says about how long we should wait to . . . you know . . . divorce."

"You need more time," I said.

"Just let it go, Grace—"

"Gotta run," I said, almost shouting to drown him out. "What with the holidays coming up, it'll probably be tough getting a flight to Arizona." He tried to speak, but I ran over his words with a train of my own. "I'll park the Honda at the airport. I'll be home for Christmas. Plenty of time to talk then."

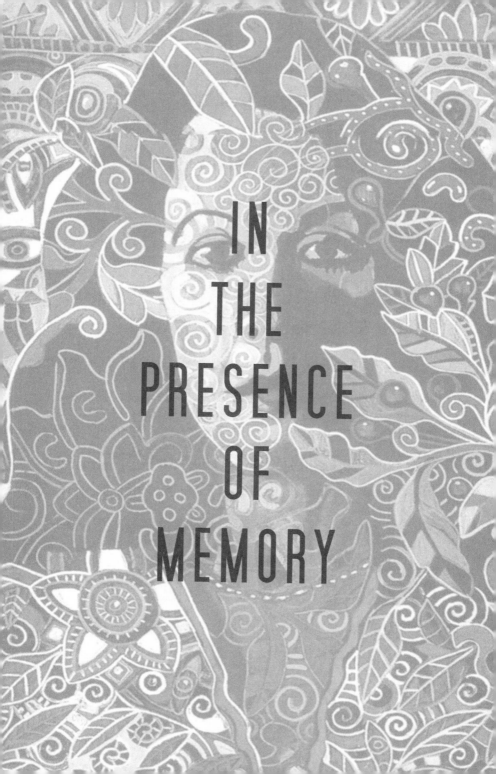

IN
THE
PRESENCE
OF
MEMORY

TWELVE

For the last mile the wind off the Sonoran Desert had increased, buffeting the Taurus I'd rented at the airport, whistling at the windows, working its way around seals, and, judging by the grit on my fingertips, into the pores of my face. So much sand wouldn't have gotten inside if I hadn't lowered the window an inch. But I'd been trying to figure out the source of the racket going on somewhere in the distance. Eerie moans and sighs had been calling to me in a siren-sweet way that gave me the shivers. The spooky sounds were sporadically interrupted by a clang or shriek.

I'd made reservations at a Holiday Inn but determined to discover the source of the babble, I followed my ears and exited the main road onto a byroad. The noise increased as I neared a mom-and-pop motel. For the umpteenth time since I'd gotten off the plane in Tucson, I asked myself what I was doing. I should return to Brockton and hash things out with Kenny, let him have his divorce. Maybe.

Yards ahead and to my right, a neon sign buzzed and popped in bright magenta BORDERLANDS MOTEL. As I drove onto the asphalt driveway in front of the motel office, the flashing neon cast a glow over the burnt-orange walls and lit up a looming construction: rocks of uneven sizes and shapes and what appeared to be bottles—brown, clear, green, blue—encased neck first into a block foundation topped by a hollowed dome. Another burst of light revealed it to be a cement and glass grotto with the Nativity nestled deep inside.

I gripped the steering wheel and glanced down the length of the motel units. At the far end of the wall, rocks painted fluorescent white lined a path of unconnected dots that dwindled away into the desert like an unfinished thought. I stared at those rocks for quite a while with the wind blowing all around me and that weird music playing. It seemed to be coming from around the back of the motel.

I angled my wrist so my old Timex could catch the moonlight: 10:30. No point in heading back to the Holiday Inn. Why not just stay here? It was bound to be cheaper, although I doubted I'd be staying the whole two weeks before Christmas like I planned. And according to the road signs this motel *was* closer to the border, meaning a shorter walk from the American Mesquite into its Mexican twin. But now that I was so close, I no longer felt an urgency to look for my roots. Well, they weren't roots anymore. I'd been cut off from them, hadn't I?

During the drive from the airport I'd had the sensation of traveling through an Old West movie, but now as I stepped out of the car, wind whipped from around the side of the motel with a clank and a whistle, and peppered me with sharp-edged sand that brought me back to reality. And to make matters worse, the wind, no longer broken by the car's shell, hit me with a directness that reminded me of javelinas, the wild boars of my nightmares, snouts pushing, snorting blasts of dry air into my ears.

A gust of wind caught me off balance, and I stumbled against the Taurus. As I twisted my head against the force, I caught the watchful gaze of a middle-aged woman standing ten feet away, arms behind her, at the glass door of the office. The woman had the same expectant face as the figures in the Nativity, and for reasons I couldn't name, I was immediately drawn to her.

The woman pushed open the office door. "Nice, eh?" she said, and indicated the Nativity with her chin. "Saw how you was looking earlier. I was just behind the curtains." She pointed toward the office and the green drapes hanging behind the front desk.

"Constance made them—the statues, not the curtains. She's an artist, get lots of artists here at The Borderlands. She brought them all the way down from Michigan. Her art teacher back there says they didn't come out right. But Constance, she says they come out just like she wanted." The woman tilted her head back when she laughed.

Still chuckling, she walked toward me, the top half of her body pushed forward and wide hips snug in stiff denim twisting from side to side, a cowgirl. One foot away, she stopped. "Josefina Sandoval. Call me Josie," she said, and offered her hand. "You lost? Wrong turn maybe?"

"I'm not sure." Josie's strong grip and kind gaze felt like a cozy embrace. "Any rooms available?" I said.

"Maybe one. Or six, or so." Josie grinned and hooked her thumbs in the loops of her unbelted jeans. "Took me years working at the Greyhound—grill cook at the lunch counter—saving up enough pesitos to buy this place. Then *boom!* Just like that, they build a new highway and here I am off the main trail. Kind of like Norman Bates, but border style, eh?" She laughed. "It's a joke."

Anyone who appreciated the value of a good movie was OK with me. A breeze whined, and brought from behind the motel the tolling of tiny bells. The hairs on my arm shot up, shivered like alerted antennae. I glanced at Josie to gauge her reaction to the noise, but she only told me to pop the trunk. "I'm gonna give you a room just a few doors down," she said. "Let's get your luggages."

We each rolled a suitcase to the office, and Josie continued speaking. "Here on the border," she said, "we're all the time getting folks who're looking for who knows what. Sometimes they know what it is, sometimes got no name for it. Then there's those that got others looking for *them*, but they ain't wantin' to get found." She glanced over her shoulder at me.

"Nobody looking for me. More the other way around."

Josie stopped. "You're looking for nobody? Or nobody ain't looking for you?"

"Just taking a break." I liked thinking of myself as honest, and mostly I was.

Josie pushed open the door to the office. "Taking a little vacation, eh? Not that it matters, not really. Me, I mind my own business, like everybody staying here. Nope, I don't listen to gossip."

She planted the suitcase on the floor next to me and rounded the registry counter. "OK," she said with a grin, "maybe I listen—nothing wrong with knowing what's going on. But I speak up if I don't agree with what's being said, and I don't spread no mean stuff. It's only I like a good story, you know? Marc, he says life ain't nothing *but* a story."

The melodious up and down of Josie's voice dipped into my memory. Grandmother had tried so hard to break me of that lilting intonation, making me repeat my sentences until I sounded more refined, which to her meant an accent from the interior of Mexico. As Grace I'd broken myself of that lilt years ago.

Outside the wind swept past the office, and the sighs from the tree worked themselves beneath the door. I told Josie how that outside music had drawn me to the motel. She rolled back her shoulders, proud as if she were speaking of her own child.

"I call it my tree of sighs. Just a little arroyo willow, but I got it all decorated real nice with all kinds of wind chimes. People tell me they like the sound when they're out there in the desert. Lets them know old Josie's here. But now, they listen real good, they can hear things."

I was about to ask her what sorts of *things* people could hear, when footsteps sounded from behind the curtained doorway. I glanced up from filling out the registration card. A man lifted one panel of the curtain and stepped into the space behind the desk and to one side of Josie. He stood a bit over six feet, with most of his height and mass in his upper body. Although I guessed his age as early or mid-thirties, a few years younger than me, a crescent-shaped Robert De Niro crease between his eyebrows gave him an older first impression.

"I washed up the coffee cups." He spoke to Josie, but his gaze flicked over me, and he nodded slightly in my direction. "I'm taking off now," he said to Josie.

"Excuse my manners." Josie glanced at the card. "Grace Thornberry, my friend, Marc Delint. His room's at the other end. He's on his winter break. Teaches there." She pointed to the black tee shirt stretched tight across his chest and the white print that read VALPARAISO COMMUNITY COLLEGE.

Delint sounded French, but in his face and physique, I detected traces of Indian blood, a mestizo, mixed race like so many of my childhood friends. Like me. When Marc reached out his hand, I hesitated. My palms had turned moist, but I shouldn't have worried. He held my hand only briefly before his long fingers slid away.

"You're stopping by the Descanso tomorrow, right?" Josie said to Marc. With a side glance to me she added, "Casa del Descanso," then translated, "The House of Rest."

"Look," Josie said to Marc, "under the counter, the box of clothes I told you about? Don't forget to pick them up in the morning, in case I get busy and don't remind you."

Marc clicked his tongue in exasperation but I could tell he didn't really mind. He approached the counter, bent down across from me, and when he stood, box in arms, released a whiff of beer and end-of-the-day notes of a musky aftershave. Something awakened in my mind, a fleeting memory of ladies' nights with Inez at The Parlor. I backed up a step.

"Don't forget about little Félix, either," Josie said. "Anybody knows where he's gone to, they should tell him I want to see him, you got that?"

"Sometimes," Marc said, as he walked out the door, "it's better to just let it go."

"Just let it go," I murmured after the door closed behind him.

"How's that?" Josie said.

"Someone said that to me recently." I shrugged. "It's nothing." That was my usual reaction when a subject I didn't want to discuss came up. A shrug and "It's nothing," or sometimes "It's not important." To move the conversation on a different path, I commented that Marc's accent didn't sound especially southwestern.

"You got a good ear. Born right here in Mesquite—I known him since he was a kid—but then his family moved, traveled a lot, following jobs, you know how it is. Always said the border feels most like home for him. Especially right here, the Borderlands Motel. Just the place for misfits, he says. Misfits," she repeated and laughed. "His word, not mine."

"Nobody has to be a misfit." I drummed my fingers on the counter. "Just takes a little adapting." Where was that prim school teacher voice coming from? Next I'd be saying words like *tardy* and *young lady*.

"Adapt. Yeah, I guess peoples could do that if they wanted to be like everybody else." Josie turned to the computer to input my information. "Brockton, Indiana, huh? Stay over three weeks, you get special rates."

I thanked her but let her know that I'd be returning home before Christmas. "Kenny—my husband—and I always spend Christmas Eve together, just the two of us, then the big day with his family." Breaking the habit of fibbing wasn't going to be easy.

Before Josie could follow up with possible questions about Kenny that I didn't want to answer, I said, "I'm from Mesquite originally, the Mexican side, though." I wasn't used to speaking the truth about my past, and here I was revealing myself to a perfect stranger. But then after I left the motel, we'd never see each other again, so why not say what I was thinking? I would only be there long enough to visit old memories.

The phone rang, and to show Josie that I wasn't eavesdropping, I leafed through brochures of nearby tourist attractions. If I had the time, maybe I'd visit Tombstone or Tumacacori. The only plans I'd made so far consisted of some vague notion of eventually crossing the border to visit the cemetery where my parents were buried. And probably Grandmother. After all, in spite of Molly Carol's lie, it didn't mean that Grandmother was still alive. She had been sick and destitute. I hated to think of what her last days must have been.

"Sorry about that," Josie said, after hanging up the phone. "What were you saying? Oh yeah, that you're Mexican?"

"Not really." I glanced meaningfully at my luggage and the door.

Josie followed my gaze then returned her eyes to mine. "How, *not really*?" she said.

"I was born in Mexico. Now I'm an American."

"I thought you was a gringa, a real one, I mean. The way you look and talk, you know?"

When I told her I'd left Sonora twenty-six years ago, Josie said, "Wow, and you haven't been back? All those years without seeing your family?"

"All dead." It felt liberating speaking the truth about my past, but the experience was still so new that I had to force myself to not look over my shoulder for eavesdroppers. "My grandmother was alive when I left, but she's probably dead now."

Josie lifted her chin in the direction of my left ring finger. "Thornberry's not your family name—blood family, I mean."

I glanced at my suitcases again. I could pick them up and return to my car and the highway. Somewhere out there my name was listed at a chain motel staffed by busy clerks who would like nothing more than to register me with as little chitchat as possible. There was something to be said for assembly-line anonymity. But then again, something about Josie made it difficult for me to leave.

"That's right," I said. "I was born Altagracia Villalobos." The authenticity of my accent surprised me.

"Villalobos," Josie repeated, and furrowed her brow.

"Maybe you knew my family?" The question had popped out of my mouth.

"Then you *are* looking for somebody," Josie said, and grinned.

"When I was a kid," I said, "my family owned a small business across the line, The Peacock Gifts and Curios. Ever hear of it?"

"Peacock. It's like I want to remember, but it's not coming to me." Josie scratched her jaw. "Nah, sorry. Maybe you can ask Marc in the morning. He's good at remembering stuff nobody thinks about. Or he could ask the Robles. You heard me say earlier about the Descanso? A place where some of the homeless kids on the other side can go in the day. Anyway, this couple, the Robles—real good people—they run it and know just about everybody across the line."

Outside the wind moaned. "That tree of yours sounds haunted," I said.

"Come on, I'll show you." Josie motioned with her hand for me to follow her behind the curtain.

"Maybe another time?"

"Sure, you're tired, and here I am talking, talking, like always."

As we wheeled the suitcases outside toward my room, I stopped at the grotto and peered in. Mary and Joseph, tanned faces burdened with weariness from their search for human kindness, reminded me of so many of the workers—although most of them had been black or white, not brown—from that nonunion factory near Teddy Bear's Diner. And the kids . . . heck, all of us were pilgrims.

"See what I mean?" Josie said. "Other artists all the time make Mary and Joseph look like they don't worry for nothing. But these, they look more true." Josie dusted desert sand off the face of the baby Jesus with the tip of her pinky finger. "Wait 'til you meet Félix. He'll be here for my Christmas party; he came last year."

"Mary looks so tired," I said.

"Yeah, but she found what she was looking for."

"Yes," I said. Did I even know what it was that I was looking for?

THIRTEEN

My body fit snugly beneath the motel-tight bed sheets, and I tried to convince myself that I felt cozy and safe. But I couldn't slow my pounding heart or silence the roaring in my ears. The darkness in the room was gobbling me up. I bolted upright, back propped against the firmness of the headboard, and reached for the lamp and then my magazine of crossword puzzles. For the first time since I'd married Kenny, I knew I needed a light burning throughout the night.

I pressed the *on* button on the remote, then clicked until I heard the drone of a taped interview from a local cable channel. I hugged one of the extra bed pillows to the side of my head. It was small and squishy, not square and solid like Kenny. Outside the Borderlands Motel, the wind howled, the tree cried, and coyotes bayed.

Children giggled as they ran, sneakers slap-squeaking on cement. Morning light crept into the room from around the sides of the drapes. Kids called out in a mixture of Spanish and English and the combined languages fit perfectly with the slightly off-kilter music playing in the background. Today I would see Josie's tree.

With a wingspread of arms, I pulled free from the tangled sheets. An image of a butterfly fluttered into my thoughts, and I remembered the dream I'd had earlier in the night. Red butterflies had appeared first as a quivering cloud of scarlet. At first I'd mistaken the mass for a pool of blood, suspended, floating in the heavens over the Borderlands Motel. Individual drops separated, and I made out the rippling of tiny wings. The butterflies, attracted to an orange tree, dipped and waved as they fluttered toward the whispering branches. I couldn't remember what had happened after that; the dream had simply drifted away on wings of red chiffon.

My stomach whined then rumbled. Before going to bed, I'd noticed the card on the night table offering a free Continental breakfast in the motel office. On the flight to Arizona, I'd been too nervous to eat dinner and now just the thought of coffee with a croissant or a Danish—and maybe fresh fruit, if I was really lucky—set off the juices in my mouth. Not likely at the Borderlands Motel, though. I could almost hear Papi's "ha, ha." It had been so long since I'd lingered on memories of him. Now I tried to form a mental image of his face, but could not. Without photographs to nudge my memory, I could only picture his white teeth clearly.

In the office, children crowded around a table that held the self-serve breakfast: a plastic pitcher filled with an artificially orange liquid; boxes of supermarket donuts, powdered sugar, cinnamon, and chocolate-iced; and a thermos labeled *café*. I had to smile at my hoped-for breakfast. The kids loaded up trays with filled foam cups and donuts stacked on paper napkins, then argued with each other about whether their parents preferred the chocolate or the cinnamon. It had been a long time since I'd been around kids who were so solicitous of their parents. Back home—and it hit me that I'd been thinking of Brockton as home—it wasn't cool for teens to treat their parents with such respect.

A young woman behind the counter leaned forward. Small dimples formed on either side of her mouth and softened a face made harsh by lips outlined in brown pencil and eyebrows shaved into uneven arches. "Make a little room for the señora," she told the children and smiled at me.

Josie stuck out her head from between the curtains. "Morning," she said. "You meet Mercedes? Mercy, for short." Josie lifted her chin in the clerk's direction. "Just like my own daughter, this one. Been my right-hand woman here in the office, but this is her last day. She's getting ready to take classes next quarter at Santa Cruz College." Josie turned back to me. "Bet you're a college woman too; I can always tell."

I told her I wasn't but that I certainly believed in the value of education. Years ago I had secretly bought one of those GED study guides. I'd gone to the library and hidden behind the stacks to cram, and after I'd taken the test and received my certificate, I hid it deep inside one of my sweater drawers. Kenny had always just assumed I was a high school graduate, and I'd never told him differently, so when I received my certificate I was afraid that he might start asking about other things he'd assumed.

Someone coughed in a theatrical way from the back of the apartment. "Marc," Josie said. "You want to ask him about your family, yes?"

She waved for me to follow her, then led me through a dimly lit room with an overstuffed sofa and armchair facing a television; a short, even dimmer, hallway; and finally into the kitchen, painted lemon-yellow and so bright that it seemed to be the sun around which the other rooms thrived. A table, folded piece of paper under one short leg was flush with the wall, and Marc sitting at one end, peered through the vapor rising from his lifted coffee mug. His eyes, no longer bloodshot, were puffy with sleep. His gaze seemed more relaxed than it had last night, but lingered, I thought, for a few seconds too long on me. I tucked my hair behind one ear with my left hand, wedding band visible, reminding him—or myself—that I was married.

"I was telling Marc about your people and The Peacock Curios," Josie said, as she offered me a seat next to him.

"Not a lot to say," Marc said. "I was a kid, only vaguely remember the store. Across the street from a tortilla place?"

I nodded, and recalled the corn tortillas that the women hand-patted and slapped onto wood-burning stoves at the Tortillería Mendoza. The scent had wafted out onto the street, floated across to the Peacock Curios and our house in back. One of my chores had been to buy the family's daily stack of tortillas. While I waited for the order, Eugenia, behind the counter, would hand me a hot tortilla that she'd sprinkled with salt and rolled up. Afterwards, I walked home with the family's bundle, toasty from the industrial-sized griddle and wrapped in a kitchen towel hugged to my chest. Such a seemingly insignificant moment, yet now it came back to me so strongly I could almost feel the warmth against my heart.

"I think that building where the Peacock used to be was razed years ago," Marc said. "Sorry."

"You don't have to be," I said. Considering the way I was reacting to being so near my past, I might burst if I actually had been able to enter the house.

"But, you know," Marc continued, "I can still picture this metal sign that hung over the door of the curio store. Swung like crazy when the wind blew. I used to be afraid it would fly off the hinges at me or my mom. Sort of hoped it would. You know, I'd be like Superman and save the day."

"Yeah, I remember that sign, now you're saying it," Josie said. "Way at the end of downtown that store was. But we didn't do shopping there. Well, it was a store for tourists, not real people." She scooped two teaspoonfuls of sweetened condensed milk from an open can into her coffee.

"Yes," I murmured. Although I could no longer picture the faces of my family, I closed my eyes for a moment and saw that sign inside my mind as clearly as if it were hanging in front of me. And heard it clang the way it had that night before the police had arrived to tell us about Papi and Mamá.

"When I was a kid," Marc continued, "the Peacock sold Spanish imports in a glass counter at the back of the store—perfumes, lace fans, mantillas, like that. Mom bought black soap, egg shaped, in long boxes." He squinted as if peering back into his memories. "That sign, it had a big peacock painted on it, bright colors. I'm looking at it one day, and suddenly I notice that in the eyes of the tail feathers, something hidden. Painted inside, human eyes—really blue."

"Peacock blue," I said. Outside something heavy and metal clanged. The timing made it seem as if Josie's tree were putting in its two cents on the sign memory.

"I'll never forget this older woman," Marc said. "Well, more like middle-age, but she seemed old to me then. She sat behind the Spanish imports counter on a high stool, usually crocheting." He laughed. "Freaked me out when I looked up at her, her eyes same as the ones in the sign outside." From the back patio, tiny bells jingled.

"My grandmother," I said. "She always had to keep busy."

"Passed away," Josie added.

"Well, I think so," I said.

"I'm sorry," Marc said. After a moment, he asked, "How long've you been away?" and when I told him he whistled softly. "You're going to find things really different. I visit here a couple times a year—Christmas break and summer—came back the first time maybe eight years ago, and the changes were already in full swing."

"Too many maquiladoras," Josie said. "You know, the foreign factories? You hear about them back in Indiana? Every day more, all along the border, and more and more peoples coming down here from inside Mexico. Dream fever, that's what they got."

There was a pause in the conversation. I wondered if Josie and Marc, like me, were thinking of their own dreams.

Josie slapped her thigh so hard, Marc and I started. "Hey, last night I was going to show you my tree," she said, looking at me. "Let's have one more cup of coffee on the back patio, yes?"

The scrubby tree grew out of the center of the walled-in courtyard. The tips of the willow's branches caressed the earth, and the web of shadows on the ground shifted. It reminded me of the tree that had appeared in my dreams in Brockton. Only this one wasn't covered with orange blossoms. Wind chimes hanging from the tree glimmered white in the light of early morning: tied-on tin cans, strips of waste metal, bolts, nuts, and washers of all sizes; seashells and tiny jingle bells threaded on ribbons of red satin; and finally, shards of pottery, jars, bottles. I strained to hear the individual notes of the chimes. *Clank-click*, metal scraping metal; a barely discernible *ting-ting, sh-shred* of ribboned bells; *clink-burst,* glass tinkling, splintering; and weaving through the chimes, wrapping around them, the prolonged moans and sighs of the wind blowing through the necks of bottles, whole and broken.

"Really something, isn't it?" Marc said. He lifted plastic chairs from the stack to one side of the outside wall, and handed us each one.

"What does it mean?" I said, and sank into one of the chairs.

Josie shrugged her shoulders. "Started with one wind chime, then I kept putting more. See it's like this. Nana—my grandmother—she talked too much, that's what I used to think. Anyway, she gets old, she talks even to the trees. Their branches, she says, catch whispers from God. Crazy, eh?"

I thought about the twin orange trees in our old courtyard and how Chelo said the wind's sighs through the branches were the spirits of the dead who had become lost. Now I strained my ears for familiar voices. I told myself that I was being irrational and superstitious, but I listened anyway.

"Crazy, I know," Josie said, when I remained silent. "Everybody thinks that at first. But it can't hurt to hang a little this, a little that on the tree, so we can hear all them whispers. You know, just in case. Sometimes I think I hear my nana."

"Who's to say you don't?" I said.

"Yeah, why not?" Josie said, and as if to herself, repeated in Spanish, "¿Por qué no?" She rested her forearms on opened knees, story-telling comfort. "A few years ago this woman comes to stay at the Borderlands for a week. Takes one look at my tree and tells about one she saw something like it in the South, South in the U.S. I mean. 'A bottle tree they call it,' she says. African slaves brought the idea.

"And me, I say people suffer so much like them, they got to know a little something about the soul, yes? Anyway, the Africans stuck bottles on tree branches for capturing evil spirits. The colored glass sparkles so pretty, spirits come poking around and get trapped inside the bottles. I say it catches the evil, why not the good, too?" She glanced at Marc. "Ain't that right, hermano?"

"No arguments from me."

"It's just a tree," I said too sharply, and pressed finger and thumb to the bridge of my nose. I couldn't reach the pinpoint of pain behind my eyes. "Sorry," I said. "I don't mean to be rude. I—I'm overwhelmed."

"My tree?" Josie said.

"Everything." I waved my hand to take in the surrounding desert. There was an uncomfortable silence, and I regretted having ruined the moment for everyone. "It's nothing," I said.

Marc cleared his throat and stood up. "I'm running late. Better get that box over to the Descanso before Josie starts in on me."

"That's the pure truth, hermanito," Josie said, and laughed.

"Want to ride along?" Marc said to me.

"Me?" I said stupidly. I gazed at the tree. "Maybe I'll ease into my memories. You know, start on this side of the border, work my way south."

Josie clutched Marc's wrist as he passed her. "Don't forget to look for Félix. I'm too busy with all the tourists at the motel right now to go myself. I hear he was seen around Magdalena, heading this way."

"Don't get your hopes up, Josie. It's only four weeks since the accident, give the boy time." Marc tapped Josie's fingers until she released him.

The next morning, in spite of spending the previous day in my room staring at the TV, I was exhausted. Throughout the night, I'd been awakened by either my dreams, a hodgepodge of fleeting images—metal signs whirling through the sky in giant dirt devils, javelinas with eyes of peacock blue, corn tortillas warm and salty—or by the howling and yipping of coyotes. At first I thought I was dreaming about them, but when I strained to hear better, the coyotes seemed to be in the near distance behind the motel. The wind increased, and the chimes on Josie's willow gathered momentum, clanging, whistling, stirring up a cacophony of sound that somehow blended with the noise of the approaching coyotes.

Too cranky to deal with Josie's questions, I was determined to avoid her. After dressing, I cut across the motel parking lot to a nearby Denny's restaurant in order to reach the sidewalk without passing the motel office. I inhaled the morning air for new energy, but instead it brought on a fit of coughing. Nearby someone was roasting chiles on a comal, and I'd sucked the stinging heat into my lungs. I thought of Chelo and how when she was roasting chiles for rellenos or for hot sauce, she'd warn me to take little breaths. Enough to enjoy the smell, she'd say, but not enough to choke you. Good advice. Today I'd visit the American Mesquite only. It wasn't going to be easy facing all the memories I'd been suppressing for so long. Perhaps I would never know any more about my true self than the façade I presented to others.

The melancholy melody of Josie's tree followed me for blocks, sighs and whispers lifting my hair, tickling my face. From a nearby hill, a curl of smoke drifted heavenward, and I smelled wood burning, the common mesquite tree that had given the city its name. No mesquite wood for me and Kenny. For our fireplace, we used wax and pressed sawdust logs. Cleaner and easier to control, Kenny said. We usually lit the first fire during the cool weekend mornings of fall.

How satisfied I'd been (tried to be?) last fall before I'd received that phone call from Violet. The chilly Indiana air had nipped at my nose, but I'd been content knowing that Kenny and I would build a fire that evening and sit in front of it, toasty and secure in our home. My steps were sure that day (not uncertain like now), and I'd breathed in the sharp nutty smell of fallen leaves, maple, elm, and oak; and with the dusky sweetness of roses in their last bloom, dry petals as papery thin as a lover's stationery.

A mutt darted past me now, so close that its mangy fur brushed my calf, and I was glad I'd worn jeans. I caught myself thinking that if the dog had touched my bare skin it would have been a bad omen. It had been a long time since I'd thought in terms of signs and omens. Back in the Midwest folks went in for that sort of thing even less than Grandmother had.

The dog ran off and I turned my attention to the display in a real estate office to my right. When I spotted the small fake Christmas trees in burlap bags plopped at either side of the window, I was reminded of the Scotch pine Kenny and I usually shopped for at one of those seasonal businesses set up in the corner of a parking lot. At least six feet tall, Kenny would insist, wanting to make sure that with the stand it would be taller than him.

From our freezer we'd pull bags of frozen cranberries and from the pantry, five-gallon cans of corn popped days ahead and gone stale for easy threading. Kenny and me, working together, crisscrossing garlands of white and red around the pine tree, then after Christmas draping the strands on the shrubs outside for the birds to eat. Kenny and I should be picking our tree out now.

The dog barked and ran across the street. He stopped at the wall, built alongside a cement-lined wash, and stood, peering down into the arroyo. The dog's loose skin furrowed between its eyes and the muscles knotted beneath the patchy fur. On the same side of the street as the wash and parallel with it, train tracks, like sutured wounds, cut through Mesquite. In the distance an oncoming engine shrieked a warning. The mutt barked one last time into the wash before darting off the tracks to beat the train.

It was only an engine with five boxcars, but as they clattered by heading north, the earth vibrated, and I had the sensation of plates shifting, rearranging beneath me. When Mamá and Papi were still alive, I used to lie in my bed at night and when I heard the train's whistle, I'd fantasize about the adventures the passengers would find on their journeys and imagine myself on the train heading to who knew where.

As I got closer to downtown, I began to see some of the changes that Marc had talked about. A number of businesses were boarded up: Hassan's Hardware, the once crisp black lettering fading to gray, and next to it the old Woolworth's, windows boarded up, with plywood spray painted with obscene pictures and accompanying words in Spanish. I shaded my eyes with one hand and gazed across the street.

At least the old park appeared the same. It had always been a popular gathering place for children. The adults used to group on the nearby benches chatting while children played tag or hide-and-seek behind the few trees or watched the goldfish in the pond. As a girl, when I'd come shopping with Grandmother, I sometimes sat on the low stone wall that closed in the rectangular pond in the center of the park. From a bag of day-old bread, I'd pinch off pieces to toss on the water and watch the fish as they broke to the surface.

Now two women wearing Mexican Indian rebozos and an old man with a battered straw hat sat on the bench. Inside the parameters of the fish pond wall, three children ran, stirring up clouds of dust, not water. In spite of their yelling and mad dashes down the length, something dull in the children's facial expressions painted them as inert as the adults.

At the edge of the park, five or six men clustered. Dressed in hand-me-down shirts and pants that bagged to the shape of someone else's body, the men huddled together, heads bowed, as if they hoped to form an anonymous brown blur. Their dark eyes cast furtive sideways glances before they rushed to a pickup truck slowing at the curb. The driver stuck out his head and one arm, and pointed to the chosen ones, who hopped into the bed of the truck. Maybe these workers were some of the overflow that didn't get one of the dream positions in the maquiladoras. I thought back to those days with Molly Carol, and afterwards on the street. Had I looked as defiantly guilty as these workers?

I ducked my head and hurried on. I wanted to revisit the string of shops where Grandmother and I had once shopped for clothing every year. But when I spotted that stretch, the wrought-iron Eiffel Tower that once hung from a pole in front of La Ville de Paris was gone, replaced with a painted sign that read CHUCHERÍAS. And on the sidewalk in front of the storefront were tables stacked with cheap plastic toys and cardboard boxes. From the boxes, women customers pulled out articles of loose clothing—slinky brightly colored blouses, flip-flops, children's jeans—and examined them beneath the watchful gaze of a Korean store clerk standing in the doorway. Farther down, the building that had once housed the Roxy Cinema was gone, and the former hairdressing salon operated by the movie-star-beautiful Noriega sisters had been gutted and was now a replica of Chucherías.

I was reminded of a little town in Michigan that Kenny and I had once driven through on our way to Detroit. The difference was that in Michigan, the town seemed to have been deserted by everyone but a few old-timers who couldn't or wouldn't move on. Here, the closer I got to town and the border crossing, the more crowded the streets were, and the people were young, intent. The old Mesquite was dying but the new hummed. My head was spinning, and I wasn't certain if it was from the sun, steadily rising, or from the part of my past that had died while I was away.

I would walk on to the Greyhound Bus Depot, only on the next block and only yards from the border. Surely it would still exist. It once had a little snack shop where Papi and I came after movies at the Roxy. In those days, I'd be glad that my grandmother thought movies a waste of time and that Mamá spent most of her days hidden away in her bedroom. At the cinema I had Papi to myself. I thought I saw the unlit Greyhound neon sign ahead, but my view was impeded by two opposing currents of people on the sidewalk directly in front of where I thought the entrance should be. I craned my neck, tried to see beyond the pedestrians streaming to and from the border crossing. The crowd increased and individual words became indistinguishable, blending until my head seemed to be filling with the buzz. Again I had the sensation of the earth rearranging itself beneath me.

"Excuse me," I said to those standing at the edge of the crowd blocking the door. All of the people, I saw now, were turned to face the entrance, bodies tense and expressions staring ahead, straining for the future. From inside the loudspeaker announced the arrival or departure of a bus—I couldn't understand which through the boom and crackle of the speaker. The mass of bodies strained in preparation. The surge of energy built, the smell of sweat intensified. I allowed the crowd to carry me through the opened grease-smudged doors, then I broke away.

Beyond the archway of the new passageway, the snack shop remained in its original location, and seemed to have had little redecorating. I crossed over green and white vinyl tiles, and wondered if the counter and stools were the same ones that Papi and I once sat at. "Orange soda and a hamburger," I ordered from the waitress, but the young woman smiled shyly and said, in Spanish, that she spoke no English. She pulled a plastic-covered menu from the aluminum holder and with her pencil indicated the bilingual lists of food and drinks, and I understood that I was to point to what I wanted.

"Soda de naranja y una hamburguesa, por favor," I said.

The Spanish words had sounded strange coming out of my mouth, and I spoke quickly, afraid that if I stopped to think, I wouldn't be able to finish. I glanced at the waitress to see if she'd understood. When the young woman nodded, I grinned with foolish pride. I had managed to pull a piece of the past out of myself.

The rat-a-tat-tat of Spanish ricocheted off the walls and ceiling, but most of the people did not speak the Chicano Spanish of the border. These were the accents of native speakers, but not all of them Mexican, perhaps Central Americans. So many changes. Yet there I sat in the very space my father had once occupied. But Papi was gone. No one left to validate the memory. I stared into the orange of my soda and had a flash of the coral gladiolus Grandmother and I had bought outside the gate of the Lourdes Cemetery for Papi's grave. Tomorrow I would cross the line into Mesquite, Sonora.

That night at the motel, I lay in bed for hours trying to will myself to sleep, but although my body ached with exhaustion, my brain churned, spitting out over and over all I'd seen during the day. Outside the motel, the coyotes' din was even louder than it had been the night before. I threw off the covers and pulled on jeans and a sweater. As I headed to the back of the motel to find out what the racket was about, the beauty of the starry sky almost made me forget the coyotes. I stopped. Someone stood behind a palo verde at the very back of Josie's courtyard wall. The shadow stepped away from the small tree.

"Grace?" the man said.

"Marc," I said, relieved. "The coyotes keeping you awake, too?"

When I reached him, he pointed to a wooden box beneath the palo verde. "This is probably what's attracting them." He lifted the hinged lid to reveal plastic jugs of water and stuffed plastic bags. "Josie," he said. "She leaves food and water for any who might be passing by."

"Entering illegally, you mean?"

"Let's say pilgrims," Marc said. "I suspect this load's supposed to attract Félix."

"The boy she keeps asking about?"

Marc nodded. "Josie has this Christmas party every year, and she's positive that Félix will show up for that. For the gifts, if nothing else."

"Who *is* Félix?" I asked, glad for the opportunity to think about something other than myself.

"It was Josie's tree that drew him and his older brother Chano here," Marc said, and gestured with his chin toward the inside of the courtyard. "They'd slip across the border, make a stop at Josie's before hopping a train to Tucson for a day or two of begging. Or stealing, to be honest."

I looked inside the iron gates of the courtyard walls. Ground lights shone up into the willow, and the chimes bathed in moonlight, glowed silver. The wind had died down, and now the lighter-weight chimes tinkled softly as Marc told me the story of the two brothers.

Chano and Félix had originally come from a small village in Mexico. Their father had traveled to the U.S. in hopes of finding a job so he could telegraph money back to feed his hungry wife and six children. When the money stopped, Mom took the kids out of school and got them jobs shining shoes and selling Chiclets or molded gelatin. Mom soon met a tamale vendor who wanted Mom but no kids. She sent the kids off to relatives, but Chano, a thirteen-year-old man, struck out for the border, bringing eight-year-old Félix with him. Like most of the Mexicans who came to the border, Marc said, the boys hoped to find work.

Chano realized that they were too young for the maquiladoras but hoped the streets would be kinder with the generosity of the lucky ones who did get the jobs. Too many people had the same idea, and that's when the boys took shelter in the tunnels beneath the two Mesquites like so many of the other homeless kids running the streets of Mesquite, Mexico.

Marc softly thumped his fist against the wrought-iron gate. "Four weeks ago Chano jumped the train—he was by himself that trip—fell off, and was killed. Félix ran away after that, and no one's seen him since."

While Marc spoke, I had flashes of my short time on the streets, of Tara, Sweet William, and most of all, funny Stan. It had been a hard life, but I suspected that these tunnel kids had even fewer choices than the street kids I'd known in Dayton. But then, maybe once a kid feels unloved and unwanted, a few more material comforts didn't make a whole lot of difference.

"Josie loved those boys," Marc said. "She had dreams of adopting them and forming a family with her partner."

"Constance?" I asked.

Marc told me how Josie and Constance had broken up not too long ago when Constance's grown kids wanted her to return to Michigan. "According to them," Marc said, "Constance wasn't really a lesbian. It was only Josie's bad influence." Marc shook his head. "People believe what they need to, I guess. Me, I think the truth's always best."

"In theory anyway," I said, and looked away from his eyes. His gaze was too intense, too direct. He saw more than I wanted to reveal. Before he could respond, I tapped the box with my shoe. "Do you think leaving this food and water out here does anything other than attract coyotes?"

"I keep telling Josie she's slapping an itty bitty band-aid over a cut-open artery." He grinned. "I guess she's like me—You gotta try, you know?"

"What do I know?" I said.

"Yeah, I guess we could all ask that," Marc answered.

I passed my hand over my face. On the wind floated the faintest aroma of something sweet. The hairs on the back of my neck stood up. "What's that scent?" I asked, and thinking of the vanilla pod that my mother so often clasped in her hand, I shivered.

"Ponderosa pine bark," Marc said. "The Olsons—down the road—they're burning it in the fireplace. Smells different from other pine. Their son brings them logs when he visits from up North. You don't remember that smell from when you lived here?"

"Sort of," I said, and remembered the murals on my parents' bedroom walls, the orchid fields of Papantla.

After I returned to my room, I dreamt of wrought-iron bars that locked me in, then locked me out; I dreamt of flower vendors outside cemetery walls. A young girl bought armfuls of gladiolus, bright and bold corals and crimsons for Papi, pale and tremulous whites and pinks for Mamá. Although I sensed the girl was me, I saw her from a distance, outside of her.

I dreamt of javelinas who howled like coyotes and charged into my head, hooves thundering. The boars poked into the wet folds of my brain and turned up a sliver of glass, blue and sharp; a blue so cold that ice crystals formed in its tumble through my brain. I tried to escape the dream, told the javelinas I knew they were only a figment of my imagination. They snuffled louder, pushed harder, pricked me with their bristled snouts. I awoke in a sweat, fell back asleep, and dreamt of orange trees, a drift of orange blossoms on the ground beneath it; of a man's tanned and bare feet shifting among the fragrant petals, releasing a faint citrus smell. "Come walk with me," Marc said from behind the branches.

FOURTEEN

The phone trilled next to me on the end table, startling me out of my half-awake state. Before I managed to get the right ends to ear and mouth, Josie chirped, "Don't tell me you're still sleeping."

I started to explain how I'd tossed and turned all night because of all those howling coyotes, but Josie interrupted to invite me to lunch at her apartment. She told me that Marc would return in a few minutes, that he'd just run out to buy a box of pencils. "He promised to take some when he goes to the Descanso," Josie said. "He's got news."

"News?" I said, trying to stall for time to think of an excuse to turn down her offer. An image of high-arched feet walking through blossoms had flashed into my mind. A dumb dream brought on by stress. It meant nothing. I was already reliving memories repressed for so long, and that was emotion enough.

"Thanks," I said, "but I don't think I can make it."

"Come on, now. Marc says it's important. And hurry or the food will get cold." Josie hung up the phone so fast that she almost cut off the end of her sentence.

Once I hopped into the shower and awakened myself with the cool spray, I told myself that I was being silly. Marc meant nothing to me. And Josie had been so excited that the news was probably about Félix. So enthralled with the little boy, she seemed to assume that everyone else was too. Why did people always assume that women loved stories about kids? Kids or not, seeing Josie happy would cheer me up. And I needed all the positive thoughts I could get. Today I would cross the border.

At her kitchen stove, Josie tilted a skillet so I could see inside. "Scrambled eggs and black beans. A late breakfast. I got hot sauce, pico de gallo, in the refrigerator, made fresh last night. Just plain Mexican food, maybe you can't eat it no more?"

"It's been a while, but sure."

"OK, woman, that's it." Josie rolled a stack of wheat tortillas that she said she'd made the night before in a cloth napkin and placed them on the table with a plate heaped with the beans and eggs.

"There's the salsa," she said, pointing to a small clay cazuela. "Buen provecho, like we say in Spanish. You go ahead and start. Marc, he's coming, don't worry." Although she was the one fidgeting and pacing, not me.

"Great eggs," I said, after swallowing a mouthful. "You'll have to give me the recipe."

"What recipe?" Josie said. "Scramble, throw in some black beans. So how did it went yesterday? What do you think of our little town? No place like the border, yes?"

In between chewing, I described some of the differences since I'd last been here, and although now and then, she'd murmur, Oh yeah? Josie didn't seem to be listening. Each time the bell tinkled over the front door, she'd stop with her head cocked, waiting for his voice.

He finally arrived, greeting Josie with a hug, then turning to me, he said, "Pretty amazing, isn't it?"

I must have looked confused, because he glanced back at Josie, and said with mock surprise, "Don't tell me you actually waited for me to tell her?"

"What's going on?" I said.

"Long story short," Marc said. "The Robleses—from the Descanso?—they *do* remember your family and the Peacock Curios. And the best part? Your grandmother's alive."

"Alive?" I tried to return Marc's smile, but couldn't. "She's dead," I said. "She must be. She was so sick."

"Paz Villalobos, that's her name, right?" Marc said.

"Alive," Josie said. "You heard the man."

"But I never thought. . . ." Individual words lay like pearls inside my head, but when I tried to string them together in a coherent line, the thread broke and the dots of white rolled away into the blue. I looked out the window at the tree. The wind was playful today, and the red ribbons on the branches were intertwining, working around each other, winding together. Like Grandmother's crocheted lace.

I caught the end of what Marc was saying: "Lives in a little house up in the hills."

"House? Her *own* house?" I squeaked.

"You all right?" Marc said. "I only asked around because I thought you wanted to find your grandmother."

"No," I said. "I mean yes, of course I want to find her." I was in a movie, and no one had bothered to hand me the script.

"You want, I'll run you over to her house," he said.

"An unexpected visit from me might be too much," I said quickly. "I've been away so long. She's old . . . the shock could hurt her."

Josie placed her hand over mine on the table. "You're lucky, woman," she said. "You found what you was looking for." She told me that she'd had a somewhat similar experience but hers hadn't ended so well.

"What?" My head was spinning. Josie took a chair, settled into her storytelling pose. Good. I needed a moment to let the news sink in.

"See," Josie began, "when I worked at the bus depot, well, I was always checking out folks' faces. My mother, she ran away when I was a baby, left me with my nana and tata. So, I'm thinking maybe someday Mami will slip back into town. She was like that, never wanting to stay in one place."

"And did she return?" I said.

"Nah, my mother, she wanted to stay disappeared."

I wondered if Grandmother had hoped that I'd stayed disappeared. For certain, Grandmother had made a miraculous recovery. Or maybe she hadn't been as sick as she'd claimed. But if that was so, why give me away? Poverty or not, if she had her health surely we could have managed. Things had been simpler when I believed Grandmother dead.

"Looking for your past can get complicated, can't it?" Marc said.

"It's not that," I said. But then what was it? "I had plans for the day. To visit Lourdes Cemetery. My family's—my parents'—graves." My excuses sounded lame even to me.

"No problem," Josie said. "I bet if you talk with your grandmother she's going to want to go to Lourdes with you. Why not?"

As Marc and I drove out of the parking lot, the bottles cemented in Josie's grotto caught the light from the morning sun and reflected spots of color so bright I shielded the side of my face. "Since you're expected at the Descanso," I said, "let's go there first, OK?" Why was I behaving so childishly? It was ridiculous to not want to see my own grandmother after coming all this way. Still, why rush things? Back and forth went the inner arguments.

"The Robleses say your grandmother was real excited when she found out you were here."

"I know . . . but I remember how you said the kids don't like your being late and, well, I wouldn't want you to disappoint them."

"You sure you're up to this visit?" Marc told me that he'd already called Mrs. Beltrán, a neighbor of Grandmother's who helped Grandmother out however she could. "Your grandmother doesn't have a phone," he said, "but I could call Mrs. Beltrán, see if she can get the message to her that the visit's off."

"I'm fine," I said. "Really." If I repeated it like a refrain, maybe I'd be able to convince myself.

As we neared downtown, we discussed the many changes I'd observed, and how the border had always attracted newcomers. Marc said that after World War II, immigrants came over from Europe and China, some of them settling in Mexico, others pushing toward the border with the hope of some-day coming into the U.S. I remembered the family names of my childhood schoolmates that gave testament to the mix on the border: Camou, Scrivner, Bracher, Puchi, Youngo, Wong, Maycher, Frickas, MacGregor, Medina, Elías, Paraskevas. Some of the families had branches on both the Mexican and American sides of Mesquite.

Marc said that after the NAFTA agreement was signed, a lot of foreign investors started building the maquiladoras. He said he didn't think it had worked out as well as promised. "It's brought jobs," he said, "but they don't pay much. They hire mostly women, and that leaves a lot of kids alone. From what I can tell, they're mostly making the rich richer."

As we drove across the border into Mexico, I couldn't help but think of how easily we'd crossed the line, moving from one country to another, one part of my life to another. I took a deep breath. Children with boxes of gum and trinkets pressed against the windows of the car each time we slowed in traffic. There were so many more beggars than there had been when I had lived in Mesquite, so many more vendors—a number of them Indians wearing traditional dress—with little tables set up to sell their wares.

"If you don't mind," I said once we turned onto Frontera Street, "I'd like to just sit here for a bit." Frontera was divided horizontally by the chain-link fence that marked the geographical boundaries of the two countries. La Casa del Descanso was across from us, a block building painted pink with a poster board propped in the front window announcing itself.

We sat on the waist-high wall above the wash that ran on the Mexican side, parallel with the fence. I sniffed the air, trying to distinguish the mingling scents: the familiar warm tortillas, beans simmering in clay pots, stray dogs with tongues lolling from the sides of their mouths, bakery bread warm from the oven, alcoholic vomit drying in the gutter, a whiff of perfumed memory in synthetic rose, and diesel fumes from the wall of trucks at an entry border gate farther down the line. There were so many more trucks than when I'd been a kid. My eyes stung from the polluted air. I reached my arms behind me and rested my weight on my hands. My shadow, along with Marc's, stretched in front of us, and I leaned slightly to one side so that mine met his. Realizing what I was doing, he laughed, tilted his head against mine, and pressed shoulder to shoulder. I straightened, embarrassed at being caught.

Marc pointed to the wash. "Way back when I was a little boy," he said, "kids used to ride their bikes in the arroyo bottoms. No more. The tunnel kids—'ratoncitos,' some people call them—have turned violent, huffing all that spray paint. Like another world down there—a few years back, before things got really bad, I went down."

He described descending into the high-ceilinged areas where he could stand without stooping, the cavernlike spaces that had been part of the original 1930s tunnel system. "When you get down really deep," he said, "without a flashlight, there's total blackness. It magnifies the sound of rushing water from the underground stream. The passages, darkness, water—I had the sense of returning to the womb."

I told him that his description sounded like something in a fantasy novel.

"Yeah, surreal," he said. "But you got to go through a lot of filth and nasty water to get to that level. Félix and Chano used to tell Josie how good they had it with their little house all fixed up below ground," he said. "Cardboard and blankets for beds, flashlights. They even invited her to visit, told her their home was her home."

"I guess the pretending helped them keep their pride."

"At first," Marc said, "the people on the U.S. side, even the businesses, they felt sorry for the tunnel kids, and they didn't say too much about them coming over to beg. But all that paint and paint thinner that helps them forget their hunger and pain also burns holes in their brains, turns them crazy. People get scared; you can't blame them."

He told me how criminals, a group that included some of the tunnel kids, offered their services as guides to people who wanted to enter the U.S. illegally. "Once they get them down in the tunnels," he said, "sometimes they beat and rob them of every cent they have left."

I almost said that I couldn't fathom the kids doing that to others who were as desperate as themselves. But then I thought of the street kids back in Ohio, how they'd turn on one another when other victims weren't available.

Marc must have understood my initial doubt, because he said that it was difficult for some to believe the kids would do such a thing. "You know what the kids told me?" He gave me a rueful smile. "They said that most of the people they jumped were Salvadorans and Guatemalans. 'They're not like us,' the kids said. 'They're like animals.' Always the same story, isn't it? The ones on the bottom of the heap fighting among themselves for the crumbs."

Spanish floated up from the wash, and I peered, almost a block down, at the sewage pipe. A gathering of dark shapes bumped about inside like a thundercloud moving toward the opening. Kids, all boys except for one girl, and ranging in age from maybe four to seventeen, burst out and into the dirt-bottomed arroyo. The younger kids stamped their feet in the rivulet of water trickling out of the sewer, while the older ones kept to the drier outer edges.

One small boy, light almond-brown, shaded his eyes with one hand and stared at Marc. The boy made a gang sign with his free hand and shouted, "Hey, ése."

"Félix," Marc explained, and waved. "The kids are coming for the 2:00 meal."

The kids scattered through the wash, breaking order to scramble up the cement banks. Bigger ones paused to offer a hand to the smaller. One by one, they clambered over the low wall and spilled onto Frontera. I remembered my short days on the streets and shuddered. I preferred the children on TV sitcoms who cracked adultlike witticisms, then disappeared from the screen. So much easier to forget.

The wave of children was now shifting across the street. A few of them shuffled along with heads bowed to the wind; others ran and jumped. Félix, in an oversized tee shirt and baggy khakis, spun in spiraling circles toward the Descanso. He leaped into the air as if he imagined he could take off and fly, then jerk-kicked his legs at odd angles, flung his arms up and out, elbows bent, forearms hanging. Exclamation marks in midair. His antics seemed at first like the dance of one of those curio store marionettes gone mad, but the more I studied him I had to concede a certain rhythm to his movements. Like Stan's, I thought, suddenly picturing my friend clicking his heels as we walked along the streets of Dayton.

"Wait 'til Josie finds out he's back," Marc said.

"He's so little." I wondered if any of the other kids looked after him now that his brother was dead.

Some of the kids drifted through the Descanso door, but Félix remained outside. He hopped from the sidewalk curb to the gutter, chanting words I couldn't make out. The double cowlick in his stiff hair sprang up, and with each hop, quivered like twin windmills in the desert wind. After a moment, he stopped, pulled a book of matches from his back pocket and began to strike one match, then another, each time throwing the small torch to the ground.

A small curly-haired dog peeked from around a parked car. I wanted to shout, shoo it away. I silently willed the dog to retreat, but attracted to the children's laughter, it tiptoed out, head hunkered between shoulders, tail curved submissively tight between its hind legs. Walking at an angle, it scuttled, crablike, toward Félix, who slowly looked up and away from a tiny torch still flickering in the gutter. When the dog reached within a yard of him, Félix lit all the matches remaining in the book. They caught fire with a small *whoosh*, and he flung the flaming matches at the dog.

Marc and I jumped off the wall at the same time, and yelled, he in Spanish, I in English for Félix to stop. With a frightened yelp, the small dog escaped around a corner. Félix stared at us, his impassive face revealing nothing. I'd been wrong about Félix—he wasn't at all like Stan.

A woman appeared in the doorway of the Descanso. She stood about five feet tall—counting the three inches of teased and sprayed hair, burgundy with salt and pepper roots—with small hands starfished on hips. She waved at us. "Good morning, señor Marc. And señorita Villalobos, yes?" Just as the others were doing, she was speaking Spanish. I was surprised at how natural hearing the language was beginning to feel to me after so many years away. But the thought of actually speaking it myself thickened my tongue.

I almost looked behind me, but the woman held out her hand to me. "Erminia Robles at your service."

"Look who's returned to us," Mrs. Robles said when Félix tried to rush past her. Hooking Félix's shoulder, she drew him to her. "Not so fast. How's your mother? That's where you've been, right?" She tapped the toe of one Buster Brown-style shoe as she spoke.

Félix twisted free. "I don't know nothin' about her," he muttered in Spanish. "Who cares anyway?"

Mrs. Robles sighed, glanced at Marc, and shook her head. As the children passed by us, I had to fight against recoiling at their lingering odor of black water. And when Marc whispered to me that he would try to get Félix to ride with us to Grandmother's so that he didn't take off again, I wished I had the nerve to say no. But it wasn't my car, after all.

As Marc handled the kids' bickering over who sat where at the long table covered in bright orange oilcloth, Mrs. Robles hung back to stand next to me. She touched my wrist. "Welcome to your land, pretty one."

I smiled and murmured my thanks in English. Mrs. Robles opened her arms for a hug, and when she wrapped her arms around me, her hair, smelling of hairspray and car exhaust, tickled beneath my chin. I hoped Grandmother would make me feel this wanted. But then, things were always simpler with those you don't share any history with.

When I smiled but said nothing, Mrs. Robles asked, "You don't speak Spanish?"

"A little," I answered in Spanish. The words still were getting snagged on my tongue. "But I understand everything."

Mrs. Robles slid her fingers over her mouth and tapped, as if studying the implication of my answer. "Tell me," she said, "if you'll excuse my impertinence, what would make a girl from such a nice family run away?"

"Run away?" I repeated.

"Please forgive me if I'm invading your privacy—Mrs. Beltrán mentioned about your running away. So sad. All these years you and your grandmother could have been together. Ah, well, youth; we've all made our share of mistakes, haven't we?"

"Who—who said I ran away?" I spoke louder than I'd intended, and Marc and some of the kids looked up.

"Everything OK?" Marc said, and joined us.

Mrs. Robles explained to Marc what Mrs. Beltrán had said, then turning to me said, "Don't worry, I'm sure your grandmother has forgiven you. She's old, maybe a little bitter that you left her, but she'll be so happy to see you now."

She squeezed my fingers to reassure me, but seemed flustered herself. She asked me and Marc to help her in the kitchen, explaining that her husband—her old man, she called him, was away at the moment on a mission to pick up two used computers donated by a local businesswoman. When Marc offered to return and help set them up, Mrs. Robles grinned as if it had been the response she had expected.

In the kitchen, she stirred a skillet of refried beans with one hand, and with the other, lifted the lid of a Dutch oven filled to brimming with a casserole of day-old tortillas in a thick tomato sauce. "No meat today. A bit of chorizo in the beans gives the illusion, though. And I have a chunk of cheese to crumble on the chilaquiles." She smiled, and the gold framing her two front teeth gleamed.

As we worked assembly-style, me dishing out the rice, then handing a plate to Marc, who slapped on chilaquiles before passing it to Mrs. Robles, she suddenly stopped, a spoonful of beans in midair. She fixed her eyes on the doorway. A teenage boy, maybe sixteen or seventeen, leaned against the archway between the kitchen and dining room, thumbs hooked in his front pockets, one sneakered foot crossed at the ankles. A studied James Dean posture of casual ease that didn't make it to his alert eyes, eyes the shade of green grapes, shining eerily pale in his tanned face.

"Ah, Mr. Omar," Mrs. Robles said. "Here at last. Those who arrive late for breakfast risk not having any." She slapped the mass of beans onto the plate with such force, it almost fell from her hand.

"Of course, señora," Omar answered. "I understand, very efficient. Just like the gringos say, 'Time is money.' And their money runs this place, right?"

Omar's gaze crawled down the length of my body. "Some day I'm going North, maybe marry a nice gringuita. If she's older than me, that's OK. I dated an ancient ballerina once, more than fifty years old." Then as if he thought we might not believe him, he added, "The ugliest feet I've ever seen. Toes like this." He clawed the fingers of one hand.

"Watch it, man." Marc set down the plate he'd been holding, and his pectoral muscles tensed beneath his tee shirt. "Respect."

Omar grinned and lowered his eyes. More a show of his long eyelashes, I suspected, than of submissiveness. "Yes, sir, forgive me," he said.

Félix sat at one end of the bench, his hands fisted on the table. He glanced sideways at Omar. I couldn't decide if Félix was afraid or angry.

"Eat," Marc told Félix, and set a plate in front of him. "We're going to Mrs. Thornberry's grandmother's. We need to take you with us to show us the way."

Félix shrugged, but a light shone in his black eyes.

"I could be of more help, sir, if you don't mind my saying so." Omar's pale eyes looked at some spot on the wall beyond us. "I know this town, below and above ground." His words, smooth and muscular, glided from his lips like a snake cutting through water.

"If he goes, I don't," Félix muttered.

"Don't worry," Marc said, "Omar's not getting close to you."

After twenty minutes on the serpentine road up the hills behind town, the asphalt cut off suddenly and the road wishboned: one choice, wide and deeply rutted, the other little more than a pathway cleared of brush. My gaze followed the direction of Félix's dirty finger pointing to the path. I was anxious for anything to distract my mind from a meeting with Grandmother. How could I even fathom what to say to her? What she could say to me? No point in thinking about it. Whatever would happen would happen. I stared hard at the path.

"Just a trick road the cholos made. The punks, they got their clubhouse down there by a gully, three junk cars. Take your money, watch, shoes, everything, then—" Félix sliced across the back of his knee with one finger. "Leave you flopping in the dirt like a fish."

"Cut the tendons," Marc explained to me, then to Félix's reflection in the rear view mirror, he said, "Scary stuff, eh?"

"Yes," I said, and in my mind, peacock-blue flashed neon-bright.

"Nothing scares me," Félix said, and I had a vague memory of once having said that myself. Long, long ago. I took out a tissue from my purse and dabbed at my suddenly damp forehead.

Félix bounced in the seat. "You ever go fishing, Marc? In Guaymas, they got the biggest fish in the world. And shrimp? Uuy. Bigger than my hand.

Soon I'll be going home again, maybe for Christmas." He bounced higher with the thought.

"By the way," Marc said. "Josefina Sandoval, you know from the Borderlands Motel? She invites you to her party."

"I don't need no mother," Félix said. "So don't think I do. I got one already. She keeps me in her prayers, too. Beautiful, that's what my mom is. Not like that fat Josie. High heels, long hair shiny." Félix combed his fingers along the back of the seat.

"Anyway," he said, "the tunnels are hard to get through these days. On the gringo side, S.W.A.T. All in black—man, they got some neat uniforms. Over here, the Grupo Beta." He shuddered as if taken by a sudden chill. He sat back, gazed out the window, shrugged. He wasn't afraid of anything.

"Maybe I'll go visit Josie someday," Félix said. "But don't say nothing. Better she don't get her hopes up."

"Well, I hope you stick around this time," Marc said.

"Better close the windows," Félix said. "The wind blows the stink from over there." He pointed up the road and pinched his nose with the other hand.

As the car, bottom scraping on rocky ground, edged forward, shacks seemed to sprout out of the dirt. Makeshift dwellings teetered on steep hills, incomplete squares of concrete blocks, shanties thrown together from combinations of tar paper, cardboard, burlap, tin, and dried cactus. Children and dogs scampered and rolled in the dust. The stench of open sewage drains invaded the car. I tried to be discreet as I held a tissue to my nose.

To our right, a preteen girl picked up an infant wearing only a too-small tee shirt, the torn hole in the center stretching across his chest like a gaping mouth. She straddled him on her hip. Face blank, she watched the car, her eyes drifting until they met mine. I looked away. This, I thought, had surely been what Grandmother wanted to save me from. Who could blame an old woman for that?

The car had reached a summit, and Marc pointed across the valley to a far hill on the Mexican side dotted with new houses. One, a concrete monstrosity with an outside wall of glass. The fiery red of the sun reflected off the glass and shone into my eyes. Félix stirred, and sliding forward, pushed his upper body into the space between the bucket seats. I leaned away from him and his smell of putrid water.

"Those houses," Félix said, "are like in the movies. Can they see us, too? Probably not, 'cause we're too small, right? You ever been in there?" He glanced at Marc.

"I don't travel in those circles, my friend."

"How about your grandmother?" Félix said to me. "Is she rich?"

I was doing well enough to try to focus on the conversation, but when I was drawn into it by his direct question, it startled me. I shook my head, no, although I had no idea what to expect. I alternated between hoping that Grandmother didn't live in a shack like the ones we'd just passed and that she did. I was trying so hard to not think, to not doubt her reasons for giving me up, but I was having trouble reconciling her independent living with the poverty that I'd left her in. Had she sold me to Molly Carol? Was that how she'd manage to survive?

"I haven't seen her for many years," I said, glancing back at Félix. "Not since I was just a few years older than you." I continued to speak in English, and when Félix didn't understand everything I said, he looked to Marc for translation.

"Maybe she's not gonna be there." Félix scratched his scalp, studied the scabbed flakes beneath his fingernails. "Maybe she found a boyfriend and took off, didn't even leave one little bean behind. Sometimes it happens like that. So what, who cares? What's your grandmother's name?"

"Paz Villalobos," I said.

I caught Félix's reflection in the mirror and wished he would quit watching me with those too-bright eyes. I felt guilty for being repulsed by him—he was only a kid—but with the windows up, his odor was almost overwhelming.

"Don't expect too much." Félix rocked back in the seat. "Granny's probably not there. Or maybe she doesn't want to see you, then what?"

I plucked another tissue from my purse, dabbed at the moisture on my forehead.

"Enough," Marc said. "Mrs. Thornberry's already been told that her grandmother's excited about seeing her granddaughter."

"Sometimes people lie," Félix said.

FIFTEEN

That one over there must be the Beltráns' house," Marc said. He pointed to a bungalow on the slope of the next hill, then turned back to study the house closest to us. From our viewpoint we could glimpse the top side of a coral-colored stucco with windows freshly trimmed in turquoise blue. Fuzzy cactus trees grew around the nearest border of the yard and blocked much of the house.

"Looks like your grandmother's doing OK living alone. A relief for you, I'll bet," Marc said.

"She's doing great," I said, and wadded the tissue I'd been holding. My breathing became labored, and I released broken huffs of air.

Félix, who had returned to his space between me and Marc—either not aware of or ignoring my leaning away from him—frowned at the ragged sounds coming from my nose and mouth. He quickly lost interest though, and craned his neck to look at the driveway to my right, a forty-five-degree bank of packed dirt eroded with furrows.

"How're you doing?" Marc asked.

"Fine," I said. I'd been remembering years ago when I'd pictured Grandmother wrapped in a lace mantilla and huddling against the wall of the church, begging for alms. So much for the prophecy of that image. Unless, of course, some generous soul had dropped a bagful of gold coins into Grandmother's outstretched palm.

Marc inched the Mustang beneath the shade of a triangle of mesquite trees at the foot of the driveway and eyed the deep ruts. "Cars haven't made it up there for a while," he said.

"Aren't you coming with me?" I felt foolish even before I'd finished the question, but I didn't take it back. I swiped at the beads of sweat on my nose with the damp tissue.

"Got to go back to help with those computers at the Descanso. I'll come back in an hour or two, take you both to the cemetery. Don't worry, Grace, your grandmother's expecting you, but if you want, I'll stick around to make sure she's there."

"Uuuy," Félix said. "We're not going up, are we? All this way for nothing. Want I should go with you?" He doubled over the console and twisted sideways across my lap to reach for the door handle. Marc grabbed a fistful of tee shirt.

"No, please, it's OK," I said. "Both of you come. Maybe she doesn't speak English anymore. And my Spanish is rusty. And she won't recognize me. I was only thirteen, after all."

"A grandmother living here all by herself," Félix said. "Bet she's been praying for somebody to keep her company. Men, we don't mind being alone, but old ladies, well. . . ."

The wind carried away Félix's last words as he ran up the concrete steps along one side of the driveway, his arms held straight out to the sides, making a point of not using the metal rail. Men apparently didn't need the support of human companionship or stair rails. At the top he called down, "Better watch out up here with them cactus, they'll grab you."

Glad for the distraction, I laughed too loudly. Marc misunderstood and thought I didn't believe Félix. "No joke," he said. "Teddy bear chollas. Only the name's cute. That furry-looking stuff? Barbed spines. Like Félix said, keep your distance. Get close and those suckers'll jump right on you. Hard as hell to get free of them, too. But you must remember them from before."

"Sort of," I said, and wondered silently what kind of person would have such a cactus near the front door of the house.

Félix stood with both hands clasped behind his head and studied the house. "Somebody peeked from behind the shade," he said when we reached the hilltop. "I saw a finger."

Once I passed the chollas, the front of the cottage came into view—blue door in the center and windows on either side—a blue-nosed face.

"Again with the finger," Félix shouted. "See?" He sprang toward the window.

"Quiet." Marc placed his hands on Félix's shoulders, scooted him to one side.

My hands were mottled with cold, and I rubbed them on my khakis. I rapped on the door with such pressure that I broke the skin on my knuckles. I started to suck at the scraped skin, but wondered if the paint might contain lead. When I knocked again, the finger inside drew back from the blind, but the V it had created remained in the heavy material.

Feet shuffled inside. An image of myself as a child flashed through my mind, that last morning hiding beneath the brass bed while Grandmother called to me to come out. Standing at Grandmother's door now, I thought, Come out, Grandmother, I know you're in there. Let's face the inevitable.

"Mrs. Villalobos," Marc called and stepped forward, close enough that his breath warmed the back of my neck, now as cold as my hands. "We're friends of the Robleses, from the House of Descanso. Your granddaughter's with us. Mrs. Beltrán told you we would visit, yes?" The barking of dogs echoed from somewhere in the valley below.

"Is she deaf, your grandmother?" Félix pulled out of Marc's hold and pressed his nose, face cupped in the parentheses of his hands, to the window. "We know you're in there," he hollered.

I lifted my arm, watching it as if it belonged to someone else, and knocked once more. Pulling back my fisted hand, I turned it toward myself and stared at the blue flakes imbedded in my knuckles. Different house, different door, but I felt as though I were looking at a child's hands, my hands twenty-six years ago.

I leaned my ear to the door, held up a finger for Félix to be quiet, and concentrated on the raspy breathing on the other side of the wooden panel. Without thinking, I matched the rhythm of my breath to that of Grandmother's. "Grandmother?" I whispered to the door.

A cry from the back of the house shattered the stillness.

"Holy shit." Félix pressed his back to the wall. "Some kid's getting tortured."

"Calm down," Marc said, but shot me a look that said he was unnerved, too.

"You calm down," I said, and ignoring Marc's warning to let him go first, I ran to the side of the house, swung open a chain-link gate, followed the winding path to the back. There, the patch of dirt yard was raked with tine marks broken by smooth swoops that disrupted the lined design. A chicken coop, patched roof saddled in the middle, stood at the far left side, and around the perimeter of the property, a barrier of overgrown maguey cactuses hid the encroaching shantytown only hills below.

Félix wiggled in between me and Marc. "Man, what a neat house." He pointed to the coop.

"Let's check here." I gestured toward the back of the stucco house, the built-on addition, bottom half constructed of fitted stones and top screened in with mesh wire. He yanked the screen door and two security latches popped loose from the dry wood. "Mrs. Villalobos, you in there?" I said, and ignored the odd look Marc gave me. I didn't understand myself why I'd called her by her name. Maybe I was afraid that she'd changed her mind about wanting to see her granddaughter.

"Maybe it was the old woman got murdered," Félix said.

"Enough with the crime dramas." Marc motioned for Félix to stay back, but I had already pushed into the room and Félix followed me. After traveling through all the miles and years, would I be cheated out of seeing my grandmother? No way.

"It's like a jungle." Félix widened his eyes as he looked around the room.

Like the jungles of Veracruz, I thought, but at the same time remembered how much Grandmother had always loved plants and lavished almost as much attention on them as she had on Papi. Potted plants hung from the ceiling and covered the floor: a garden of succulents, flowers, and herbs in terra-cotta crockery, wooden buckets, and rusting tins advertising coffee beans from plantations long left to ruin. I inhaled deeply and the inside of my nostrils tingled with the scent of the herbs—mint, rosemary, laurel, chamomile, basil, oregano; and potted roses in miniature—essence of tea and spice.

"God." I swayed from the rush of scented memories. Home, it smelled of home.

"You're trespassing." The old-woman voice came from the main house. From behind a curtain of hanging greenery, the door appeared to be cracked open a few inches.

Another shriek from outside the room curdled the air, and the three of us whipped our heads towards the sound.

"Look, look." Félix pointed toward the yard. "A peacock."

The bird strutted from around the right side of the house, lowered tail feathers brushing the dirt behind him, erasing his new tracks. One eye, black and small, beaded on us strangers, the gaze direct, penetrating, and yet indifferent. The eye of God, I thought.

"Man, I always knew it was a peacock making that noise," Félix said. "And you guys so scared of a bird. Not me. Birds like me." As he ran back toward the screen door, he tripped and knocked over a five-gallon can of geraniums, and I thought again what a mistake it had been to bring Félix. All he did was cause trouble.

Marc hurried to Félix's side, lifted him to his feet. "You OK?" He patted Félix's chest. He allowed Marc to brush the geranium petals, blood-red, from his tee shirt. For the first time since I'd met Félix, his eyes were unguarded, childlike. He glanced up, caught me watching, and the vulnerability in his eyes crystallized beneath a glaze of anger.

"I didn't feel nothin'," Félix said, and pushed away Marc's hand.

Hinges creaked. The black space beyond the plants widened as the door opened, and every muscle in my body tensed. I swallowed hard to ease the tightness in my throat so I could speak. "Abuela?" I croaked in Spanish.

Pale fingers separated the trailing stems of Wandering Jew and baby's tears, and Grandmother stepped out. Seeing her standing there was like being slapped in the face with my past, and when I swayed, Marc stepped closer, pressed his chest to my back, steadying me.

"Híjole," Félix said. "Look at those eyes, blue-blue like the peacock. I bet you used to be beautiful."

Grandmother made a grunting sound that may have been intended as a laugh. "I saw you out front," she said, "but you can't be too careful these days." She edged away from the hanging plants.

"You OK?" Marc whispered in my ear, and I nodded. It was all I could do.

Félix muttered that he was right, she *was* deaf, hadn't she heard us calling her? Marc hissed at him to shut up or he'd never take him anyplace again. For a moment, we were all silent, even Félix. Grandmother and I stared at each another. How old she had become. The proud spine that once inched her head high above the rest now curved into a question mark. Her black shirtwaist dress hung in baggy folds gathered by a belt at her waist. A gold chain around her neck disappeared into the top v-cut of her bodice. Did her beloved locket hang from the end of that chain? Her hair was styled into a smooth cap of gray, and on the blond down of her cheeks powder clung like a gauzy veil. At least the color of those eyes had remained true to the woman Grandmother had been.

What thoughts, I wondered, lurked behind that amazing blue? What was she thinking about me?

"Did you close the gate behind you?" Grandmother said. Her words broke the silence, and it was as if a film had been stopped and now returned to motion. I released my breath, not realizing until then that I'd been holding it.

"He was the last one through," Félix said, pointing an accusing finger at Marc. "Not me."

"Don't be afraid to tell all you know," Marc said, but chuckled.

"Sorry," I muttered, and immediately was angry with myself. Why should I apologize to her for anything? I stepped away from Marc, embarrassed now at the way I'd been leaning back into him.

"I need to get a lock," Grandmother said. "An old woman can't be too careful in these difficult times."

"You already said that," Félix said. "Anyway, this is your granddaughter. "The one you haven't seen in many, many years." He pressed his hands on the crown of his head, flattening the whorls of out-of-control hair.

Grandmother's eyes darted around the room, making certain, it seemed to me, to avoid me. She stared at Marc.

"He's Marc Delint." Félix jerked his thumb in back of him to Marc, now standing behind him and putting a squeeze on Félix's shoulder. He squirmed loose, and with a little duck of his head introduced himself. "Félix Riofrío López, at your service, señora."

Marc laughed at Félix's formality, and in spite of myself, I joined in. He did have something of the comedian in him, even if it wasn't intentional.

"Is that so?" Grandmother said in a serious voice, but one corner of her mouth twitched. When she looked more closely at Félix, her eyes lit on the uprooted geranium, and her lips flattened into a downturned line. "Look what you've done."

She wagged a finger at Félix, then walked a familiar path around the pots to the overturned geranium, her shoulders working like unbalanced scales. I knelt beside Grandmother, helped her replace clods of earth into the rusted can. The warmth of her body brought out the scent of chamomile from her hair, and my knees turned so weak I held onto the can to keep from falling.

When Grandmother tried to stand, she trembled with the effort, and I held her elbow, perhaps steadying myself as much as her. She lifted her arm from my cupped hand, and her entire body quivering with the effort, she braced herself on the floor with one hand, held onto a nearby supporting beam with the other, and pushed herself back up. Upright again, she tilted her chin and hiked one shoulder at an angle, as if trying to give the impression of height.

"Maybe Félix and I better take off and leave you two alone," Marc said. I pretended to not hear him. I felt as though I were holding my breath again, waiting for something to jump out of the darkness at me.

"I'm happy to see you again, Abuela," I said, and stood. "I never thought this day would come." The words sounded so trite, but what do you say to the past you thought dead and buried? I'd spoken in Spanish and the effort worked my jaws, facial muscles, and lips into unfamiliar positions. Félix stared at my mouth, the way children do when they hear a foreigner speak.

"You have a bit of an American accent," Grandmother said, and studied me as if she wasn't certain I really was her granddaughter.

"Makes sense," I said. "Where do you think I've been for the last twenty-five years?" I hadn't meant the question to come off so sarcastic. Grandmother's cheeks flushed.

"Uuy," Félix said. He stared at me with widened eyes. "You don't have no respect." He turned back to Grandmother. "That's a big problem she's got, your granddaughter. Me, I respect old people."

"Mrs. Villalobos," Marc said. He reached out to grab Félix's shoulder but Félix was too fast. "The boy and I are leaving now."

"That's what you say," Félix said. The screen door slammed behind him.

"So . . . in a couple of hours?" Marc said to me.

When I agreed, Grandmother said, "You're not staying the night? It's up to you, of course. But you're welcome to stay for as long as you wish." She was still avoiding looking me in the eye, the way she had done since all the years ago after the accident.

"I didn't come prepared for overnight," I said, and opened my arms to show I wasn't carrying a bag. Grandmother assured me she had a brand-new toothbrush and plenty of toiletries and extra nightgowns. Oh, and a washer and dryer. She spoke casually, as if my decision was not important to her, but the faint tremor in her voice and the rapid pulse at her throat gave her away.

"All right," I said. Of course I should stay. Wasn't she my only living relative? Surely we'd eventually be able to have a real conversation. Or maybe there was too much to say, and I wasn't certain I wanted to hear.

"Tomorrow afternoon, then," Marc said. "Just let me get Félix." He laughed. "I can guess where he is, too. Tough guy really likes that bird."

"I'll help," I said. I knew I was being a coward but I wanted to put off being alone with Grandmother for a bit longer.

"You were right," I said, after Marc and I stepped outside. I pointed to the chicken coop close to the maguey. Félix was on his hands and knees, the front half of his body inside the coop, backside sticking out. He clucked his tongue and called in baby talk for the peacock to come out. "Pavito," he called, already assigning the bird a name.

Pebbles crunched beneath Marc's feet as he walked toward the coop, and Félix cut off his sweet words. He scuttled backward on all fours before hopping to his feet and dusting the knees of his jeans.

"Time to go," Marc said.

"Nah, that's OK. Go ahead without me." Félix crossed his arms, leaned back at the waist, and surveyed the chicken coop through narrowed eyes, an imitation of a grownup. "This house needs repair. My dad was a carpenter, you know. He's probably getting rich doing work for the gringos. Taught me and my brothers. Chano, if he has the materials, he can build anything." Félix's defiant stare dared Marc to correct his use of the present tense with his brother.

As Marc neared, Félix shouted, "You can't tell me—" Before he finished the sentence, Marc grabbed Félix's arm and pulled him toward the car. When Félix twisted and kicked, Marc lifted him into his arms.

"Put me down." Félix arched his back—a rainbow of brown skin, dingy white tee shirt, and khaki pants—and rolled his eyes back to keep his gaze on the coop. "Help, help!" he yelled; then looking annoyed with himself for his moment of weakness, he bucked and screamed obscenities.

When Marc held tight, Félix spit in Marc's face. "Shit," Marc muttered and set Félix down to wipe his face with the back of his sleeve. Félix broke away, half-running, half-bottom-scooting down the hill. He tripped, somersaulted in a ball of dust and gravel, then righting himself, turned to face us.

He cupped his hands around his mouth, and yelled, "Go to the devil, all of you! Except for the peacock. And the old woman." He darted away, yelping the Mexican grito.

"Does that boy come from the shacks?" Grandmother spoke from directly behind us, and Marc and I both started.

I shrugged, and when Marc told her Félix lived in the tunnels, Grandmother nodded slowly. She told us her house had been burgled the year before. "They never found the thieves. All they got was my metal box of photos. They realized it was valuable—it was locked, you see. What they didn't realize, it was valuable only to me."

"And me," I said softly.

If she heard me, she didn't show it. She passed her hand over her eyes, and her composure returned. "Maybe," she said, "it wasn't such a good idea to bring that boy here. Did you see how carefully he was checking out my property?"

I glanced at Marc. Even thought I'd never really put up an argument about bringing Marc along, I felt so guilty about being repelled by the boy that I felt like saying, "See, I'm not such a horrible person. I'm not the only one that doesn't trust him."

"My fault," he said. "Félix is having an especially difficult time these days. I didn't think."

Grandmother placed her hand over her heart. "Still, Félix cursed you two, not me and my peacock. Pavito, isn't that what he called him? You know, that peacock appeared in my yard out of nowhere and decided to stay." A trace of a smile pulled her thin lips into a barely curved line.

"*Grace*?" Grandmother said to me, once Marc had driven off. "Is that what you're called nowadays? You've anglicized your name?"

"My name was changed for me," I said, and tried in vain to lock eyes with her.

We were inside the screened room again, and when Grandmother suddenly pivoted toward the house, she teetered. She quickly regained her balance, and said with excessive dignity, "Please come in." She parted the waterfall of plants, and as she passed through the greenery, tendrils of baby's tears brushed across the bony wings of her back.

The house smelled of dust, drying flowers, candle wax, and old age. "Sit," Grandmother said, and pointed to the table and chairs in the center of the kitchen.

On the table, draped with a starched linen tablecloth, sat a bowl of roses. The rose petals had begun to brown at the edges, as if they'd been too long waiting for company. Grandmother pulled a plate from the refrigerator and lifted the plastic wrap to reveal the sweet breads.

"Conchitas," I said. I dabbed at the top of the bun, pressed my finger into the powdered sugar design of a shell. "My favorites. Did you happen to have them or did you remember?"

"Of course," Grandmother said.

I wasn't certain which part of my question she was answering, and afraid of what her answer might be, I didn't ask. She moved to the stove, and when she stretched to one side to pull the coffee can from a nearby shelf, her arm trembled with the effort. I offered to help, but she shooed me away. "No, no," she said. "I've been doing for myself for a long time."

"Yes, me too," I snapped. This was as good a time as any to get to the heart of my visit. "I wish I could have been here to help you," I said. "But that was out of my hands." I tried to soften the bitterness in my tone. After all, I didn't want to shut her down.

Grandmother hummed an unfamiliar tune and continued making coffee. Had she truly not heard me or was she playing at being hard of hearing? I counted silently to ten before speaking, more loudly this time. "Grandmother, I need to know the truth."

Grandmother pressed upper teeth to lower lip and aspirated. "*Phht*. The truth? If you see it run by, catch it, will you?" She turned on the faucet full force, rattled an aluminum saucepan from off a hook, then dropped it (intentionally?) into the sink with a clank.

"Between the both of us," I said, "I think we can come up with some semblance of truth." I was having a hard time keeping my voice level.

At the stove, Grandmother struck a kitchen match with such pressure, a piece of the match head flew away like a tiny comet. The gas flame lit with a *whoof*. "I assume you take your coffee the same way," she said.

"Whatever's easiest," I said. I had no idea of which *way* Grandmother meant. But what did it matter?

Moments later when the water and coffee grounds came to a boil, Grandmother poured the mixture through a cloth colander. "Oh, I see," I said. "You meant you're making the coffee the way Papi liked it."

"You drank it this way, too. Strong, black, lots of sugar."

"No, that was Papi. For me Chelo heated milk and stirred in just a pinch of instant Nescafé. You remember Chelo, don't you?"

"*Phht*. Of course I remember her. My problem is I remember too much, child."

I didn't know how to ask my question, so although I softened my voice to remove the edge, I plopped the words out without the prettiness of tact. "Why did you tell Mrs. Beltrán that I ran away?"

Grandmother held onto the chair back with one hand as she eased herself down. I could see how pale she'd gone, but I had to continue. I felt as though I were pushing through quicksand, that I would be swallowed up if I didn't finish my thought.

"We both know," I said, "that you sent me away. Why?"

"I said that?" Grandmother's hand shook so much that she had trouble spooning sugar into her coffee. "No, she must have misunderstood. She's a nice woman, but like me she's not getting any younger. With the years, the mind . . ." She fluttered her fingers as if her mind had sprouted wings and floated away like a butterfly.

"OK, let's assume the runaway business was a misunderstanding." I almost added sugar into my own cup, although I never drank it sweet. "But you told me you were sick, destitute. So I don't understand all this." I swept my hand to take in our surroundings.

The kitchen faucet leaked, and for still moments the *plink-plink, plink-plink* bounced off the sink bottom, ricocheted off the walls. Grandmother shifted sideways in her chair and offered me her profile. She angled a glance my way. "You know," she said, "you remind me of my favorite sister, your namesake."

"My *namesake*?" I set down my cup before it dropped from my icy fingers. "You never spoke of having family." My thoughts buzzed erratically as I tried to make sense of what Grandmother was trying to tell me. I envisioned the fruit trees in the backyard in Brockton and the wasps, drunk on the overripe apples and pears of fall, zip-zapping in paths of broken Z's.

"Altagracia," Grandmother said, and her blue eyes turned to the opened slats of the venetian blinds over the kitchen sink window. "She was my older sister, the one like a second mother to me. I never spoke of my family," she said, "because I was dead to them a long time ago." The wattle beneath her chin trembled.

As a child I'd known next to nothing about Grandmother's past. She'd only spoken vaguely of having come to Mesquite years before when Papi was a small boy. Her life before that had been off limits. How could I lose this opportunity? "Yes, tell me about your family. My family," I said.

"La Joya," Grandmother said, "that was the name of our hacienda."

Outside the sun was setting, and the dying rays shone through the venetian slats, one bar of light shining directly into her eyes. She blinked and moved back out of the light. The loose skin of her eyelids drooped, and her eyes glittered like chips of glass caught in a web of fine wrinkles.

"We grew blue agave," she continued. "Fields and fields of those plants surrounded our house. Even now I can see their fleshy leaves. When I was a child my sister Altagracia told me that the thorny agave leaves were the unsheathed sabers of Moors. Thousands upon thousands, ready to defend us from outside evil." Grandmother chuckled.

The sound startled me, and I realized that I didn't have any memories of Grandmother laughing when I was a child. She must have, but my mind hadn't stored that sound or image. She'd always been worried about the business, the household, bills, propriety. She'd wanted what was best for all of us. How could I doubt her intentions now? She was silent now, studied her hands as she clasped them as if prayer. She winced and unclasped them once more and dropped them into her lap, staring at them with a quizzical look on her face. As if she wasn't certain they belonged to her.

"Go on, Grandmother," I said softly, afraid of breaking the spell that seemed to have come over her. She said nothing for a moment, and I was afraid she would say no more. But then she sighed and her gaze lifted from her lap and stared at something I could not see.

"Altagracia," Grandmother said, her voice soft and slow as syrup in winter, "often entertained me with her curious descriptions. But all those lovely stories came to nothing. Do you know what happens to agave? Their fronds are stripped away and the hearts cut out. Thousands and thousands of hearts ripped out. All for what?"

Her expression suggested the question was rhetorical, so I didn't bother answering. *Plinkity-plink*, the faucet dripped onto stainless steel.

Grandmother held up a finger. "Nothing is lovelier than the sound of running water. Our rooms opened to a portico that ran around the courtyard, and in the center, the fountain. Altagracia added oil of orange blossom, and with the water's circulation the scent filled the air we breathed, day and night. We lived in heaven, I tell you."

"That's why you planted those orange trees in our old courtyard," I said.

"When I was a girl," Grandmother continued, as if I hadn't spoken, "my hair—so blond it was then—hung past my waist. My maid Inocencia brushed my hair one hundred strokes every day, but often she was rough with the tangles. But on one particular day she was gentle as a lamb. And usually such a serious girl, that morning she laughed and joked."

I closed my eyes to hold the image of Grandmother as a young girl in my head. How lovely she must have been before worry set her face in frowning creases. "And then," I whispered, even though encouragement for her to continue was no longer necessary. It was as if she had been waiting to tell this story, and now, after so many years, nothing could stop her.

"I asked Inocencia why she was so cheerful," Grandmother said.

"'I had a dream last night, señorita Paz,' Inocencia answered me. 'You see, every night I have been asking the Holy Virgin why some have so much and others so little. But last night, she appeared to me and said that in the end, all of us—poor or rich, proud or humble—we will all get what we deserve.'

"I told Inocencia she was being foolish. And that I had more important things on my mind than her silly dreams. Later, just as I had for the last three months during siesta, I slipped out of my bedroom of white Belgian lace and dashed out to the stables. I told the boy to take off the English saddle, and I rode Flor bareback that afternoon, for I wanted to feel the power of her muscles. As if her strength could be mine." Grandmother stared down at her hands again, and with a fingertip touched the brown spots on the back, first one hand then the other.

"You felt the horse's power as your own," I said, when she paused too long.

"Hmm," Grandmother said. "Selim Mena." She released a long sigh that whistled through her nostrils. "He was from a family of shopkeepers, you see, and not even Catholic. It goes without saying that he wasn't suitable for someone of my blood. I was too much woman for him, as the saying goes. Ha.

"Well, that day I pushed Flor hard, wanted to arrive to the little grove of trees by the bank of the Santiago River before Selim. I planned for him to find me sitting on a fallen tree, profile to the sun, my blond tresses freed of their ribbons. You see, my Selim, a poet of sorts, was fond of romantic pictures. I often struck poses that he imagined were natural."

I pictured the young and lovely Paz waiting for her lover, and my eyes moistened. But I refused to cry. Somewhere along the line, I had taught myself to hold back the tears—what was the point? Now, I was determined that those tears so denied would not fall for this woman who had destroyed my life. For whatever reason.

"So," Grandmother continued. "When I slid off Flor that day, a chill came over me." She rubbed at the gooseflesh on her arms.

I massaged my own arms.

"I saw the shadows among the trees and thought Selim had beaten me to our spot. But instead the shadows that moved towards me were those of my father's workers. I had been betrayed. Where were the sabers to protect me?"

"Inocencia betrayed you?" I asked.

From the back of the house, Pavito cried out, but Grandmother only tilted her head to one side, her eyes far away, as if listening to something inside herself. "When I was a girl," she said, voice dreamy, "my mother kept peacocks. I have never stopped hearing their sweet cry calling me home.

"But I digress. Even after my shame had been revealed—I was pregnant, you see—I thought that because I was my father's favorite, he would give in to my tantrums. But my father was not one to allow tradition to be weakened by love.

" 'From this day forward, you are dead to the family,' he said, and not even my dear Altagracia could bring herself to defy his decree."

Grandmother paused. The ray of light through the window was slowly making its way down her body. Her mind seemed to be drifting, but I had to hear the rest. "After your father banned you from the family," I said, "what happened? Was Papi the baby you were carrying?"

"As it turned out," Grandmother said, her voice hoarse now, "Selim—for whom I gave up heaven—already belonged to another. He was married to a woman in Puebla. So years later when I was feeling myself again, I threw the name 'Mena' into the Santiago River and left with my little Salvador. A predictable ending to a sordid story, yes?" She released a breath so long that it must have come from somewhere deep, deep inside her.

"I don't know what to say," I said.

She brushed imaginary crumbs from her lap. Then almost shyly she said, "It is my story. Do with it what you will."

We sat for long moments in the gathering shadows, each lost in the memories lingering like ghosts in the dusk. Finally I reached across the table and touched her forearm with my fingertips. "We can't change the past," I said.

"No," Grandmother said, after a long pause. "I suppose life is for the living, memories for the dead. Isn't that what they say?"

"I don't think you believe that any more than I do."

Grandmother stood with a groan. "I'll show you to your room."

"Before we do, Grandmother. . . ." My words faded, but I gathered my courage. "I'm so happy that you told me about your—our—family. And I want to hear more." I paused. "But I'd like to hear about how you've made out so well. After I left, that is." Was it cruel to push Grandmother when she seemed so weak and tried? I didn't care, I had to know.

"Oh," Grandmother said. "My brain can only handle so much. We have tomorrow."

Grandmother headed toward a curtained archway to one side of the kitchen. She lifted one of the flowered panels and pointed to the left end of a shadowy hall. "The bathroom," she said, and pointing to an open door next to it, "Your room."

I glanced farther down to a shut door. Grandmother made a slight involuntary movement that seemed almost to be an attempt to block my view, and I made a mental note to check it out if I had the chance.

The room I was to stay in smelled of Pine Sol, as if the tile floors had been recently scrubbed. The space was small, a large portion of it taken up by a rollaway bed, neatly made with a chenille bedspread. A crucifix hung on the wall over the head of the bed, and the side table held a lamp and a clay water carafe and cup. A nightgown was folded neatly at the foot of the bed with a fresh towel, washcloth, and a new toothbrush still in the box.

"You've gone to a lot of trouble for me," I said. I couldn't help but wonder if it was all because Grandmother genuinely wanted to spend time with me, or if she were trying to assuage a guilty conscience. Most likely, I suspected, a bit of both. I thought of Félix, how he reminded me of my own lost childhood, of all the children who had lost their innocence. I remembered little Travis, left to suffer. I was a child myself when I'd left. There wasn't much I could have done. But in spite of all my good intentions, I'd never made that call to social services. Maybe it wouldn't have helped. But then again, maybe it would have. Yes, I understood guilt.

"In the bathroom, you'll find anything else you need, I think." Grandmother told me to bathe before her, but I could see the small water heater through the opened door of the bathroom and knew how quickly the hot water would run out. I insisted she go first, and she reluctantly gave in.

While Grandmother was in the bath, I tiptoed down the hall to the closed door to what was apparently her room. Not to rummage through her things;

I hoped that looking around the surface would reveal something of her. The new information had only piqued my curiosity. I twisted the knob gently although I knew she wouldn't hear it over the running bath water. The door was locked. My face flushed. She'd suspected that I'd try to get in. I was angry at her opinion of me, and embarrassed that she'd been right.

I left my own door open so that when Grandmother came out she could see that I had nothing to hide. No locked doors for me. She paused in the doorway of my room, and asked me if I needed anything before she retired. The lamplight reflected off the gold locket on Grandmother's chest, and the soft gleam teased me.

"I recognize that," I said, and pointed to the locket. "You always wore it back then too, Papi's picture on one side, yours on the other."

Grandmother's hand fisted around the locket. She flattened her lips, worked her mouth from side to side.

"May I see it?" I walked towards her.

"Why?" Grandmother put out her free hand in a stopping gesture and stepped back into the hallway.

"I had no pictures to carry with me when I left." I spoke softly to calm her. "You see, the memories refuse to leave even when I want them to—but the faces elude me."

"Nothing to see. I forgot to take it off in the bath one day. Well, you can imagine. The pictures are ruined—the water you know—only stained paper now. Sorry."

"You must have other photos. Could I see them?" She wasn't making it easy for me to forgive.

"I told you earlier. They were stolen when my house was burgled." Grandmother sighed and tapped one temple. "Ah, well, all the pictures are in here."

"I wish I could say the same," I said.

Later in bed I didn't realize I'd been crying until I tasted the unfamiliar wet saltiness at one corner of my mouth. The sheets smelled of lavender sachet, and each time I moved, my body warmth exuded the spiciness of the Maja soap I'd bathed with. This was not the same house I'd spent my childhood in, yet scents were bringing me to the bordering edges of those memories.

Outside the peacock cried. The wind rushed at the house, and the walls sighed and moaned. Inside the house creaked and wheezed as it settled deeper into the desert earth. And from the kitchen the methodical *plink-plink* of the faucet marked time. I had opened the curtains of the window next to the bed, and the stars and moon bathed me with their silvery light. I fought to concentrate and keep all thought at bay.

I awoke from a sleep so fitful that I could not have sworn that I had actually slept. Birds chirped outside the window. Wind blew through the mesquite trees dotting the hillside, and I remembered Grandmother's story of orange blossoms and betrayal. I thought about getting up, but I hadn't worn my watch and didn't know the time. Marc had said he'd be back this afternoon, and I couldn't imagine sustaining a conversation with Grandmother for hours. I'd thought we'd finally broken down barriers, but then she'd returned to her cold selfishness with the locket. She'd probably given as much of herself as she was capable. Maybe all that talking yesterday had tired her out; I was exhausted myself. Maybe she'd sleep in.

The flush of the toilet dispelled that notion. I squeezed my eyes shut when the bathroom door creaked open and footsteps shuffled toward my room. She paused outside the door, and my first thought was to ignore her. But it was a new day.

"Good morning," I called out.

"I didn't mean to wake you," Grandmother said, and opened the door a crack to peek in. "I was just thinking, remembering you when you were a little girl. I look at you now, and I ask myself, Where has my granddaughter gone?"

I swung my legs over the side of the bed. Grandmother's sadness irritated me, and my resentment returned with a flash, settled in as if it had never been softened by the tale of her own childhood. What right had she to be so nostalgic about lost years? She was the one who separated us. She may be old and sad for the past, but there were answers I needed.

When Grandmother said she would prepare us coffee, I thanked her and offered to make us breakfast. Hadn't I learned back during my days with Molly Carol that one way to dull the mind was to overburden the body? Keep moving, keep moving, run from thought.

"I'll make you something American," I said. When I found some stale French bread, eggs, and milk, I decided on French toast, and when she joked that the name of the dish certainly wasn't American, I said that we Americans were a smorgasbord of ethnicities. "American Grace, that's me." I didn't bother to keep the sarcasm out of my voice, although hadn't I read somewhere that sarcasm was the protest of the weak?

I pushed my toast around on my plate, and tried to put my questions together. "It's the money," I said. I'd spoken so suddenly, Grandmother dropped her fork. "Sorry," I said. "Let me begin again. I mean you told me you were sick, destitute, and that's why you sent me away. Look . . . I appreciate how much you shared with me last night . . . but. . . ." As usual, when I became nervous, the words flew around in my head, and I couldn't capture enough of them to form a halfway coherent sentence.

"Yes, I understand. It's been so long since I've allowed myself to indulge in memories of my girlhood that I forgot to make my point. Or maybe it's just proof of my aging brain." Grandmother's voice thickened with emotion. She pushed her plate to the side. Neither one of us was able to eat.

"It seems my beautiful sister Altagracia never forgot me," she said finally. "When she knew she didn't have long to live, she had detectives locate me. She left me a little of her good fortune for my old age."

Was Grandmother telling me what she thought I wanted to hear? Was it all a lie?

"I wanted to keep my pride and return the money," Grandmother said, "but Altagracia had told the lawyers that I was not to receive the money until after she died. I suppose she was afraid I'd try to find her."

"Wouldn't she have wanted to see you after all those years?"

"Guilt is a horrible thing. Maybe Altagracia wanted to die believing what she wanted to believe."

"Maybe," I said. How could I absorb so many *maybes* at once? I wished I could go off someplace alone and think. For now, I needed to keep busy, keep moving. I insisted on washing the dishes, and when I opened the blinds over the kitchen window, the morning light revealed that the kitchen was not as clean as Grandmother always insisted our house be years ago. Her housekeeper was taking advantage of her aging vision. I told Grandmother that I'd straighten up while she rested. When she tried to stand, I had to help her, and this time she allowed me to support her elbow as I walked her to the front room. She gestured toward a lumpy love seat and asked me to hand her a sewing basket from a nearby table. She pulled out crochet thread and needle.

"Remember what a mess I made of that bedspread we were crocheting for Mamá and Papi's bed?" I said.

"You were always such an impatient girl." Grandmother pulled a tiny bootie from the basket. "Marta Beltrán and I make booties and sweaters for the girls at the Descanso who get pregnant," she said. "And here," she said, pulling a small square out, "are snowflakes to hang on their Christmas tree. Just imagine. In my day, we celebrated the Epiphany, and the three Magi left gifts in our shoes. Now it's all Santa Claus and snow and Christmas trees. Well, everything changes, eh?" Her still nimble fingers worked the needle in and out, linking loops of white thread into intricate designs.

For the next hours before Marc returned for me, we spoke little. When I asked Grandmother to unlock her bedroom so I could clean, she thanked me but said it wasn't necessary. Her refusal only made me more curious.

When Marc arrived, Grandmother wanted to invite him in, but I said that he'd have to come some other time because I had an appointment. Marc glanced at me, but went along with the lie. I could tell Grandmother didn't believe me, but I figured that made us even. Outside, as Marc and I walked away, Grandmother stood with the front door to her back. I looked back over my shoulder at her, and she remained so still she looked as though she were a photograph. The flaccid skin draped over the prominent bones of her face and puddled into the wattle of her neck—but, except for the thin skin around the eyes, she was marked by few lines, creating the illusion of skin melting off bone. I wanted to rush back to her, stroke the ruined face, wrap my arms around the bony shoulders, but the thought of touching the old woman somehow repelled me. I didn't want to feel that way, but I did.

"I'll be in touch," I said.

SIXTEEN

I settled back in the Mustang and turned my eyes to the road before us. The wind blew softly around the car, and from off one of the distant hills, carried the faint tinkle of a wind chime.

"I'm assuming you don't want to go to Lourdes right now?" Marc said.

I shook my head. I'd completely forgotten the visit to the cemetery.

"Want to talk about it?" Marc briefly laid his hand over mine, and when he returned his own hand to the steering wheel, the heat of his touch remained on my skin.

"Not now," I said. I'd repressed my memories and thoughts for so long; now the past had collided with present, as joined and yet separated as the two Mesquites, yet my head felt as though it were battling to split into two distinct parts.

I wished that I could turn away from Mesquite, keep driving farther out until I reached the outskirts of town and areas new to me. A fresh start, just as I'd done time after time before Kenny. Now Kenny was the one who wanted a fresh start. Without me. Soon I'd be back in Brockton and we'd straighten things out between us. And all of *this* would be forgotten. What a lie. No matter what happened with Grandmother, the borderland was inside me, a part of me.

"I used to walk through these hills when I was a girl," I said. "After I shampooed my hair, I'd go outside and sit on the bench in our courtyard until my hair dried. The sun was so warm, comforting. Grandmother used to say that lying in the sun was for lizards. Or that if I wasn't careful my skin would get as dark as a laborer's."

"Yeah, I had an aunt like that." Marc shrugged. "Leftover attitudes from the Spanish colonial times, I guess."

"Does The Three Little Pigs Restaurant still exist?" I asked.

Marc laughed and said that I should work on my transitions. The restaurant had gone out of business years ago, he said, and asked if it had been a special place for me.

"It's not important," I said. There I went again, shutting off an opportunity to reveal something real about myself. How to crack the protective shell I'd taken so many years to build?

As we neared the border crossing, the cars in line to cross into the U.S. slowed until we eventually came to a standstill. Little boys swarmed at the windows, holding up the ubiquitous boxes of Chiclets, silver chains, toys, knickknacks. One boy tapped at my window and pointed to the balero he held in his hand. With a flick of his wrist, he flipped the wooden barrel so the hole drilled in the bottom landed time after time onto the string-attached stick. I was proud of myself for remembering the name of the popular toy until it occurred to me that my Spanish vocabulary had stopped developing at the point I was taken away. I had the vocabulary of a thirteen-year-old; if I wanted to express myself as an adult, I had a lot of catching up to do.

The boy pressed his face to my window, his nose and open mouth mashed against the glass. I had my finger on the window button when Marc said softly, "If you buy something from one, what about the others? I don't want anybody to get under my wheels where I can't see them. I saw a kid get run over in this very spot."

I was saved from making a decision when the children turned to look at a car down the line, and like flocking birds, they shifted, gathered, and swooped away to the hand sticking out an open car window. The boy at my side of the car hesitated. Our eyes met, and it was like looking into Félix's cynical gaze. After he'd run off, I thought about asking Marc how Félix was doing. But I glanced at the border crossing, and the pulse in my temples pounded. How stupid I'd been to cross into Mexico without a thought of being able to return to the U.S.

After all the years of lies—at first outright and then only by omission—I had convinced even myself that I was an American (and wasn't I?). I had my driver's license with me, but none of the fake documentation that I kept in our safety deposit box back in Brockton. No one in Brockton doubted me, but the customs agents, they'd recognize a fake gringa when they saw one, wouldn't they? My stomach was twisting into such tight knots, I was afraid I'd vomit.

"Why so jumpy?" Marc said. "We don't have anything to worry about. Just say, 'American citizen,' remember?" I watched the suspicion creep into his eyes.

"Take it easy," he said. "Act natural, or they'll ask a lot of questions."

I felt like a kid again back on the streets of Dayton with Stan and Sweet William warning me that staring at the cops was a sure way to draw them to you. Was it Stan who had told me to keep my hands where the police could see them? I unfisted my hands, dropped them into my lap, concentrated in order to keep them from clenching back up.

The border guard leaned down, and Marc lowered the window. "American citizen," Marc said.

The guard nodded, as if Marc were familiar to him. But when he glanced at me, I must have hesitated a moment too long to respond. His head inched into the window. "Where were you born?" he asked me.

"Brockton, Indiana," I said.

"How do you like living in the buckeye state?" His eyes didn't leave my face.

"That's Ohio. Buckeyes. I'm a Hoosier. And proud of it." I tried to push my wobbly lips into a smile.

The guard held my gaze for another moment, then slapped the roof of the car with his hand. "Welcome home, folks," he said, and waved us through.

Once we'd crossed the line, I was the one to break the silence. "I could do with a drink," I said. "Or two."

Marc laughed. "I got that impression."

Marc squeezed the Mustang into a space between a pickup and a rusted station wagon, and now pointed his finger to a building a half-block away. "Tip Top Bar & Lounge, down there between Puchi's Computers and Youngo's Treasures."

I sucked in my breath.

"What?" Marc said.

"As a kid, Grandmother sold some of our things to Youngo's. It's just weird seeing the place, knowing that it still exists."

I lowered the window just as a gust of wind *whooshed* down the sidewalk, passing the Tip Top on its way toward us. From the toothless yawn of its open door, the wind sucked chance words in Spanish and English, and a halitosis of cigarette smoke and spilled beer on musty carpet, and swept both sounds and odors past the Mustang.

"Not as bad as it smells," Marc said with a grin. "A neighborhood joint, mostly working folks. Some in between jobs, some getting off shift or drinking up the courage to return. Small space, bad ventilation, but I like the people. And they make the best cheeseburgers in town. But if you want, I can take you outside of town to a more family-oriented establishment."

"I can appreciate a good cheeseburger," I said. Although it was drink, not food on my mind. I'd pretty much stopped drinking after my ladies' night days had ended. But now I felt as thirsty as I ever had. I needed to wash away . . . what? I couldn't say exactly; I only knew I wanted a drink. Marc was compassionate, intelligent, and, like Josie, I wouldn't see him again once I returned to Brockton. Another potential confidant.

Marc paused in the doorway of the Tip Top with me behind him before turning sideways so I could step forward. Letting the insiders know, I understood, that although a stranger, I was with him, a regular, and could be trusted. In spite of his body language, the murmuring hushed, and I could sense rather than see the curious eyes.

From the darkness, cigarette tips burned in a helter-skelter scattering of lights, and to the left a long mirror behind the bar caught the glare from the streetlight. A northern Mexico tune on the juke box ended in a flourish of accordion harmony, and a ranchera began, a sad song of love and betrayal. I was entering a film noir, border style. A woman only feet from me burst out in laughter, and although cynical, the sound was also contagious. Marc and I laughed.

His hand encircled my upper arm to guide me to a table in a far corner. I hoped that nothing on the outside of my body gave away the tiny current of electricity inside, zip-zipping along the nerves from my arm to my spine. I told myself it was only static electricity. But I knew that it was much more. I thought of Kenny's eyes, so calm, so placid, but the half-formed image disappeared into the hazy smoke trapped in the Tip Top Bar and Lounge. Anticipation neon-buzzed inside me, filled me with the sense of nearing the mountain's summit.

If it hadn't been so dark inside the bar, or if the beat of the music hadn't vibrated through the floor and entered via the soles of my shoes, or if Marc hadn't been so near . . . perhaps then I would have felt more like the me I'd been for the last fifteen years—sensible Grace Thornberry. I was nameless, a woman in a dim bar full of anonymous bodies and next to a man who radiated too much heat. My senses were sparking and snaking like a live wire torn down by a storm.

At the table, the waitress, a young woman with large breasts and a small blouse, crouched on the floor next to Marc. "What's it going to be tonight, handsome?"

When he said, "Let's see what the lady wants first," I was pleased that he'd let the waitress know I was with him. I wasn't, of course, but I liked the thought. Maybe a few moments of escape would help me put all that had happened for the last weeks behind me. At least for one night.

"Diet Coke," I said to the waitress, but when Marc ordered Corona beer with lime and salt on the side, I said, "What the heck, make it two."

We shared a nervous first-date kind of laughter. I couldn't remember the last time I'd laughed so much. I fell back on the Grace from ladies' night days and told myself that when in doubt have another drink. I had several.

Marc scooted his chair close to mine. Was it merely the darkness dilating his pupils, or was there a bit of desire in there too? "Hard to hear with all this racket," he said.

"Boy, that's the truth," I said. Sitting on stools at the end of the bar, a middle-aged man and woman leaned slightly toward one another, shoulders touching but faces turned to the mirror over the bar. The man played at the hem of his partner's short skirt before working his hand inside and up. The woman parted her plump thighs slightly.

Marc tilted back his head, swigged deeply from his bottle of beer, his throat muscles pushing the liquid down. I pressed the cool bottle of Corona to my flushed face.

"So, tell me about yourself," I said.

"Not much to say." He shrugged, but I could see in his eyes that he was pleased with my interest. Maybe he'd been waiting for someone to talk with too.

I encouraged him some more, even though it was more a matter of being polite than interested. My pulse was throbbing to the beat of the music. I'd pretty much given up on coming up with any intelligent conversation. But he'd been so nice to me. The least I could do was to try and listen. I must have sounded convincing because after another swallow of beer, Marc started telling me how he'd begun his studies in business although what he'd always wanted to do was write a novel.

"Why don't you?" I said. How sure I sounded of my advice. Even if I didn't have clear dreams for myself, I liked it when someone else did.

Marc ripped the label from the beer bottle, piling a small heap of paper strips as he continued speaking. He said that his parents, father from Mexico and Anglo mother from the United States, had believed in the American dream—the financial part of it. "It was all about moving up economically for them," he said. "But thanks to them, I didn't live through the hard times they had, and ironically I lost some of their need for making money."

I nodded. I appreciated his confiding in me, but at the same time it made me nervous. Desire I could deal with; emotion was something else altogether. I had to keep reminding myself that Marc and I wouldn't see each other again after I left Mesquite.

He was saying that he'd once worked days at a bank while occupying his nights studying for his master's in English rather than the MBA his parents would have preferred. "As soon as I completed the program, I applied for a teaching position at Valparaiso, and have been there ever since." He said he liked working with non-traditional students, but the teaching load was so heavy that he had trouble finding time to write.

"Take off for a while," I suggested. "Get that novel started. It's important for your dreams." I was so heady with alcohol, my advice no longer felt hypocritical to me. I sounded wise, intelligent.

"Maybe I will," he said, "maybe I will. And you, you've already achieved your dreams?"

"My husband and I have our own business, Thornberry Dental Laboratory." Even as I said the words I felt foolish. The lab had been Kenny's dream, not mine. My lips were going numb from the alcohol, and I may have slurred my speech because Marc suggested that I might want to slow down on the Coronas. But my inhibitions were softening, and I knew deep down that was why I was keeping those beers coming.

I pressed my shoulder to Marc's. "Will you be honest with me?" I said.

"I've been told I'm too honest."

"No point in going overboard," I said. My comment struck me as pretty damn funny, and I laughed too loudly. I'd wanted to ask him if he found me attractive, but he looked so serious that I couldn't bring myself to form the question. "Can't remember what I was going to ask," I said. "Maybe it'll come to me later."

He pushed his pile of beer label strips around. "Grace," he began slowly. "What was going on back at the crossing? Can I help?"

"What are you, everybody's savior?" I demanded, then immediately apologized. "I shouldn't have said that."

"No, I'm sorry," he said. "I just got the feeling that you wanted to talk." His face was so full of compassion, so nonjudgmental, that the gates to my heart opened a crack.

I laughed nervously, and without thinking, said, "I don't have documents to be in the United States. Not legitimate ones." Marc looked at me calmly, as if he had heard that statement a hundred times.

"Already figured that out, didn't you?" I said.

I'd seen scenes in movies where the therapists sat back and let the patient rattle on, only offering an occasional encouraging word. That night at the Tip Top, Marc was my therapist. In my rush to get it all out before the alcohol buzz wore off, I tripped over my words and sometimes had to backtrack and start again in order for him to understand. I told him, in alternately halting speech and rushed spurts, about my last days with my parents, Mamá's fears, Papi's lilies, and finally the accident.

"It wasn't your fault," Marc said, understanding the parts I wasn't articulating. "You were only a kid." He squeezed my hand.

I told him of the exchange at The Three Little Pigs with Mr. Genaro, Molly Carol, Grandmother. Except for the slight slurring, I sounded fairly calm. But inside me, pressure was building. I fought the urge to scream.

"And why couldn't you stay with your grandmother?" Marc asked.

I repeated all of Grandmother's reasons. "Why're you looking at me like that, Marc?" I said. "You're thinking my grandmother lied, aren't you? But, see, the thing is, she inherited some money. That's why she's doing so well."

"I'm not accusing anybody of anything." How gentle his voice was. "I'm just sorry doña Paz didn't inherit the money sooner, so you could have stayed put."

Marc had laid out the very thought that I'd been pushing from my mind ever since Grandmother had told me about the inheritance. When *had* she received the money? My head was splitting, the impulse to scream returning. Movement, I needed movement. "Let's dance," I said. I stood and tugged at his arm.

A ballad had begun. "And don't even think I'm trying to seduce you," I said. It felt good to be silly and flirting, to pretend that I hadn't a care. When we reached the patch of vinyl-tiled floor next to the jukebox, Marc wrapped one arm around my waist, brought me within inches of him. My legs trembled, and I leaned against him for support, mashing my breasts to his chest.

"So smoky in here." I turned my head toward him, rested my forehead against his jaw. In the shallow at the base of his throat, his pulse thrummed. Each beat released heat and with it his faint scent of musk and citrus. A young couple joined us on the floor, and the girl, teetering on high heels, fell back into us. I held on tighter to Marc.

"The beer," I mumbled. "Sometimes, later on?—can't even remember what I do."

"You're safe with me," he said.

"Not too safe, I hope," I whispered.

"Don't do something you'd only regret tomorrow."

"What do you mean?" I said. My cheeks burned. I knew he knew I understood what he meant. Before he could answer, I added, "Anyway, I don't regret anything."

"Lucky you," he said, and smiled in such a sad way, I danced harder, faster. After I'd stepped on his feet a couple of times, Marc suggested that it might be time for both of us to take a break.

"One more toast before we leave," I said, when we reached the table. "Here's to my divorce."

Marc glanced at my wedding band.

"Decided this very minute," I said. But had I really decided to give Kenny his freedom, or was I trying to say whatever would convince Marc to stay the night with me? And if that was the case, was it lust or the fear of being alone motivating me?

"I want to hear about it," Marc said. "But maybe when you're sober?"

Outside the blood-red sun hung low on the horizon, and its burst of dying light bathed the dusty hills in a rosy glow. The evening breeze off the desert chilled, and as Marc opened the car door, I leaned back into him, searching out his warmth. His hand brushed against my arm as he helped me in, and my elbow jerked as if he'd hit my crazy bone.

As Marc started to get into the car, a passerby called to him. From what I could hear, the man was an acquaintance who hadn't realized Marc was in town, and they were making arrangements to meet the next day. As I twisted, getting comfortable in the bucket seat, my knee hit the glove compartment and the door plopped open. I was trying to stuff back some fallen papers when a folded piece of newspaper caught my attention.

I opened up the sheet and held it at an angle to catch more light from the streetlight. The grainy color photo covered one quarter of the page, but it took me a moment to make out the image on the yellowed paper. A mutilated body lay on the railroad tracks, split at an angle from crotch to collarbone, halves butterflied so that one leg and arm lay inside the tracks, the other beyond, and between the red wings, a rail reflected the sun into the camera's lens. I'd forgotten how graphic some of the Mexican newspapers could get.

"Don't look at that, Grace," Marc said, as he dropped into his seat. He reached across the console and took the paper from me. "It'll give you nightmares."

"Who is it?" I asked, and immediately wished I hadn't. Did I really want to discuss the photo now?

"Chano, Félix's brother. Remember, I told you he was killed by a train? Can't bring myself to throw the kid's picture away." His voice was sharp, bitter. "The press played up the roving pack of man-eating-dogs angle. Gets people's attention when they think the horror might get personal. You know, like, 'Who knows if next time the wild dogs appear, maybe they snatch one of the decent folks from the safety of home and family?'" He thumped his fist on the steering wheel.

"Well," I said, without commitment. All this ugliness was bringing too much reality into the moment.

"You should've seen Chano in life, a face like an angel," Marc said as he pulled onto the street. "Maybe that's why the bastards couldn't leave him alone."

"Who wouldn't leave him alone?" In spite of myself, I wanted to know more.

"Chano and Félix bore a family resemblance," he said, "but Félix, you've seen him, sturdy little guy, lots of energy. Chano was delicate, didn't seem like he was built for the long haul. Looking at him, you just kind of held your breath waiting for disaster to hit. Anyway, the theory is the little guy had gone back to huffing paint, got high, fell off the train. It happens."

"What can one person do, Marc? It's like Josie putting out water and food. What good does any of it do?" I pressed fingers to temples, massaged little circles. I didn't want to hear any more details.

"If everybody said that, where would we be?"

"Better off, maybe," I mumbled, and avoided looking at him.

"You left your TV on," Marc said twenty minutes later when we stepped into my motel room.

"Did I?" I giggled, impressed with how innocent I'd sounded, as if I hadn't made certain that it would be on when I returned, voices to fill my loneliness.

He told me that he didn't want to rush off, but he had to get up early. "Lots of work at the Descanso tomorrow."

"Sure you won't come in for a minute or two?" My voice was so needy that I couldn't look him in the eye.

"I don't think that's a good idea," he said. "Maybe some other time?"

"No big deal," I said, and shut the door quickly before he could see the hurt on my face.

The wind had picked up, and the chimes on Josie's tree were in motion, calling shrilly, without harmony, each vying to be heard over the other. I locked the door. As if I could keep chaos away.

SEVENTEEN

In the shower, I bent forward, head bowed. Hot spray pounded the crabbed muscles at the back of my neck. Dizzy, I straightened and braced one shoulder against the shower wall. I lifted my face to the needles of water. Hard, sharp, stinging. But they were neither strong enough nor hot enough to drive all thought from my mind. The events of the last weeks swirled inside my skull, pieces of memories caught in a dirt devil.

How to make sense of my broken marriage, the past? Grandmother? Myself? I'd told Marc I was getting a divorce. Was I? I turned up the hot water. My mind steamed. Married woman reveals her past to her husband and is consequently dumped. Reunites with grandmother who has suspiciously prospered since giving granddaughter away. Gets the hots for young, single guy who rejects attempts at seduction. Grandmother's blue eyes glitter cold. Turn up the heat, keep away cold. Water scalding. If I didn't watch out, I could drown in self-pity.

I fumbled for the washcloth and scoured my heat-pink skin to a bright red, then lathered my hair with shampoo, knuckled rose-scented bubbles into my scalp. The more I scrubbed, the stronger the aroma. My mind played tricks on me, transformed roses into chamomile and greenery. Baby's tears and Wandering Jew. I rinsed, pressed skull with spread fingertips (keeping my head from exploding?). The day was over. Don't dwell on it, not Grandmother, or Félix and Chano, or Marc. Red butterfly splayed on railroad tracks. Black eye of the peacock. Blue, blue.

Stepping out of the tub, I tried to avoid the mirror. But when I reached for a towel, I caught a glimpse of my reflection, gauzy beneath a film of condensing steam. A tear track ran down the center of the glass eye.

In pajamas and towel-turbaned head, my skin pulsated, but the heat failed to reach the frigid core inside my heart. Before sitting on the bed to watch TV, I pulled on thick socks then stared at the small screen, but couldn't concentrate long enough to figure out what I was watching. I needed to talk to someone. Maybe Josie—but I didn't know the woman well enough to risk waking her for a session of *poor little me*. Kenny had been the closest thing I'd had for a friend for years. (And for his kindness and loyalty, I had betrayed him.) I reached for the phone and dialed the house in Brockton, but when there was no answer I tried the lab.

On the eighth ring, Kenny picked up.

"Hi," I said, voice high with false cheer. Struggling to form a sentence and wishing I'd prepared a dialogue before time, I said finally, "Uh, I only called to give you the name and number of the hotel where I'm staying you should see it it's so colorful—"

"You already gave me that info, Grace," he said, interrupting me. "Remember? You wrote it down before you left?"

"Did I?"

"Holiday Inn?"

I pushed out a chuckle because he couldn't see my smile, and I wanted to be certain he understood that I was keeping things relaxed, casual. "I changed motels. Can you believe it? I'm seeking adventure."

"Adventure. OK." Kenny was tapping his fingers on the mouthpiece the way he did when he was irritated. "I got a pencil and paper. Shoot."

I gave him the name and address of The Borderlands, and listened for the sound of lead scratching on paper. At least he was writing it down.

Country music played in the background, maybe one of his Reba Mcentire CDs. I was never certain if it was Reba's singing or her looks that Kenny liked more. In the past, he had wondered aloud what I would look like with curly red hair, but I'd always ignored the hint and left my hair brown and straight. I was confused enough about identity.

Tap, tap. "Look, I don't want to be rude," Kenny said, "but I got another porcelain crown to build before calling it a night. Christmas, New Year's, you know how it is, people wanting to wear their new teeth for the holidays?"

"I left at a bad time, didn't I? What was I thinking leaving during our busiest season?"

"Grace. I haven't changed my mind about . . . the divorce." Why did he have to sound so kind? I felt pathetic, needy. I didn't love him, or at least I wasn't *in* love with him. Why couldn't I just let him go?

When I didn't answer, he made a sound deep in his throat and said, "Anyway, the office is fine. Lorene wouldn't be much of a secretary if she couldn't keep the office under control." *Tap, tap.*

I forced my voice back up to perky. "Well, then . . . hope you're taking care of yourself. Bet you're not eating enough fruits and vegetables. And your vitamins—on the little shelf in the kitchen. I'll go ahead and pick up your Christmas gift from over here, something southwestern."

God, how low would I sink? Why not just come out and ask him to remember to buy me a gift? But I just couldn't bear the thought of arriving in Brockton only to discover that he'd forgotten me.

"We didn't get a Christmas tree this year," I said, when his side of the line stayed quiet.

"I did—actually that reminds me of something. The office Christmas party. I'm going to throw it at the house this year."

The wind rushed down the outside corridor, carried interrupted melodies from Josie's willow. I hugged the pillow to me as I spoke. I imagined the surrounding desert, its vastness. "Why the change?" I said. "What's wrong with having it at the office?"

"Lorene and her boys," he said. Was I imagining things, or had his voice gone velvet-soft?

Lorene, the divorcée with three stair-step boys, all red-headed like their mother. She'd begun working for us last summer and had brought the boys to an office picnic. Now I tried to remember when Kenny's fascination with red hair had begun.

"What's Lorene got to do with having the party at the house?" I asked.

"Meaning? I hope you're not accusing me. I've never been unfaithful to you. *I* don't lie about who I am."

"That was a cheap shot."

"It's late, and I'm tired."

"You haven't even pulled a Jimmy Carter?" I said. "You know, lusting in your heart?" I laughed to let him know I meant it as a joke.

Kenny didn't laugh. "I'm doing it for the boys. That bastard father of theirs hardly ever sees them. I wanted to give them a real homey type of Christmas."

"Like the ones we use to have? Only minus the kids, of course," I added sarcastically.

"Divorce is hard on kids. It's not like with me and you."

"You think is divorce is easy?" When he only sighed in answer, I added, "Maybe I'll get back in time for the party. What do you think, wouldn't that be nice?"

He paused, a moment too long it seemed to me. "Whatever you decide. It's your house too."

"For now, anyway. Is that what you mean?"

"Look," Kenny said. "Let's talk when you get back. Like we agreed." He'd stopped tapping. "Grace . . . I'm not going to lie to you, I'm ready to move on. You should too. Now, that's all I got to say; I'm hanging up," he said, and did.

I thought about calling him right back, but instead dug deep beneath the covers. I was positive that I would not sleep. Yet I dropped off quickly into dreams.

I stood at the edge of a precipice. Up, up, I commanded myself and sprang onto the balls of my feet, raising my arms until a puff of wind lifted me into clouds that rained bitter-tasting tears; soaring through them, above, where I could look down. An ancient voice whispered, "What makes you think you can fly?" and when I glanced down at myself saw that, unlike the Totonac on Mamá's mural, I had no rope tied to my waist. I crashed to earth, rolled off a cliff. I jerked awake, fingers clawing at the floor of the Borderlands Motel, thinking, I can learn to fly.

Even though the carpet scratched through the thin material of my pajamas, I flattened my body to the floor. Where was that sharp odor coming from? I stretched out the neck of my pajama top, sniffed inside. The acrid smell of fear. God, was I becoming Mamá's ghost-shadow? Could a ghost have a shadow? Could a ghost have an odor? Laughter ricocheted off the walls, and it took me a moment to realize the hysterical sound was coming from me.

I don't know how long I lay on the floor before the knock on the door. Soft at first, but when I didn't answer, firm. "Hey, Grace, you awake?"

I turned my face so that I looked away from Marc's voice. Why was he knocking in the middle of the night?

He knocked louder. "Did you want to go to Lourdes Cemetery today?"

Today? What had happened to the night? I stretched to see the curtains. A bar of light broke at the center where the drapes were not completely closed.

"Grace?" he called. "I can stop by for you later after I finish at the Descanso."

Marc didn't knock again, but I sensed him still there, standing yards from me on the other side of the door. I climbed back onto the bed. When the rapping came again, I was disoriented. Was Marc still there? How much time had passed?

"Cleaning service," a female voice called out. It wasn't until the maid slid the key card into the lock that I raised my head.

"Don't need anything today," I said, and when she didn't answer, I repeated myself, only louder.

I wandered in and out of sleep, sometimes floating through pleasant dreams, other times thrashing to keep the javelinas at bay.

On the second day I again turned away the maid and after undoing myself from the snarl of blankets, shuffled to the toilet. I peed a steady stream into the bowl, and still seated on the commode, stared at the pajamas bottoms around my ankles. Maybe I should get dressed, go out for breakfast. But what I had taken for energy was only relief at emptying my bladder. Tempted to collapse onto the coolness of the bathroom tiles, I eye-measured the cramped space and braced myself for the return trip to the easy softness of the bed.

Outside, the cleaning crew called to one another; children laughed and argued and their parents chided. The phone rang, but I ignored it. I couldn't think of one person I wanted to talk to. The wind moaned and intermingled with the music from Josie's tree. I squeezed my eyes shut, and on the backs of my eyelids I saw blue. Grandmother's eyes, evolving into the eye in a peacock's fan, growing darker, evolving into the black of Félix's eyes, the peacock's eye. And little Travis, the watery blue of his eyes, eyes that I turned away from to save myself. If I were to get up now, walk around the room, would eyes follow me like those of Jesus in the cheap five-and-dime framed pictures?

"Oye, you in there?" Josie yelled, and pounded on the door. "I hear you're not letting the workers do the cleaning. Oye, Sleeping Beauty, you don't answer, I'm coming in. We got to talk. You OK?"

Sitting caused me to become light-headed, and I held onto the mattress until the wave of blackness subsided. Hunger gnawed at the walls of my stomach. I cleared crusted matter from sleep-swollen eyes and ran my gaze around the walls to remind myself of where I was. I stared at framed pictures of idealized desert scenes chosen to fit the room's scheme of mauve and gray, neutralized colors and designs that wouldn't offend passers-through. A temporary home for anonymous pilgrims.

"Ready or not." Josie rattled the doorknob.

"Coming, coming." When I opened the door and blinked at the brightness of the midday light, I said sheepishly, "Hey, Josie," and realized how glad I was to see her kind face.

"What's happening?" Josie peered into the room as if she suspected someone lurking inside had been holding me prisoner. "Why you don't answer your phone, woman?"

"I'm fine," I said, and meant it. I had spent the last three days with my ghosts. And survived. I spoke with lips tight to keep my halitosis to myself. The coating on my tongue tasted as if one of the javelinas of my nightmares had curled up and died inside my mouth.

Dead, I thought, yes, the javelinas were dead. But as much as I liked that idea, if my breath smelled as bad as it tasted, one good blast would knock Josie over.

"You haven't been eating, right?" Josie said. "Already you're too skinny. You come to the office, let's get some meat on those bones." She stayed put until I agreed, then turned on the heel of her boot and tossed her final sentence over her shoulder. "I got important information for you. No joke, OK?" She stared at me until I answered that I understood. Josie walked away, the twist of her denimed hips determined, a rhythm as steady and practical as an agitating washing machine.

I tilted my face to the sun's warmth for a moment before turning my gaze to the left, toward the end of the squat building where the line of white stones began. When I'd first arrived at the motel the stones had seemed so full of possibility. They still did. I imagined myself following the path of white into the desert, connecting the dots with a trail of my footprints. Although the impressions left by my feet would sink deep into the sand, they would soon be erased by the desert wind. But that was the way of things for everyone, wasn't it? I wasn't the only one trying to sort out the mess I'd made of my life.

I felt emptied. Purged of so much poison. I was ready to face the day.

EIGHTEEN

Soup's good for cold days," Josie said as I walked into her kitchen. "But maybe you don't mind. It's more cold in Indiana, yes?"

Conversation usually came easily to Josie, but now her voice was as strained as the expression in her eyes. I suspected that I had reason to worry about whatever it was she really wanted to discuss. "Josie," I said, "could we not wait for Marc this time? I mean for you to give me the news?"

"Marc? Oh . . . no, that's not it." She placed a steaming bowl on the table in front of me. "Sopa de albóndigas, meatball soup," she said.

"You don't need to translate for me, Josie."

"I keep forgetting you're one of us."

"Me too," I said, but wondered if I was really a part of any *us*. Or maybe I was a part of a more inclusive *us*. I liked that idea.

Outside the kitchen window, a gust of wind swung a branch weighted with a large steel bolt. On the upswing, the bolt smashed into an amber-colored bottle, ribbon-tied to a higher branch. Metal shattered glass, spraying an arc of golden brown. Félix, I thought, struggling in Marc's arms at Grandmother's.

"How's Félix?" I said.

"Why you asking for Félix?" Josie said. "Somebody call you about him?"

"I haven't been answering my phone. I think you know that." I pushed my soup to one side. "While this cools, why don't you tell me what's going on?"

Josie exhaled. "This is it. Doña Paz went to the hospital—hold on. She's OK. They took her to Santa Isabel, in Mesquite, across the line."

It was the hospital where Papi had died. I don't know if it was shock or if I half-way expected the bad news, but I remained calm. Maybe it was my fault. I'd put a strain on Grandmother's heart by pushing her into telling me about the past. Yet I hadn't forced Grandmother; she'd wanted to talk, as if she'd been waiting for years to share herself so the memories wouldn't die with her.

"Heart attack?" I said, so quietly Josie studied me, forehead furrowed.

"No, no, nothing like that. She got scared, that's all. I swear." Josie pressed her thumb to curved index finger and kissed it as one would after making the sign of the cross. "Now she's home, and Mrs. Beltrán is going to stay with her until you get there."

I asked Josie to please tell me the whole story, that I could handle the truth. Her gaze shifted from me to the window. The panes rattled as if the wind would take them away any minute, and on the tree some of the larger bell chimes rang clearly above the muffled chorus of the scrap metal, pottery, and bottles. Josie sighed and turned back to me. "You eat," she said, "I will start at the beginning of the story."

She explained that Marc had called early that morning. He'd called my room first, she said, but there'd been no answer. She paused to allow me the full weight of the implication of not answering one's phone before settling into her forward-leaning storytelling position.

"Last night," she began, "the Beltráns are sleeping like angels in their bed—well, it's midnight so where else, yes? They hear a loud banging on their front door and some kid screaming like the world is ending."

"Félix?" I asked, although by the way Josie's eyes lit up I assumed it was him.

Josie shot me a sharp look. "They open the door," she continued with a loud voice, letting me know she didn't appreciate interruptions. "So, standing at the door is a little boy—the blood is dripping from his nose right into his mouth. He says they got to call for an ambulance cause somebody broke into doña Paz's and hurt her. He's hurt bad hisself, understand, but he only worries for her."

She paused as if giving me time to grasp the full bearing of the boy's courage. "That little kid," she went on, "he won't even answer no questions until Mr. Beltrán picks up the phone and starts to dialing. This," Josie said, "is what the boy says to Mrs. Beltrán: "I was taking a walk along the road and all of a sudden I hear a scream and I run to the house of doña Paz. 'Cause even though I'm so small I got to help." As Josie quoted the boy, she widened her eyes, portraying the look of innocence she obviously wanted to project onto him.

I wondered how likely it was that a boy telling this story would comment on his own size. Or more importantly how likely was it that he just *happened* to be taking a walk past Grandmother's at midnight? But I also knew that if I spoke my thoughts, Josie would stop the story to go into his defense.

"Oh, my," I said.

"Exactly," Josie said, "that's the same like I say. He could ignore the screams and save hisself, but instead he goes to the back of the house. Good thing, too, because the real criminal already broke that lock, which makes it more easy for Félix to get in now."

"Then it *was* Félix."

"Félix that saves her—not Félix that did nothing bad. He's a hero, that one. And nobody can't tell me nothing else."

I pushed a meatball around in my soup. "Very heroic," I said, "but by any chance is Félix, well, maybe suspected of being involved in the break-in?"

"See? I knew you was going to accuse him. You got to understand, midnight don't mean nothing to homeless kids; they don't keep no schedule, and they take walks all over the place." She waited for me to nod in agreement.

"OK," she went on, "see this picture: Félix gets inside, he hears all this noise in the bedroom. There's too many candles burning in there, and he sees this big vato wearing a mask like the Mexican wrestlers use. The vato has his hands right around your nana's neck." Josie clasped her hands around her throat in a choking gesture.

Without thinking, my hand flew to my own throat.

"Exactly," Josie said, "very scary. So, Félix, he wants to fight mano a mano, but the other one's too big. Félix starts throwing everything he can to keep the guy off him. Candles, books, and the—what you call it?" Josie snapped her fingers as she tried to think of the word. "Chamber pot, that's it. Which—forgive my manners—was not empty. And that pot hits the big guy right in the face—*pow,* and the orín splashes all over his mask, probably in his mouth. Off the vato runs like the coward he is.

"And on his way out he punches Félix in the nose." Josie sat back in her chair and crossed her arms at chest. "And that's the way it happened."

"Did the police catch the one who broke in?"

"The police keep saying, Félix, Félix." Josie's voice quavered. "Find the masked one, I tell them, but they say it's easier to find a little one. *If* there is a big one, they say, Félix can lead them to him."

"So the police don't believe Félix?" I said.

"The biggest problem? Your grandmother. She won't say nothing. I know she's scared, but she has to talk. In Mexico, it ain't like on this side of the line. Over there it's not innocent until proven guilty; it's guilty until you prove you're innocent."

I had vague recollections of Grandmother and Papi years ago discussing a local crime and Mexico's Napoleonic Code. "Maybe they just want a statement from Félix," I said, without even convincing myself.

Josie harrumphed. "Mexican police—local, federal, whatever kind—they don't mess around. You know that. The tunnel kids always say they're more scared for the Grupo Beta than even the SWAT team from here. And here I am, can't leave this motel. Mercy's gone, and Marc, he's already left for the Descanso. . . ." She left the sentence hanging, stared intently at me, as if waiting for me to pluck her incomplete thought from the air and finish it.

When I stood and told her I would go across the line and do what I could, Josie almost pushed me towards the door. She warned that if I took a taxi to Grandmother's—better not drive up those roads—that I should be certain I got into only an official taxi at the stand. "Just to be careful," she said.

"Hey," she added, as I was leaving. "You invite your grandmother to my Christmas party. Ask her if she likes menudo." Her voice rang false with optimistic cheer. "My friends the Olsons are bringing potato salad and ham—I know, sounds like a gringo picnic but it tastes good. We don't want nothing too formal. And this is the borderlands, so we got our own way of doing things. Oh, and my friend Paquito, he's doing tamales, all kinds, even some of those little canarios."

Canarios. When I was a child, Grandmother had ordered the sweet tamales with tiny bits of pineapple every year for my birthday. "I'll tell her," I said. "And Félix, too, if I see him."

While I waited at the stand in the Mexican Mesquite for the next available taxi, I breathed in the settling afternoon fumes of traffic exhaust and the burnoff of an unknown chemical that was probably coming from one of the maquiladoras. I'd already sneezed until my diaphragm muscles ached, and I pictured the Taurus and the insulation of its metal shell. I'd thought about driving to Grandmother's on my own, but when I'd first arrived and rented the car, I hadn't applied for the expensive insurance for driving into Mexico.

A tap on the shoulder startled me. Omar laughed and leaned in, his face inches from mine, pale green eyes glittering. His cologne and breath of alcohol, tobacco, and peppermint gum almost overpowered the stench of the maquiladoras. When I pulled back, I bumped into a parking meter, and Omar reached for my shoulders to steady me. I shrugged out of his grasp.

"Don't be scared," he said, and laughed.

"I'm not." I hoped that my bravado convinced him more than it did me.

"You remember me, yes?" His coy smile assumed I did.

I stepped off the sidewalk and turned my head to one side, then the other, squinting into the distance in obvious search of a taxi. Let Omar see I had no time to chat with teenage gigolos. He hopped off the pavement, stood behind me, so close his hot breath chilled the back of my scalp and his cologne wrapped around me with a dizzying heaviness. Years ago a young customer at Teddy Bear's had used the same scent—Brut, that's what it was.

I glanced around, but no one seemed to be interested in the gringa and the teenage masher. I told myself I was being silly, blowing things out of proportion. After all, he hadn't done anything to me. My reassurances didn't work; there was just something about Omar that made me feel like I needed a bath. But if I pushed out any farther into the street, I risked being hit by one of the bicycles, buses, cars, or trucks, swerving, brake-slamming, dodging, all with no concern for lanes or traffic laws.

I angled my head so I could glimpse Omar in my peripheral vision. How could I have ever found him humorous? Maybe it had only been Marc's presence (and his compassion?) putting so much space between me and Omar that had softened my view.

"I wish you was waiting for me," Omar said. "You have been in my dreams since that moment I met you at the Descanso. I'm tired of this place. I'm moving on today. Maybe with you?"

Omar's eyelashes were so long they matted at the corners, and when he lowered them the movement somehow fascinated me. I stared without speaking, wanted to say something, anything to take his mind off me. He blinked, breaking the spell.

"Have you seen Félix lately?" I said, because I felt as though I needed to speak, show I had some control over the situation. "Josie, from the Borderlands—know who she is?—she's looking for him."

A glimpse of something fleeting and dark flashed across Omar's pale eyes. He grinned a little wider and shifted his weight. "I don't play with children," he said. "I'm a big boy."

He raised his arm. When I flinched, he laughed and shook his head, as if my jumpiness confused him. He put his hand to his mouth, stuck two fingers beneath his tongue and blew. His whistle pierced what was left of my reserve, and I lunged forward.

Omar pulled me to him and out of the path of the taxi that swerved to a stop in front of us. I grabbed for the Volkswagen door but Omar reached around me, beating me to the handle, and when I looked down, an unexpected sadness bubbled up inside me. His hand was so young, flesh-padded, and the skin hairless and clear except for a sprinkling of scars: starburst circles, some small, some large, with smooth, raised centers surrounded by puckered skin.

I had seen burns like that, long ago, on Jesse, the grill cook at Parker's. Jesse had said that during his drinking days, he used to play a version of chicken. He and a challenger would place their bare forearms on a table, then each guy would press his bare arm to the other's. A lit cigarette was laid where their flesh met, and whoever pulled his arm away first, lost. The winner received a free drink and scars for life. But although Omar's burns looked similar to Jesse's, Omar's were rounder, scattered, more haphazard.

I hopped into the taxi and almost caught my foot in the door as I slammed it shut.

Omar knocked on the passenger window. "You missed your chance for happiness," he hollered over the roar of the broken muffler. His laughter rang false.

"That way," I yelled at the driver.

"I'm not deaf, lady, are you?" the driver said, and held my gaze in the rearview mirror.

The woman who answered Grandmother's door reached for my hand and introduced herself as Mrs. Beltrán. "You don't need to tell me who you are," she said. "You don't have your grandmother's blue eyes—what a pity—but you have the same pretty face."

"Thank you," I said, because I knew it was meant as a compliment. Yet I was already detecting more of Grandmother in myself than I wanted.

In the kitchen, Mrs. Beltrán told me that there was caldo de res on the stove, but that she hadn't been able to get Grandmother to sip the beef broth, much less eat the beef or carrots and chayote. "See what you can do," she said. "Such a shock is hard on us old people. But don't worry. Doña Paz will be fine now that you're here. She keeps asking for you."

"I understand it was two boys," I said, feeling a little guilty for checking on Josie's version of the story. I couldn't erase the picture of Félix tormenting the curly-haired dog that first day I'd met him.

"Two boys, yes," Mrs. Beltrán said. "The police suspect Félix was involved, but I told them, why would he come pounding on my door if he's the one who did it? Still, you never know. Félix did disappear afterwards as well as the masked one. The elderly are the victims of today."

"I'll talk to my grandmother," I said, "and see if she can give me more information."

"Maybe she'll tell you. She won't talk to me," Mrs. Beltrán said. "Well, at her age, the horror of this situation cannot be overemphasized." She crossed herself, and began gathering her purse and sweater, draped over the back of a kitchen chair, all the while apologizing for having to leave so soon. "But you know how husbands are," she said, and smiled. "Gustavo and I have been together for forty-five years. When I'm out of his sight, he says it's like he's missing a part of himself."

"Yes," I said, and realized I hadn't thought of Kenny once since I'd awakened.

As she left, Mrs. Beltrán told me that she'd double-checked all the locks and that I should make certain to bolt the front door behind her. In the hallway to the bedrooms, the dim overhead light had been replaced with a high-wattage bulb. Under the harsh glare, I noticed for the first time a hairline crack that ran through a series of ceramic tiles on the floor. As if the foundation beneath them had not been properly prepared.

I stood outside Grandmother's closed door, half surprised when I found it unlocked. I walked into a heavy smell of rose-scented paraffin. Flush with the wall across the room and in front of me, the dresser mirror was draped with a dust cloth, as you might find in a house of mourning. Votive candles of all sizes were arranged on furniture tops and wall sconces. The bed—a brass bed—was pushed to one dim corner, and the headboard caught the light from the flickering candles.

I flattened my back against the cool wall to keep myself steady. Maybe it wasn't my parents' bed, only a replica. Grandmother had sold the last of our furniture before I left with Molly Carol. I'd left in the early morning hours, and Youngo's was to come that afternoon to pick up the bed and the rocker. I distinctly remembered that. My gaze roamed the room. At the far end of the dresser, and next to a heavily shaded window, was the rocker. Dizziness made me sway, and I pressed my head and back harder against the wall. If the inheritance had arrived in time to save the last of the furniture, why not in time to save me?

A sigh drifted from the direction of the bed. Grandmother lay in the center of the bed beneath a blanket. She was no more than a traffic bump, a passing interruption created to slow—but not stop—ongoing movement. For a moment I imagined it was my mother's tiny body beneath the covers. I could almost smell the vanilla that had both attracted and repelled me. The mix of present and past swirled around me like a thick fog. I was in the presence of memory.

I clenched every muscle in my body to keep from going soft, but I couldn't pick up my feet. I shuffled across the wood floor toward the polished gleam of the bed, as I had when I was a child moving toward my mother's waiting hand. I eased down onto the edge of the bed, and the springs groaned almost imperceptibly beneath my weight. Grandmother remained still.

The bedspread, folded midway down the bed, was of white crocheted squares. Grandmother *had* completed the bedspread from so many years ago. I worked my fingers into the lace. Grandmother's breathing was labored, her lips making tight puckering motions. Her eyelids fluttered open (heart-stopping flash of blue). She looked both startled and irritated.

She struggled to raise her head from the pillow. "You returned," she said. She pointed to the clay carafe on the side table and gestured for me to pour her a glass of water. Her free hand slid up to her chest and hovered an inch above it. She dropped her hand to the blanket and clutched the border. "I thought you had left, that you had returned to the United States." She took a sip of water from the glass I held to her lips. "That's what you're going to do, isn't it?"

"Yes," I said. "I have problems that need to be cleared up." I pressed her hand around the glass, and pulled my own hand away.

"And a family waiting?" She glanced at my wedding band.

"No children. And my husband and I are separating." How easily the words came, as if I'd known all along that I was moving toward this end. I *would* give Kenny his freedom. And I would have mine. I would have to begin again, but this time it wouldn't be in order to lose myself. It would be to find myself. How simple it seemed. But I understood the journey would not be so simple.

"And then?" Grandmother sipped more water. "You'll return?"

"Maybe . . . yes. I will. But I don't know for how long."

Grandmother's hand trembled and I took the glass from her. I wanted to reach out and take her in my arms, comfort her. At the same time, my arms and compassion weren't strong enough to push aside the question about the bed and the rocker. I looked down and as Grandmother leaned forward, I had a view of the top of her head. The lacquered clumps of gray separated in spots and revealed from my height, roots sprouting from a pink scalp. Such a vulnerable shade of pink.

"I heard about what happened," I said, "the assault." I tried to put the compassion in my voice that I couldn't make myself show physically.

"He stole my locket," she said, and her eyes widened as if she saw the incident all over again. "Tore it off my neck." Tears streamed down into the grooved skin on her cheeks. "It's like losing my son all over again. I can't live without my locket."

Grandmother's head dropped back, the weight too heavy for her stem-thin neck. I placed a hand behind her back only long enough to steady her. But when I tried to draw away, she clutched at my arm. Her ache for human touch was palpable. My arm stiffened but I allowed her to hold on. "Did you recognize the intruders?" I said.

"A big boy wearing a mask," she said. "He grabbed me. I was still half asleep. He ripped the chain from me." She closed her eyelids, and I could see her eyes jittering beneath the crepelike skin.

"If you couldn't see him," I said, "how do you know he was young?"

She opened her eyes and stared into the shadows. "I don't know. He felt young. He smelled young. And his hands—" Her eyes widened slightly as if she'd suddenly seen something. "His hands," she said, "were a boy's. But covered with scars of some sort. Maybe burns."

I wasn't really surprised. No wonder Omar was leaving town. I asked Grandmother if she'd given the information about the scars to the police, but she said she'd only now recalled seeing them.

"How is Félix involved?" I said.

"Such a little man. He came running in, screaming like a wild thing. He beat on the bigger one, kept calling him a murderer." Grandmother shook her head slowly from side to side as if she still couldn't believe what had happened. "The big one threw Félix off. And when he—the big one—ran out, he dropped the locket. I saw it. On the floor. Right there. Félix took off after him. I don't know, I think I fainted for a moment or something. I can't remember. The next thing, Mrs. Beltrán was here. But Félix never returned. And the locket, no one could find it."

"Are you saying Félix took the locket?"

"I didn't tell the police that," she said. "And, really, I can't be certain."

I told her that the police suspected Félix. "No, no," she said. "It's safe to say he saved my life." She promised me that the next day, with my help, she'd go to the police station and make a statement.

"Now, you need to eat," I said. I told her I would bring her the caldo de res, and that I expected her to eat. When I stood up, the bedsprings squeaked, and I couldn't stop the words from coming out of my mouth. "I'm so glad that you were able to hold onto my parents' bed." I tried to keep anger and accusation out of my voice. "Your sister's money came in time to save the furniture?"

Grandmother stared into the middle distance and clamped her jaw tight, emphasizing once more her under bite. If she ever answered, it would be on her own time. I wondered if I would ever know the truth. Did Grandmother even know any more what the truth was? Or had it become too painful for her to bear?

I was in the kitchen getting a bowl down from the cupboard when Pavito cried several times from the backyard. I sat down the bowl and eased open the door leading to the back screened room. Dusk was falling, and the yard was shrouded in shadows. The wind moaned through the screen. From the hills the leaves of the mesquite trees and dry brush rustled, and in the distance, near and far, the coyotes howled. Was that a male voice muttering something? Was the voice from nearby or carried on the wind from the distance?

NINETEEN

I stood as still as possible in the screened room and hoped that if anyone were in the backyard, I would be hidden by the hanging plants. Pavito screeched again. I stepped outside. When I was young, Mesquite kids often picked up the ever-handy rocks as weapons. Now I did the same before making my way to the coop. At the opening, I bent over and whispered, "Anybody in there?" I didn't expect an answer and didn't receive one.

Something crunched softly on the outside of the coop. I jumped back so fast I almost fell. The peacock strutted from around the side. "It's only me," I said stupidly when the bird eyed me. I peered into the darkness beyond but saw nothing between me and the cholla cactuses that lined that corner of the yard. I angled myself so I could survey the brush and cactus-dotted hill that sloped down to the winding road.

At the foot of the hill and near the road, the wind slipped through the triangle of mesquite trees that Marc had parked under during our first visit. The dry branches and leaves stirred, *ssh-rrush, ssh-rush*. The trunk of the tree farthest from me seemed to have a huge knob on one side. I squinted. A bird hooted, flew out of the top of a mesquite, and the knob became a moving silhouette that darted from the tree to a nearby saguaro cactus. Animal or human?

Above me, the stars were just beginning to twinkle into view and in the distance a wind chime tinkled, delicate notes echoing off the valley slopes. As a child I'd loved the desert. I hadn't been allowed out after dark by myself, but now here I was: an adult, free to do as I wished, and surrounded by the promise of a cool and starry night. How odd to think that in those faraway days, I'd detested all the rules that adults imposed on me and yet, through the years, had found comfort and safety in regulations and stagnancy. Who would I have become if my life in Mesquite had not been interrupted?

Those kinds of thoughts were pointless, I knew, but just for a few moments I wanted to sit alone in the desert. I'd try not to think of what could've, what should've been, and instead become one with the moment, as if I could stop time and exist forever in the now. I looked around me one last time, told myself that the noises had only been the peacock, the wind, and an awakened sensitivity brought on by so much discussion of the past. Down the hill and across the road a huge boulder with a scooped-out place on one side seemed to be the perfect place for sitting.

The hill was steep, and afraid that I might slide into one of the cactuses, I walked through the side gate and took the concrete steps to the road. At the boulder, I first made certain there were no holes where tarantulas or scorpions might be hiding, then climbed up onto the ledge. I studied the skies for a shooting star. What might I wish for? The possibilities now seemed endless.

In the far distance below, contained flames leaped from the side of the road. Someone must have lit fires in the metal barrels I'd seen when we'd passed through the shantytown. Some of the folks down there were probably staring up at the same stars, wishing, wishing. Or were their hopes too dead for wishes? Maybe not. The human spirit was difficult to snuff out. Did the shanty families drift outside after nightfall the way I remembered doing in Mesquite when I was a kid? Or as the twins and I used to sit on the porch at Molly Carol's? At Barb and Rose of Sharon's we hadn't had a porch, but we'd taken folding chairs out in the scrap of front yard and sipped lemonade or Cokes, speaking to each other in hushed tones, sharing the events of the day. The need for quiet communion among the growing shadows must be universal.

A pebble crunched near the road and to one side of me. I whirled to face the sound. A lizard darted through the brush. Did those gangs that Félix told me and Marc about venture up to these parts? Or maybe Omar had returned. Why had I strayed so far from Grandmother's? How quickly darkness was falling.

I slid off the rock, and, glancing over my shoulder every few steps, made my way back up the hill. I walked fast but resisted the temptation to run. If someone were right behind me, they'd have no difficulty in taking me. And after all these years, I still remembered Sweet William's advice about not walking like a victim. I straightened my spine as much as I could and brought my feet down more solidly onto the ground. Let all the hidden eyes in the surrounding desert see: I was somebody going somewhere.

Was that a giggle? "Who's there?" I demanded, and tightened my grip on the rock that I'd had the good sense to keep with me. If I landed a shot, maybe I'd have time to beat whoever it was to the house.

"Omar?" I said.

"Fuck Omar." Félix sprang from behind a maguey. "Never saw me, did you? I'm like a ghost. Super Ghost, that's me." He pursed his lips and *whooo-whooled* like a lost wraith.

"Are you alone?" I asked.

"I don't need nobody," he shouted. "How many times I told you?"

"*Shh.*" I stepped behind a spreading prickly pear cactus.

"Scared, huh?" With his walking stick, Félix pointed to the hills below. "Don't worry, they can't see you from down there," he said. He moved toward me, *tap-tapping* his stick before him like a blind man.

"I'm not hiding."

"Oh, yeah? They're only people. Same like you."

"I know that," I said. "I'm not afraid."

"Liar." He scratched a drawing that I couldn't make out in the sand. "I saw you and that puto together earlier."

"Puto? Who's a whore? Are you still talking about Omar? At the taxi stand?" My gaze darted from brush to tree to cactus. Could Omar be watching us now? "Look," I said, "why don't we go up to the house? The night's turning so cold. I'll make us some hot chocolate. With extra cinnamon, OK?"

Félix hopped from one foot to the other, faster, faster. "I know about that puto and his lies. He killed my brother." He screeched the last words, and from Grandmother's yard, the peacock responded.

Félix looked so small and his anger seemed so futile that I wanted to protect him. I reached for him, but he jumped away. He was yelling, saliva spraying from his mouth. I had trouble understanding what he was saying, but I did manage to make out something about the police.

"Don't worry about them," I said. I hoped my calm voice would affect him. All the while I edged up the road, and he moved along with me, partners in a lopsided dance. Earlier I'd felt as one with the desert, now I felt alien, an outsider being watched by millions of glittering heavenly eyes.

"Grandmother says you helped her," I said. "We're going to make sure the police know that."

"What are you talking? I hate cops. They say Chano raped some girl in the tunnels. Liars. I hope the devil takes them." Félix turned his face to the sky and a scream ripped from deep inside him.

I sputtered, trying to think of something to say.

"They dragged us," Félix said, gasping between words. "Me and my brother, into the station. Omar was already there. Well, he lets that fat cop mess with him, doesn't he?" Félix popped his finger in and out of mouth, making obscene sucking noises.

"Everything's going to be all right," I said.

"Because of what Omar *did* that night at the cop station," Félix shouted. "That's why Chano sniffed the paint. The paint made him fall off the train."

I tried to pat Félix's back, but he arched and jerked away.

"What do you think, I'm a fuckin' girl?" His sobs turned to blubbering, and snot ran from his nose. He wiped at it with the back of his hand, smearing green slime across his face. I had a vague memory of reading somewhere that mucus that color suggested infection.

"Come on," I said, trying to nudge him with my soft words. "Up the steps. See? We're almost there."

Félix ran up the steps, holding onto the rail this time. When he reached the top, he turned. "Listen to me," he shrieked. "They tied me to a chair. My brother, they put a dress on him. Like he was a girl. Made him dance with Omar. 'Do it to him,' the cops say to Omar."

I wanted to shout him down, cover my ears, run away. But this time I wouldn't turn away. I was an adult, and this child needed me.

"Then they say, 'Now you will know what it's like. To be a girl who gets screwed. When she don't want it.'" He was bawling now, wet gulps from deep inside him.

"But . . . but," I stammered. I felt sick to my stomach. The rock I'd been clutching dropped to the ground. "But why?" I said. "I mean, why did Omar go along? Was he part of the plan?"

"Don't tell me it's not his fault." Félix tried to scream the words, but his voice had grown hoarse. "A few little burns with a cigarette? A man has to endure pain."

We were in Grandmother's backyard now, and the peacock watched us with his obsidian-black eye. I reached for Félix. This time he allowed me to hold him. His tiny body trembled, and his heart raced against mine. When he pulled away, he left a wet spot of tears and snot on my blouse. I clutched his hand in mine.

"Just listen to that peacock," I said. "It almost sounds like he's calling your name."

Félix hiccupped. "Yeah," he said. He nodded, and one of his double cowlicks sprung loose from the heavy pomade he'd slathered in his hair. "Pavito likes me more than anybody."

"Then come with me," I said. "After our merienda, you can come back out and feed the peacock."

"Pavito," Félix said, "that's his name."

"It's only me," I called out when we entered the kitchen. "And Félix."

I pulled Félix into the bathroom so he could clean up before we went to Grandmother's room. He blew his nose and splashed water on his face, then stood on a small box so he could check himself in the mirror over the sink. He tried to flatten his hair but the cowlicks popped back up.

"I don't want to scare the old lady," he said.

"She said you were a real hero," I whispered, as we walked down the hall.

"It's nothing," he said. His chest puffed out like the peacock's. "I told you before. That old woman needs a man around this house."

Grandmother was still in bed when we entered her room, but she'd obviously gotten up because she was wearing a robe and had brushed back the loose hairs from her face. Her jaw was set and lifted, and one shoulder was hiked at the familiar tilt.

"Thank you, young man," she said. Félix was about to respond, but she interrupted. "No beating around the bush. My gold locket. Where is it?" Her voice shook.

Félix pulled his hand loose from mine. "You see how she is? Crazy old rich woman. They don't never appreciate nothing."

"No, no." Grandmother stretched out a hand, but he ignored it.

"It's only," I said, "that her locket is missing, and it means more to her than anything."

"More than the peacock?" Félix said.

"Did Omar take it?" I said. "It was Omar that night, wasn't it? Maybe he dropped the locket . . . maybe—"

"Maybe you picked it up for me and then forgot," Grandmother said.

Félix backed toward the door. "I don't steal. And I don't lie," he screeched, his arms lifted straight above his head while he jumped up and down with both feet. Rumpelstiltskin from the fairy tale, that's who he reminded me of with all that stomping and outrage. I remembered watching a film with Tiffany and Travis, and how we'd laughed at the antics of the tiny Rumpelstiltskin after he thought he'd been duped, tiny legs thumping away at the earth while he yelled to the heavens that it wasn't fair. As if someone or something was there to hear his cries.

"All of you can go to the devil," Félix shouted. I reached for him, but he was too slippery.

I slept little during the night, waking up every few hours. I'd decided that when Grandmother and I went over to the Beltráns', I would call Marc instead of a taxi to take us to the police station. Félix hadn't said which of the police groups had been involved in Chano's rape, so I wanted to make certain that I spoke with someone who had the authority to call off the hunt for Félix. As a volunteer worker for the Descanso, Marc had surely gotten to know a cop or two. Maybe he'd know who the right person was to talk to. That morning, over mugs of strawberry atole, I explained all this to Grandmother as my reasoning for calling Marc instead of a taxi.

"Of course, it's not because you would like to see him again, true?" Grandmother smiled. "I'm not so old that I don't remember what love is."

"No, no," I said. It was too soon to know what I felt for Marc, but I did like the idea that after all these years of burying my emotions, I might be capable of falling in love. Someday. "How about going with me and Marc to a Christmas party after we finish our business?" I said, and to my surprise, she said she'd go with me as long as I brought her back early.

"No staying overnight," she said. "If I die in my sleep, I want to die in my own bed."

"Papi's bed?"

She gave me a look I couldn't interpret, before quickly shifting the conversation to worries over which dress she should wear. I looked in her closet with her, and didn't say so, but couldn't understand what the problem was in choosing from among the row of black dresses that seemed to have been cut from the same dull pattern. Would she be forever mourning Papi?

After dressing, Grandmother patted her messy hair. "Will I have time to stop at the beauty parlor? In all the commotion, I didn't keep my regular appointment."

I understood by her sly sideways glance that she wanted me to offer to do her hair, but shampooing seemed too intimate. I told myself that I was being silly, that hairdressers provide this service to perfect strangers every day. It meant nothing. Of course I could do it.

"I'll fix you up," I said, but without enthusiasm. Maybe I hoped she'd turn me down. She didn't, though, and I asked her if she had any chamomile around for a final rinse.

"No chamomile," Grandmother said. "My days of blond illusions are over."

At first her neck was stiff when she leaned back onto the folded towel at the edge of the basin, and I brushed my fingers across her tensed forehead. The papery skin was as cool as death, and it was an effort to not pull my fingers away too quickly.

I turned on the water, made certain it was warm. Gently I cupped her bony skull in my palm (how neatly it fit), and lowered it into the sink. Again, her neck stiffened, and with my free hand, I stroked her forehead again. Within moments the weight of Grandmother's head pressed deeper into my palm, and her eyes twitched beneath the lids. Her breath was shallow as my hand moved in slow massaging circles over her scalp.

"You know," Grandmother said as I was rinsing her, "sometimes people do things that indirectly hurt others. Like Félix, I mean. Maybe he did steal but he's sorry. He just doesn't know how to say so."

"For adults it should be easier." I couldn't wait any longer to ask the question I needed answered. "Grandmother," I said quickly, before I could censor myself, "about your inheritance."

Her head lifted slightly. "My neck hurts." She sat up and I patted her hair with a towel.

"Earlier," I said, determined, "you said for me to be direct."

She waited, her chest barely moving up, down with each shallow breath.

"When exactly did you receive your inheritance? Was it before you took me to Mr. Genaro's? Are you able to explain why you got rid of me?"

An odd sound escaped from her throat. "I was sick. Destitute. Alone."

"I want to know the truth."

"The past is gone, Altagracia." Slowly her gaze met mine. Her eyes had never been a clearer blue. "Please, don't be like me."

"As in we've both been trapped by a past we have tried to deny?"

Her eyelids lowered, the blue disappearing beneath the folds of ruined skin. Perhaps I would never know if Grandmother had given me away because she had wanted to or because she had to. Had the inheritance come at the last moment when the plan was already in action? Had she found it unbearable to be near the child whose interference had caused her son's death? Did Grandmother herself know anymore? But then, how often do any of us truly understand, or even recognize, the motivation for our own actions?

Once Grandmother was styled and dressed, she stood in front of me, waiting for validation. Her purse hung from one arm. The clasp had come open and the purse dropped open, gaped like a mouth, revealing the near emptiness inside. "Well," she said, "what do you think?"

"I guess we're as ready as we'll ever be," I said.

TWENTY

The exterior of the Borderlands Motel blazed with lights that winked at us as we drove up in Marc's Mustang. Multicolored bulbs framed the plate glass window, and a constant string of blue, a shade that matched the Madonna's robes, wove around the opening of the grotto. The bottoms of the cement-encased bottles caught the blue lights and sparkled more than ever, and somehow Mary and Joseph looked more rested, less sad.

Grandmother held onto Marc's hand as he helped her out of the front passenger seat of the car. Her face tensed as she cocked her head to one side in listening concentration.

"It's Josie's tree," I said, and offered her my arm. "Special wind chimes. That's what's making the music."

"I don't know that I would call it music," Grandmother said.

"It does sound a little off balance today, doesn't it?" I said, without looking at Marc. I had trouble meeting his gaze.

Earlier, when I'd called him from the Beltráns', he'd immediately agreed to pick me and Grandmother up, had even sounded happy to help. I had a flash of myself trying to seduce him a few nights ago—and being rejected. I tried to apologize for my behavior at the Tip Top and afterwards, but he wouldn't allow it. Come on, Grace, he said. It's no big deal. What *I* keep thinking about is how close I felt to you, and how easy you are to talk to. And how much we shared. Both of us.

I wanted to tell him I felt the same, but became tongue-tied like a schoolgirl with a crush. I turned the conversation to Félix and how we needed Marc's help at the police station. In whispers, so Grandmother and the Beltráns wouldn't hear, I explained what had happened to Chano and Félix. As it turned out, Marc had already heard the story.

There have been rumors, he said. He told me that he and the Robleses had been working to find a way to keep Félix off the streets. If he could save at least one child, Marc said, all the hours and heart he'd put into his volunteer work would be worth it. "Yes," I'd agreed. One child at a time.

At the police station, Grandmother's frail hand fluttered around her heart as she wrote out her statement. She'd told me and Marc of her plan to lie and say that the locket had been found, pushed under a rug in all the commotion. It was the best way, she said, to keep the cops from concerning themselves with Félix.

"So this is doña Paz," Josie said, and opened the office door wide for us. She had dressed for the occasion: stiff new jeans, red cowboy shirt, sprig of mistletoe stuck through one buttonhole. "My home is your home, señora. And I must say you're as beautiful as Marc told me."

"Nonsense," Grandmother said. But she lowered her eyes coquettishly at Marc. I had a flash of the young coquette Paz posing by the Santiago River for her Selim.

Earlier, after we'd left the police station, we'd stopped so I could buy Grandmother a cell phone. Now I wanted to make certain that she and Josie exchanged numbers. Marc had already provided his, both at the motel and then for after New Year's, his home and office at Valparaiso.

We were early and the first to arrive for the party, so when Grandmother commented on the wind chimes, Josie didn't miss a chance to show off her tree. She held Grandmother's arm tenderly and led her through the apartment and to the courtyard.

Cathedral-like shadows had begun to gather with winter's early gloaming, and the lights that Josie had strung on the arroyo willow twinkled as brightly as stars.

"What a miracle," Grandmother said, and clasped her hands. For a few moments, we all fell silent. Finally Grandmother said, "Maybe you should adjust the wires. See, over there." At one side, the strings of tiny white lights crisscrossed each other in a tangle around the tree, confining the movement of some of the branches.

"I knew something didn't sound right today," Josie said, and walked toward the tree.

Grandmother sank into a chair. When I asked her if she wasn't cold, she waved me away, said that she hadn't worn a coat just for looks. I stood next to Marc. The sides of our arms were not touching, but the heat of his body pulled at my blood like some sort of magnet.

"Will you be coming back this way?" he whispered. "I want to stay in touch. I know people always say that. But I'm serious."

I wanted to be honest with whatever I told him, so I waited a moment before going on. "Right now, I feel suddenly free," I said. "It's a little scary." I laughed, still embarrassed by my new directness. "I've been hiding behind a mask for so many years that I can't say for certain anymore who I am. Or what I want."

"Can I help?" Marc brushed the back of his hand against mine.

I shook my head. "I need to do this on my own. At least for now. First, I return to Brockton, and from there. . . . I will stay in touch, though."

"Híjole," Josie shouted. She was craning her neck and now veered away from the tree and headed toward the gate. She pushed it open and pointed to the box she had filled with water and food.

"Everything's gone," she hollered. "That travieso Félix, he's around. Has to be."

Grandmother insisted on going with Marc and me to investigate. She took his arm, and I followed behind. As we were passing the tree, a spark of gold caught my eye. When I reached out I did so cautiously, expecting to find nothing more than a shard from a broken bottle. Instead, partially hidden behind a rusty bolt, Grandmother's locket swung in a gentle breeze.

When I reached for it, Grandmother turned, and gasped. I dropped the locket into her upturned palm. She closed her fingers over it and tears pushed through the lashes of squeezed-shut eyes. When she opened them again, the blue shimmered. "Open it," she said, and held out her hand to me.

"Thank you," I whispered.

"I'll leave you two," Marc said, and went to join Josie.

My fingers trembled so much it took me two tries to pry open the locket. On one side, a picture of grandmother when she was a young teen, beautiful, the light eyes almost faded to white in the sepia-toned photo; facing her, Papi, Salvador, in his early thirties. In the photos, son was older than mother. As I studied his wavy hair and broad smile, I remembered how his smile never made it to his hazel eyes.

I closed the locket with a small click. "Here," I said, and clasped the necklace around Grandmother's neck.

She nodded. "When you return, it will be for you," she said.

I took her arm and led her to stand near Marc and Josie.

"Maybe I can adopt him," Josie was saying.

"Why should he leave his land?" Grandmother said, interrupting.

Marc started to say something, but Grandmother held up a hand. "There's no need for that boy to abandon his country," she said. "After all, I have an extra room. The boy and I can help one another, that's all."

"We'll see," Josie said.

Grandmother turned her anxious eyes to the desert. "Is he out there?"

A gust of wind rushed at the tree. A ribbon, caught on a branch, broke free, furled away on the music of the chimes. I could almost hear the tune of the Totonac's flute.